ILLEGAL ENTRY

When Forsythe reached Martha Simmon's office it was dark. There was no movement inside when he rapped. Just what impulse made him turn the knob he did not know, but the door swung open onto the darkness beyond, and he stepped inside.

Martha Simmons had said nothing to him about leaving town. What had happened, then, to change her plans? Was she afraid? he wondered. Or was she so deeply involved in the Collier case that she was obliged to escape? In other words, had she meant to kill Collier and only accidentally shot Anne?

It took only a moment to realize that someone had been there before him. Both the safe and the drawers of the steel cases were standing open, and one of the folders lay empty on the desk.

That was when he saw Martha Simmons. She was lying on the floor partly behind the desk, and she was dead.

MARY ROBERTS RINEHART
THE FRIGHTENED WIFE

ZEBRA BOOKS
KENSINGTON PUBLISHING CORP.

ZEBRA BOOKS

are published by

Kensington Publishing Corp.
475 Park Avenue South
New York, NY 10016

Third Zebra Books printing: December, 1990

Printed in the United States of America

CONTENTS

The
Frightened
Wife

1

There was nothing to indicate anything unusual that Tuesday morning in the life of Wade Forsythe II, ex-lieutenant of Marines in the late if not the last war and now member of the bar. There was no poetry in his soul, no particular love in his heart. There was, on the contrary, a look of concentrated hatred in his good-looking face as he sat down at his desk and glared at the red-bound book which was the *Revenue Act of 1951*.

His secretary, Miss Potter, accustomed to the Ides of March, was unperturbed.

"Take that mail out of my sight," Forsythe more or less snarled. "And see that I have a free morning. Do you know what date this is?"

Miss Potter indicated she did, and picked up the wire basket of correspondence.

"You understand, Potter. Nobody sees me. I'm out of town. I'm sick in bed. I broke my leg. And tell Stella, in case you have to powder you nose."

Miss Potter told Stella. That is, she said she hoped she would come through the next ten days without a heart attack or possibly mayhem on the person. And for heaven's sake why didn't the Government stagger its returns? This giving the whole country jitters one day in the year was an outrage.

"And if I'm out, don't let anybody in the office," she warned. "Not unless you want your nose bit off."

Which makes the more unusual what followed.

Forsythe was studying something concerning a collapsible corporation, which need not interest us here—or ever—when he heard someone rapping rather desperately on the door leading to the hall. He was about to ring furiously for Miss Potter when it ceased to be necessary. The door opened and a young woman projected herself into the room.

For a moment she said nothing. She stood listening intently with her back to him. Then she turned and came toward him. She was breathing hard.

"I'm sorry," she gasped. "I thought this was the reception room."

"The sign on the door says 'Private,'" he told her coldly. "If you have an appointment—"

She shook her head, and as though her legs would not hold her she sat down suddenly. Forsythe thought she was about to faint, but she rallied. She tried to smile.

"Just let me get my breath," she said. "I—I suppose I hurried, rather."

She was still pale, however, and he saw she was trembling. Something had frightened her, and frightened her badly. And since he was, outside of tax cases, a rather amiable young man, he got up hastily.

"Wait a minute," he said. "I'll get something to fix you up. Just sit still."

He disappeared into the small lavatory off the office and came back with a bottle and two glasses. Into one he poured a fair shot of brandy and held it out to her.

"Down with it," he ordered peremptorily. "Then the water. You'll be all right."

She choked a little, but obeyed him, and after a moment or two her color began to come back. Her voice, too, was stronger.

"Do you mind locking that door?" she asked. "The one where I came in?"

"Of course not. It's supposed to be left locked. These night cleaning women—"

She watched him as he fastened the door and then went around to sit behind his desk. She perplexed him. She was rather lovely, he thought dispassionately, in spite of her evident terror. In spite, too, of her shabbiness, the worn gloves and handbag, and the inexpensive suit. It was quite clear also that she did not have taxes on her mind.

"Now," he said, as her color came back, "what's it all about? The police aren't after you, are they?"

"The police?" She looked surprised. "Why the police?"

He smiled.

"Well, when a young woman bolts through a door marked 'Private' and then tries to faint, I wonder a little. That's all."

"Just because I came through the wrong door!" she said indignantly. "Actually I came to see you professionally, Mr. Forsythe. I—I have a problem. You see, I want to draw up a will."

It was the last thing he expected, although he was rapidly revising his opinion of her. Shabby or not, she was a lady. Her voice was cultured, her diction impeccable, and had she not been too thin she might have been beautiful. Nevertheless, the idea of a will made him smile again.

"You look pretty healthy," he said. "Pretty young, too. Why a will?"

"I can't tell you," she said flatly. "And I'm not so young. I'm twenty-seven. Everybody should make a will. You're a lawyer. You know that."

He eyed her dubiously.

11

"It depends. Sometimes a will is a nuisance. Of course, if there's considerable property at stake—"

"There is, and it's mine, Mr. Forsythe."

"What sort of property?"

"Money. Quite a lot of it." And seeing his puzzled face, she went on. "The trouble is, it's not deposited in my own name. I've used my pen name. Now I don't know what to do."

He smiled.

"That's not indispensable. Certainly it's hardly frightening. Who were you escaping when you ducked in here?"

"My husband," she said defiantly. "If you think that's funny, it just isn't. I thought I had lost him, but I hadn't. He wasn't far behind me as I got into the elevator."

She meant it. He saw that. Moreover, she had commenced to tremble again. She clenched her hands together to steady them.

"Maybe you'd better explain," he said mildly. "You've written something under a pseudonym, and it has made you some money. Where does your husband come in? Does he want the cash, or what?"

"He doesn't know about it, or at least he didn't until a few days ago. Now I don't know. He's suspicious. Perhaps someone in our apartment building heard me typing and mentioned it to him. Or he may have followed me to Central Park."

He looked slightly puzzled.

"Central Park? What about it?"

She did not answer him directly.

"I don't suppose you listen to the radio much," she said. "I've had an afternoon program running almost ever since the war. You know, a soap opera about a family. The sponsors call it *Monica's Marriage,* and they pay well, especially if the stuff is popular. I began it after my husband came home from France. Only I didn't use his name. I didn't tell him about it at all."

She looked at him still rather defiantly.

"Why not? You weren't ashamed of it, were you?"

"I suppose it's all right. I'm dreadfully tired of it, of course."

"And your husband?" he insisted.

"I wanted him to be a man, if you know what I mean, to get work and settle down. If he knew I was earning, it would be bad for him. Even as things were he didn't try to get anything to do for a long time. He drank a lot, and I think he gambled. But we got along. I have an aunt in Connecticut, and he thought she was keeping us. I was having a baby, too. He didn't want it."

He felt a certain admiration for her, for her determination to make something of a worthless husband. And something else was tugging at his mind, a feeling of familiarity, as though sometime in his life he had known her.

"He works now, I suppose?"

"He sells secondhand cars. We live on what he makes, but sometimes I wonder—" She did not finish that. "I don't blame him entirely," she said. "You were in the war yourself. It changed a lot of men. And after my baby came, I wanted to keep the money for him."

"Where is it? Where do you keep it?"

"In a bank downtown. My agent takes her ten per cent, and after that she deposits the rest to my account under my other name. I call myself Jessica Blake."

"And suppose your husband finds the bank deposit receipts."

"They're in my agent's files. It's the Gotham Trust Company."

13

He sat back, thinking hard. He knew little or nothing about radio programs, but he thought they paid very well. Great Scott, he thought, after seven years this girl might have a considerable fortune. His eyes fell on the book on the desk in front of him.

"What about taxes?" he asked.

"I don't know," she said vaguely. "I suppose my agent pays them."

"If she doesn't, God help her," he warned her. "Some day the Government will catch up with you, and all hell will break loose." And when she made no comment: "You say you want it to go to your son?"

"In trust. He's only six now. And I've sent him to my aunt. It seemed better, the way things are."

Things must be pretty bad, he thought, to make her do that. He felt uneasy. There might be real trouble in the making. The husband was evidently a bad egg. Suppose he learned about the money and decided to do away with her. It would be easy, a push under a bus or taxi or beneath a subway train., But of course that was ridiculous. He was building something out of nothing, and since she seemed determined to move the Jessica Blake account to her own name, he told her that she and the agent—and himself, if she wanted him—could do it easily whenever she cared to do so. It was a simple matter of identification.

"Which reminds me," he said. "You haven't yet told me your name. I may want to call you, you know."

She looked frightened again.

"Please don't," she said. "I'll call you. But I want a simple will. As little as possible to my husband, although I expect he would have to have a third. The rest is to go to Billy, my boy."

"Billy who? What's his full name?"

14

"William Blake Collier. I think you knew my husband in France. He's Wilfred Collier, if you remember him."

Forsythe felt a cold chill down his spine. Fred Collier had been a sergeant in his company when he first joined it as a green young lieutenant. And Fred had been the typical sergeant of fiction, hard, unscrupulous, and even murderous when drinking. He had a wild inclination to tell this girl not to go back to her husband. If he ever learned that she had been holding out on him—

"I remember him, yes, Mrs. Collier. He's no man to fool with. If you're worried, how about going to this aunt in Connecticut? He might not bother you there."

She was not listening. A man was walking along the hall outside, and evidently she recognized the heavy footsteps. She did not move, but all her color was gone again, and the fingers gripping the bag were white with tension. A moment later they heard a man's voice raised in the outer office.

"I want to see Forsythe," he said arrogantly. "And if my wife's with him I want to see her, too."

"Your wife's not here," Miss Potter snapped. "There's no woman here except the two of us. And Mr. Forsythe is out."

"I think you're lying, sister."

"I wouldn't bother," she said contemptuously. "Go and hunt your wife somewhere else. This is a law office and if you want trouble we have quite a few husky young members of the bar around on this floor to give it to you."

"I've handled young punks before this. I don't scare easy."

In spite of this, however, a moment or two later the outer door slammed and Collier started back along the hall. At the door marked "Private" he stopped and tried the knob, then finding the door locked and hearing no sounds within he went on. Neither the girl nor Forsythe spoke until they heard the elevator stop to pick him up.

"I guess that's that," Forsythe said. "I don't like the idea of your going home to him, Mrs. Collier."

"I'll be all right," she told him. "I don't think he's sure yet, and until he is—I only hope I haven't got you into trouble. May I stay a few minutes, if I'm not disturbing you?"

He glanced at his desk. In front of him was his morning's work, still barely started. He shoved it aside.

"Stay as long as you like," he said. "Just try to relax. Want another brandy?"

"I'm all right, thanks."

"You know," he said conversationally, "your boy's name—William Blake. I knew a Bill Blake at college. And I have an idea I've seen you somewhere before. You look vaguely familiar."

It was the right note. She even managed a faint smile.

"I didn't think you could possibly remember," she said. "It's years ago. I went to a prom at Yale, when you were going to law school. You'd played football, of course, and I almost died with excitement when you asked me to dance. I always thought Bill asked you to."

He remembered her then. Queer, too, with all the girls he had danced with that night, and innumerable nights since; a scared, very young girl with amazingly long eyelashes and in a badly fitted white dress, with her brother desperately working on the stag line for men to dance with her.

"Of course," he said amusedly. "Bill Blake's little

16

sister, Anne! Do you know, you still have the eyelashes!"

"It was my first real party," she said rather shyly. "And my dress was too long. I kept stumbling on it. But that's one reason I'm here. I knew you and Bill were friends."

"So we were. He was a grand guy. I'm afraid I've lost touch with him since then." He said it tentatively. It was as dangerous these days to ask about men as it was to inquire about a husband or a wife, and he was not astonished when he saw tears in her eyes. She opened the bag and got out a handkerchief.

"I'm sorry," she said. "You see, he was killed in the war. If only I had him—"

Unexpectedly she dropped her head on the desk, her shoulders shaking with repressed sobs. He got up and put an arm over her thin shoulders.

"Don't cry, Anne," he said. "Let me be Bill, and see what I can do. There are plenty of ways of fixing this thing up." And one of them, he thought, was to throw the fear of God into Wilfred Collier. "Why did you marry him, Anne?"

She did not lift her head.

"Why does any girl marry any man? Maybe it was the uniform. I don't know. Bill brought him to see me before they went overseas. I was working as a secretary then, and I suppose I was lonely. He wrote me all through the war, and—well, that's all. We were married as soon as he came back."

She got up then, and once more he repeated his suggestion about the aunt in Connecticut. She shook her head, however.

"I can't go anywhere until I've straightened things out and made the will," she said. "After that I'll feel free to take young Billy and go wherever I want."

17

"Can you come back tomorrow morning?"

"I can try," she said. "I'm sorry if I've involved you in anything, Wade. You don't mind if I call you that, do you? Bill always did. But you heard Fred. He's in an ugly mood. He'll try to make trouble. I know him."

At the door he was surprised when she stood on tiptoe and kissed him lightly.

"For being wonderful to Bill's sister," she said and was out the door and out of sight before he had recovered. Of course the elevator had gone when he reached it. He took the next one down, only to see her being put in a rather battered Ford, with a man holding tight to her elbow. It did not require another look for him to recognize the big hulking figure of Fred Collier.

So the fat was in the fire, he thought apprehensively. Evidently Collier either knew or suspected what she had been doing, and Forsythe had a feeling that no time ought to be lost. The very thought of Collier's inheriting his wife's hard-earned money was revolting. But it was not only that. It would be easy, he realized, knowing the man, to get her out of the way by faking some sort of accident.

It was out of his hands, of course, at least until and if she came back the next day. He should not have let her go, he thought worriedly. And he had even, he remembered, forgotten to ask the name of her agent.

He picked up the red-bound book on his desk and absently read a paragraph where it opened. It read: *Redemption of stock to pay death taxes. The provisions of this subsection—*

He flung the book across the room and rang for Miss Potter. She came in with her notebook, a substantial woman in her forties, looking prepared for anything, from ugly citizens like Fred Collier to

18

the dull routine of taking dictation. He waved the notebook aside, however.

"Know anything about the radio business, Miss Potter?" he asked.

For once she look astonished.

"Radio?" she said. "I've got a set, if that's what you mean."

"The business," he said shortly. "The scripts, if that's what they call them. How do they get them? Who writes them?"

"I'm sure I don't know. One of the elevator men here keeps trying. I don't think he's sold any."

"Well, find out as soon as you can. Get a list of the agents who handle that sort of stuff. The town must be full of them."

Miss Potter took it in her stride.

"Anything you particularly want to know?"

He hesitated.

"I'd like to know who handles a serial called *Monica's Marriage*," he said. "By a writer named Jessica Blake. But be tactful, Miss Potter. You've heard it and liked the stuff. Maybe you're scouting for a sponsor, but be sure you keep me out of it."

Miss Potter refused to look surprised. Very little surprised her, but she was not unaware that a small white handkerchief was on the floor in front of the desk, and to her experienced eyes it was definitely moist. So maybe that tough guy's wife had been here after all! If so, no wonder she wept.

Her face, of course, recorded none of this. She said she would do her best, and retired with her usual placidity. In the rest room later, however, she found Stella, powdering and lipsticking for the lunch hour, and queried her.

"Ever hear of a radio program called *Monica's Marriage*, Stella?" she asked.

"Mother lives by it. Hears it every day. What about it?"

"Know who sponsors it?"

"Listen," Stella said, working with an eyebrow brush, "I wouldn't be caught dead listening to that truck. What's your interest in it?"

"Nothing much," said Miss Potter, preparing to leave. "Have an idea the boss may be going into radio. That's all, and I say God bless him. Anything but taxes."

And left Stella staring after her.

2

Miss Potter had not located the agent for *Monica's Marriage* by the time the office closed, and Forsythe felt more and more uneasy as he took a taxi home. It was raining. And he was relieved, in his state of mind, that he had that rarity among well-to-do young New York bachelors, a free evening.

He lived with his widowed sister, Margery, in an old high-stooped house in the Thirties, the home in which he had been born and which, except for some necessary modernization, was much as it had been built. Margery had refused to change it, or to move to an apartment.

"I like to eat looking out on the garden," she said, the garden being a euphemism for the small plot back of the basement dining-room. "And I really can't see Thomas Carlyle with a sandbox and without his lady friends. It would be sheer cruelty to animals."

Forsythe always grinned at that. He was confident that due to Thomas Carlyle—so named because of Margery's reading of *The French Revolution*—the district was swarming with unwanted kittens, and he frequently stated to Margery that quite commonly, coming home late at night, he met stealthy gentlemen, carrying squirming bags and on their way to the East River.

He was not grinning that night, however. Margery, plump and easygoing, looked at him with a speculative eye as she came down the stairs.

"Tired?" she asked.

"Hellish weather," he said, handing his raincoat to a neat maid. "Thank God I'm in tonight. I need a cocktail. How about you?"

She agreed, and they went back to the big living-room at the back of the house. He did not relax, however, while he mixed and shook cocktails at the portable bar. Being a wise woman, Margery simpy waited, sipping her drink. She was ten years older than he was, and in a sense she had reared him. So not until he had downed his second cocktail did she speak at all. Then: "What's bothering you, Wade?" she asked. "Anything wrong at the office?"

"No. Not exactly. Just something that happened. I didn't handle it very well. Maybe I'm scared. I don't know."

She gazed at him. He was not easily scared. In fact, she thought he probably never had been.

"What's frightened you?" she asked placidly. "Is it the Government? You're always jittery this time of year."

He hesitated, but having gone so far he went on, grimly.

"I let a girl leave with a husband who has a lot to gain if he can manage to kill her. If he knows what I think he may know."

"Wade! You didn't!"

"Well, what was I to do? Call a car and chase them? Notify the police? So far as I know he hasn't lifted a hand against her as yet."

Margery stared at him.

"I don't understand," she said. "Who is she? And why did she come to you?"

"She wants to make a will. Or she wanted to. I

22

don't even know if she got home today. Maybe he sent the car over the Palisades somewhere.''

"Perhaps that's only her story. Is she pretty, Wade?''

"How in God's name do I know? She's thin as a rail and she looked desperate. If it was acting it was damn good acting. Besides I knew the man in the war. He was a murderous brute.''

He was about to make himself another cocktail when Margery stopped him.

"You don't need that,'' she said sharply. "You need what brains you have if you're really worried. Why not call up, if she has a telephone, and see if she's there?''

"And have him suspect who it is? He followed her to the office today. Potter got rid of him, but he was suspicious as hell.''

"He wouldn't know about me. What's her name, and where does she live?''

"I don't know where she lives. She rushed out in a hurry. She's Mrs. Wilfred Collier, and if you remember Bill Blake from my college days, she's his younger sister, Anne. That's why she came to see me.''

"Then she may be in the *Social Register*. The Blakes used to be, at least until the crash.''

"Better try the telephone book,'' he said dryly. "I don't imagine Collier rates the *Register*, or Dun and Bradstreet, either, But I'd like to bet the police have his record somewhere. Look here,'' he added in some alarm as she began to look up the number, "you might get her into trouble.''

"Why?'' Margery said practically. "If he answers, I can pretend it was a wrong number. If she does, you'll know she's all right. In the East Fifties, Wilfred Collier. That's it, isn't it? All right, and don't look as if you'd like to choke me. If I didn't know you better I'd say you'd fallen for the girl."

She dialed deliberately, to have a male voice answer in a loud bellow. "Well, what the hell is it?" it shouted.

"I'm very sorry," Margery said politely. "I'm afraid I have the wrong number. You are certainly not the gentleman I am calling."

The immediate reaction was a string of abuse, and she was slightly flushed as she hung up.

"If that was Wilfred Collier," she said, "I'd hate to meet him in an alley on a dark night, or at any time or place. He's raging about something." Then, seeing her brother's face: "But he can't have done her any real harm, Wade. If he had, wouldn't he be out somewhere, establishing an alibi, or whatever they do?"

In spite of his state of mind he smiled at this.

"Nicely reasoned, my dear," he said. "As a matter of fact, he probably doesn't know about the will, or anything else. Just now he's only suspicious and ugly. In a day or two he'll probably have dug up the whole story. Then there may be real trouble."

He did not elaborate on that. Dinner was announced and, with the neat maid serving, the talk was casual. He was aware, of course, of Margery's burning curiosity, but in these comfortable familiar surroundings some of his own anxiety seemed rather absurd. With the after-dinner coffee Tillie, the maid, was excused, and he sat back looking through the French doors at the wet garden, with its sundial in the center and its still bedraggled March shrubbery.

"Funny," he said. "I seem to have worked myself into a fit over a girl I saw but once before, and that was ten years ago. I danced with her at a prom, and she remembered it."

"Why wouldn't she?" Margery said proudly.

He grinned at her.

"She was pretty young, and Bill almost broke his neck showing her a good time. Then, before they went overseas, he brought this Collier to see her, and when he came back—Bill didn't—she married him. He was a bad egg, but there was no one to tell her. Now she has a boy, and you can imagine how things are when she's sent the kid to an aunt in Connecticut."

"She must have money, or why a will? The Blakes didn't leave anything."

He lit a cigarette before he answered. Just how much to tell Margery was a question. But she had a hard core of common sense and in the end he told her the story. Not too much, for fear of alarming her. He left out Fred Collier in France, merely saying he had known him there, but at the mention of the radio program Margery sat up.

"I often hear it," she said. "It's really good, Wade. And it's been going on forever. She must have made pots of money. Is that what the will is about?"

"I told you she has a child. She wants the money in trust for him. Collier's not to touch it. He doesn't know about it yet. She's used another name, and I gather she only works when he's out, which is probably most of the time. But something has happened to make him suspicious. He was certainly tailing her today."

It was a relief to talk about the case. Nevertheless, he was still restless when they went up to the living-room. Usually on his few evenings at home he caught up with his reading, while Margery knitted and listened to the radio. But he could not settle down. There had been something almost sinister in the way Collier had held Anne's arm that morning and almost forced her into the car, and the thought that she was alone with him now, virtually at his mercy, was not conducive to peace of mind.

He took to pacing the floor of the long room with its faded Aubusson carpets and its comfortable Victorian furniture. His hands were in his pockets and clenched into fists until he realized it and drew them out. Margery watched him.

"Thinking of killing him yourself?" she inquired blandly. "I wouldn't blame you."

"It wouldn't be the first time I've wanted to," he said. "Mind if I go out? A little air will do me good."

She didn't mind. One of the pleasant things about Margery was that she seldom minded anything he did; a reason perhaps why a good many mothers of daughters resented her bitterly. But he had a faint qualm himself. He knew how she liked the few evenings he was at home.

He agreed not to stay long, and picking up his hat in the front hall stepped out into the night. The rain had finally ceased, but the gutters were still running, and a passing taxicab splashed water from a puddle over the pavement. From the areaway below a light streamed out from the kitchen, and he saw Thomas Carlyle, daintily lifting his paws as he surveyed his sodden world.

Forsythe looked down at him.

"Not a good night for love, Tom," he said. "Better stay home for once."

Tom, however, disdained him and, tail high in the air, moved away.

At first, Forsythe had no definite objective. It was not until he was well up Lexington Avenue that he decided to go on. The exercise plus the fresh air had their usual effect, and he began to rationalize his situation. Why get into what Margery would have called a tizzy because ten years ago a young girl with eyes like stars and fabulous lashes had gone to her first dance in a badly fitted dress, and had remembered him? Or had put her head on his desk that day and wept for her dead brother? And why in the name of heaven believe that her husband was potentially a deliberate, cold-blooded murderer?

He swung along briskly. The rain had swept the streets clean and even the air had lost its customary mixture of smoke and fog. He liked New York at night, the lights in the tall buildings where some late office worker or cleaning woman was busy; the shop windows extravagantly showing their prodigality of clothing, of food, of the vast resources of the country, as against the poverty of the Europe he had left after the war. But this last made him uncomfortable.

The poor devils, he thought, and was surprised to find that he had reached the street which housed the Colliers. He stopped at the corner. Why go on? She was certainly all right. Sheer curiosity, however, decided him in the end, and he found the number only a block or two from the East River. The building was a small apartment of the walk-up type, but with a smartly painted red door and a general effect of being rather better than its neighbors.

On the ground floor the tenants were having a party. One of the windows was partly raised, and he could hear laughter and the clinking of glasses. But as there was no one in sight on the street he stepped into the foyer and looked at the cards above the bells.

The first floor was *Kerr, Joseph H*. The second, neatly typed, was the Colliers. The third merely said bluntly *Jamison*, and the fourth was evidently empty.

He was still looking at the names when a small, middle-aged man, neatly dressed and carrying an

27

umbrella, stepped in from the street.

"Looking for somebody?" he inquired pleasantly.

Forsythe had to think fast.

"I was trying to locate a family named Blake," he said. "The William Blakes."

The stranger stepped forward and peered nearsightedly at the board.

"Don't see them," he said. "They may have moved out. The fourth floor's empty. I've only moved onto the third floor a week or so ago. Name's Jamison. That's my card there."

"I see. Well, thanks, Mr. Jamison. It isn't important anyhow. I was just taking a walk. I can call Blake in the morning."

He was about to leave when a door slammed above and someone started down the stairs. Forsythe had only time to turn his back when Fred Collier reached the foyer. He brushed roughly past the two men and out into the street, and Mr. Jamison looked annoyed.

"That's my only objection to this place," he said. "The man who just went out. He lives just below me, and when he's drunk he's nasty. The floors are thin, and I can hear him quarreling with his wife night after night. Bellows like a bull. I'm afraid he'll hurt her some day. Nice young woman, too."

Forsythe had a wild impulse to take advantage of Collier's absence to try to see Anne, but Mr. Jamison showed no inclination to move.

"I'm a bachelor," he said. "I have no family left, so I go to the movies most evenings. They fill in the time." He looked up at Forsythe. "I was wondering—if you're only taking a walk, perhaps you'd have a drink with me. The stairs are bad, but I'm only two flights up."

"I might at that," Forsythe agreed, anxious to stay in the building if possible. "Sure you want me?"

"My dear boy, if you have ever lived alone you realize what a visitor means."

The apartment when they reached it turned out to be rather bare but extremely neat. Forsythe learned that all in the building were the same, a small living-room, three bedrooms, a kitchen with a dinette, and a bath.

"A little large for me, of course," Jamison explained, bringing ice from the kitchen, "but you know how things are today. Anyhow, it will look better, too, when I bring in my books. I'm waiting to have the shelves built."

He was a talkative little man. He said he was a bookkeeper for a real estate company downtown, and seemed not to notice Forsythe's abtraction. Forsythe was listening for sounds from the floor below, and finally they came. The door banged again, and he could hear Collier's voice raised, although not what he said.

"You see what I mean," said Jamison. "He's been out for a drink or two and probably brought a bottle back with him. Now he'll be really ugly."

Forsythe sat listening. He could see Anne in the room below, watching the great hulking brute who was her husband, but if she spoke at all he did not hear her.

"Probably locked in her own room," said Mr. Jamison, an ear cocked to the floor. "The superintendent says they don't live together. Maybe things would be better if they did. No peacemaker like a pillow," he said, and gave a cackling laugh.

All at once Forsythe disliked the little man, with his prying and spying, and disliked him intensely. He got up abruptly.

"Well, thanks a lot," he said. "My sister will wonder what's become of me. That was good Scotch,

Mr. Jamison."

Jamison smiled.

"I don't drink much, but Dawson's *is* a good Scotch. By the way, I don't think I know your name."

"Wade," said Forsythe, and got out as fast as he could. He would have stopped on the second floor on his way out, but Jamison was seeing him off from his landing. There was nothing to do but go on and out.

He slept badly that night, but when he reached the office the next morning he found Miss Potter waiting for him.

"Found the agent," she said, placing a neatly typed memorandum in front of him. "Got it from some clerk or other at the sponsor's. It's a cereal company, and her name's Simmons. Martha Simmons. That's her address there. She was kind of upset when I called her. Said she had an ironclad contract, so just to make it interesting I said there wasn't such a thing. She almost bit the telephone."

"Thanks, Potter," he said. "That's fine. I'll ring for you a little later. If a message comes for me put it through, will you?"

When it did come, however, at eleven o'clock, it was disappointing. Anne's voice was tense and hurried.

"Listen, Wade," she said. "I'm at the grocer's. Fred's outside, watching for me. I've just seen him. I don't dare to come to your office today."

He swallowed his disappointment.

"It's important. I needn't tell you that. But it's more important to know that you're all right."

"Of course I'm all right," she said, a little wearily. "He was bad last night, but he still doesn't know anything. He found my typewriter, so he thinks I'm writing a book. And he's afraid I'm getting a divorce.

I'll come as soon as I can, Wade."

He worked on the tax return of the corporation the rest of the morning, indicating among other things that its salesmen itemize their expense sheets. His heart was not in it, however, and after a quick lunch he went to the address Miss Potter had given him for the Simmons woman. It was in a midtown office building, and he found her name on the directory. Her offices were on the seventh floor, a small anteroom with a covered typewriter which looked as though it had not been used lately, and beyond it a somewhat larger room with a desk, a safe, a row of steel files, and two or three plain chairs.

Miss Simmons was behind the desk. A carton, which had contained coffee, and crumbs and waxed paper indicated that she had just finished a frugal meal, and he felt rather puzzled. After all, the agent's percentage of the Jessica Blake income over the years must have been substantial, but there was no evidence of it here, nor in the woman herself. Martha Simmons was a woman in her late thirties, rather slovenly in appearance but with a pair of very sharp eyes. She surveyed him without interest until he gave her his card.

"A lawyer!" she said. "What on earth have *I* done?"

He smiled.

"Perhaps you know that better than I do," he said pleasantly. "Personally I doubt if you've done anything actionable, but it makes things rather confusing. It's the Jessica Blake matter, Miss Simmons."

She gave him a hard stare.

"So what about it?" she said, her voice cold. "It's the way she wanted it. I told her at the start it was silly. She had some idea of making a man out of that

31

hulk she married, as if even the Creator could do that! He's a total loss, if you ask me." Then she brightened somewhat. "Don't tell me she's come to her senses and is getting rid of him."

"I don't know about that," he said. "Actually, she wants to make a will."

She was jolted by this, profoundly shocked. She went pale.

"A will? For God's sake, why a will?"

"She didn't say, but I understand she has earned a rather large sum from her program." And when she merely nodded: "You see, there's a slight complication. The money was deposited under a pseudonym. That's a fact, isn't it?"

She had pulled herself together somewhat, although she was still uneasy.

"I've told you she wanted it that way. I can show you the bank deposit receipts if you like."

She got up and going to a steel file brought out a bulging folder.

"She's made plenty," she said dryly, and shoved it across the desk to him. The receipts were there, made to the account of Jessica Blake, and she watched him as he went over them.

"She left them here," she said. "Afraid her husband would find them. I wish to high heaven he'd never come back from the war."

He smiled, remembering the times he had wished the same thing.

"Well, that's out of our hands," he said. "The thing to do now is a simple matter of identification. I expected her today but she couldn't come. She says the checks were made out by you and deposited to the Blake account, so we'll need you, of course, at the bank."

She nodded dully.

"Does this mean the end of the program?" she asked.

"I don't see why. It's up to her, of course. I gather she's rather tired of it."

Her mind, however, seemed to be far away.

"Why does she want a will? she asked. "Is she afraid of Fred Collier?"

"Most people with a hundred thousand dollars or more have wills, Miss Simmons."

"I suppose so," she said, her voice bitter. "Isn't it just my luck?"

"I don't see how a will affects you."

"I'm not talking about the will," she said hastily. "She's my best account, what with television and everything else. And it's a success, Mr. Forsythe. It's made money for years and it still goes on. What's the matter with her? Why not just leave Collier, if she's afraid he'll kill her?"

Forsythe managed a thin smile.

"I don't think it will come to that. Has he ever been here, Miss Simmons? Is there any way he could know what she's been doing?"

"Not from me," she said promptly. "Her identity is the best-kept secret in radio. She never goes to a rehearsal, she never comes here. Do you know where I meet her, Mr. Forsythe? In Central Park. Snow or rain, cold or hot, that's where I meet her. When the kid was young she brought the scripts in his pram, and believe me, one or two were wet in those days! She'd pretend to show him to me, and I'd sneak them into my muff, or what have you. Tie that if you can."

"It sounds unusual."

"Unusual! It's crazy. Don't think I just sit here and collect my commission. Know anything about radio? She's good, but who cuts if the script's too long? Who sits at rehearsal day after day? I do, Mr. Forsythe.

I do."

He felt rather sorry for her as he left. He thought his call had been a considerable shock to her, although he could not imagine why. The bank deposit receipts were in order. What really startled him, however, was the amount of money at stake, enough incentive for any crime. Even murder.

He went back to his office to work that afternoon, but his feeling of apprehension remained. Suppose he went to the police? They would laugh at him, of course. Unless they had something on Collier. Anne had started to say something about his business of secondhand cars, and then checked herself. She had said, "Sometimes I wonder—" Wonder what? Was she afraid he dealt in stolen automobiles, had them painted and with new license plates shipped them out of town? Collier had done something like that in France and narrowly escaped court-martial for it.

It was unfortunate, when he finally settled down, that he opened the red-bound book at a section entitled *Base Period Catastrophe*.

3

He dined out that evening, a typical Park Avenue dinner party, the hour set for eight and not all the guests arriving until almost an hour later. By that time he had more to drink than he wanted. And, for the first time in his life, much more than he wanted of chattering young women who rose apparently unclothed above the top of the long table. He was frantically bored as the meal went on, and for some reason increasingly apprehensive.

Over coffee and liqueurs and hot political talk with the other men after dinner he tried to think of some way to escape the inevitable bridge or canasta. And he was still debating this when a butler leaned over his shoulder.

"Sorry to disturb you, sir, but you are wanted on the telephone. Your sister, she says."

Only a real emergency would make Margery call him at such a time, and he never doubted what it was. He was alternately hot and cold as he slid quietly out of the diningroom and to the telephone in the library. But Margery's voice was calm.

"It isn't what you think, Wade," she said. "But the doctor said she had a couple of letters in her hand when she fell. One of them was to you. She isn't badly hurt, but he thought you might want to know. Her husband's out and they can't locate him."

"Where did she fall? And how?" He hardly recognized his own voice.

"Apparently down the stairs. She's badly shaken up, but that's all. Nothing's broken."

"Collier's not there?"

"No. She says he left before it happened. She doesn't know where he is." She hesitated. "I had the impression from the doctor that she wants to see you or I wouldn't have called."

He made a brief apology to his hostess and five minutes later was in a cab. He was puzzled. If Collier was gone when she fell it seemed to let him out of it. His distrust of the man was so great, however, that he did not relax. Collier could have pretended to go and been waiting somewhere in the dark upper hall. It was not like her to fall, he thought. She moved lightly and easily, even gracefully, and he remembered the long straight flight of stairs and shivered.

He found the superintendent on the pavement waiting for him, a stockily built man, wearing an old gray sweater and a truculent expression.

"I'm Hellinger," he said. "The doc thought you'd probably be along. And don't think she's got any grounds for a lawsuit against this building, Mr. Forsythe. She fell because she had a damned good reason to."

"You mean she was pushed?"

"Worse than that," said the superintendent. "Come inside and I'll show you something."

What he had to show was a longish piece of wire, thin but strong. He grinned as Forsythe examined it.

"Stretched across the top of the stairs," he said. "It was sure tight. Fellow on the third floor above heard her fall and almost broke his own neck on it when he ran down. Doc's with him now. Soon as I let you in I'm going out to get him some aspirin."

Forsythe handed back the wire.

36

"I understand her husband was gone when it happened," he said.

Hellinger shrugged.

"Nothing to prevent him leaving a little souvenir behind him, was there? Maybe he knew she was going out soon as he left. She had a couple of letters when she fell, one to her boy, the other to you. Old trick, of course, the wire. Had a kid here once almost killed his mother that way."

He left, presumably to get Mr. Jamison's aspirin, and Forsythe slowly climbed the stairs. Somehow, he thought, he must get her away from the place, to Connecticut, to a hotel, even to his own house and Margery. It was clear, however, as soon as he saw her that she could not be moved very soon.

She was lying prostrate in her bed and she turned her head slowly and painfully when she heard him.

"Sorry, Wade,", she said. "I twisted my neck and I ache all over. What a fool thing to do anyhow! I've gone down those stairs for years and never even stumbled."

"That's what you did? Just stumbled?"

She smiled faintly.

"Nobody pushed me, if that's what you mean. Fred had gone out. He was delivering a car somewhere in New Jersey, so don't think he did it. He couldn't have."

He did not mention the wire. He drew a chair beside the bed and, sitting down, took one of her hands.

"I'm sorry, Anne," he said. "Sorry and glad it's no worse. You might have killed yourself. But why were you writing me? the doctor saw the letters."

"Because I couldn't use the phone. Fred stayed here all day. So I pretended to write little Billy, and wrote you, too. I didn't know he was going out. He didn't

37

either, but he got a phone call and had to. He threatened to lock me in my room, but I'd hidden the key."

"Why? What excuse did he give for a thing like that?"

She moved wearily.

"He knows I saw you, and he's worried about a divorce. I don't think he knows about the other matter. That's what I wrote you about, that I'd have to wait about the will. He can't watch me forever. And to tell Martha Simmons I'm not renewing my contract. I'm sorry for her, but what else can I do?"

What could he do, either, he thought resentfully. Tell her her husband was trying to kill her? That he had tried it tonight, and would certainly try it again? He was strongly tempted, but she had already been badly shocked. Her face was colorless and she was clearly in pain. Her mind was entirely clear, however.

"I've been thinking," she said. "Suppose I'd broken my neck, and no will? He'd get it all, wouldn't he?"

"But you didn't, my dear."

"Why can't you draw one now?" she asked feverishly. "A holograph, if that's what you call it. Or a real will. I can sign it, and the superintendent, Mike Hellinger, can witness it. I think the doctor's coming back, too. The man upstairs fell trying to get to me, and he's up there with him."

Forsythe did not like the idea. A will was a serious matter, especially with so much at stake. It would go to probate. Judges would examine it, in case of a contest. The fact that she was badly shocked, too, might operate against it. But he felt helpless against the pleading in her face. Finally, at the desk in the living-room, he made a rough draft and was carrying it in to read to her when the hall door opened. It was Collier, astonished first, and then ugly and menacing.

"Well, for God's sake!" he said thickly. "If it ain't Forsythe! What do you think you're doing here?"

"If you want the exact facts," Forsythe said, "I'm doing some legal work for your wife. After tonight I think she needs it."

"If you're talking about a divorce, she's not getting one."

"That's hardly up to you, is it?"

"Why, you young bastard, I'll knock the hell out of you."

In the next room Anne was sitting up in bed.

"Stop it, Fred," she called sharply. "I sent for him. Don't be a fool. You're only making trouble for yourself."

Fred, however, only grinned.

"Always hated your guts," he said, "didn't I, Forsythe? Almost got me court-martialed, didn't you? Why, you—I'll smash that good-looking face of yours to hell and gone!"

He made a sudden lunge, but Forsythe countered quickly. He had a certain advantage. Collier had not only had a few drinks. He was also softer than in the war years. But he was still a big man, with long arms and his first blow landed on Forsythe's jaw and almost knocked him off his feet. It did throw him over the sharp edge of a table, which knocked the breath out of him. But his training in the Marines came to his aid. He recovered in time, and the fight was almost a draw, with chairs and a small table overturned, when at last Forsythe got in a hard blow to Collier's chin and he was out like a light.

Only then did he realize there was an audience. Hellinger, the superintendent, and an elderly man carrying a bag were in the doorway, and both of them were looking gratified.

Forsythe was panting, but he turned and called to Anne in the next room.

"Don't worry. He'll be all right. Just knocked out."

The doctor had put down his bag and was stooping over Collier.

"Nice work," he told Forsythe. "Drunk, I suppose? He'll give you no trouble for a while."

He went in and spoke to Anne.

"You've had quite a jolt," he said, "but you're lucky. No bones broken."

"What about Mr. Jamison?" she asked.

"Making the devil of a fuss. Says he's sprained his leg. Maybe he did. Claims he always said the stairs weren't safe."

When he came back the three men picked up the still unconscious Collier and dumped him on the bed. Then Hellinger took the doorkey and locked him in.

"That'll hold the murdering devil," he said with a grin. "Want me to call the cops, mister?"

Forsythe shook his head, which was unfortunate as he had suffered some certain damages himself. He felt dizzy and sat down, with a vision of Miss Potter at the office reading her morning paper and coming across his name as having been involved in a brawl. As well as his hostess of that evening, and the thousand and one people an eligible single male in New York always knew.

"No police, thanks," he said. "But I'm staying. I knew the fellow in the war. Even jails don't hold him when he wants to get out."

Anne, however, was insistent.

"He'll be quiet now," she said. "He won't

remember much in the morning, and I don't need a nurse. I'll be all right, really."

Forsythe was reluctant to leave her, but Hellinger offered to keep an eye on the place, so he finally agreed. In the hall, however, he asked for the piece of wire and was given it rather grudgingly.

"If that fellow upstairs makes trouble, I'll need it," Hellinger protested.

"You'll get it back," Forsythe promised. "I only want it for a few hours."

He wasn't quite sure himself why he had asked for it except that it had been intended to kill Anne. Nevertheless, he rolled it up and put it in his trousers pocket.

On his way out he found the Kerrs waiting in the hall. Both of them were in dressing-gowns over nightclothes, and both stared at him unbelievingly.

"Oh, brother!" the man breathed. "That must have been something!"

For the first time Forsythe stopped to take inventory of his condition. His black dress tie was missing entirely, and one sleeve of his jacket was hanging loose from the shoulder. What with one eye swelling rapidly and a split lip which had bled down his shirt front he realized he cut a rather sorry figure. Also that Mrs. Kerr was trying hard not to laugh.

"I—I'm sorry," she gasped. "Can I—can I pin up your sleeve?"

"Thanks," he said politely but with care, because of the lip. "I have my overcoat. Anything you know about tonight?"

Kerr was a tall thin boyish-looking individual, probably in his mid-thirties, with a pencil mustache and a conspicuous Adam's apple which moved up and down as he spoke. His wife, however, was attractive, in spite of the cold cream on her face. It

41

was Kerr who answered.

"Only that Collier came home and raised hell, according to Mike Hellinger," he said.

"Was either of you at home when his wife fell down the stairs? She had rather a nasty fall."

He suspected Hellinger had told them about the wire, for he was aware of a quick glance between them.

"Went to the movies," Kerr said. "Only been home an hour or so. Those stairs are bad, mister. That's why we live down here."

Forsythe said good night and took a taxi home. In the cab he tried to rationalize the situation. Men did not usually murder their wives to prevent their getting a divorce. If Collier had actually placed the wire on the stairs, it looked as thought he knew about Anne's money. It was possible, of course, remembering what Martha Simmons had said about Central Park.

If he had followed Anne there and seen her meet the Simmons woman, what was easier than to trace the agent to her office? And Martha Simmons had been scared that day when he visited her. Why? Suppose she had told Collier the facts, and was now afraid for Anne as well as her program? She had been badly frightened when he talked to her. He realized that now.

Margery, of course, was waiting for him when he got home. All he wanted was a hot shower for his aching muscles and to get to bed, but she took one look at him, opened her mouth to yelp, thought better of it, and dashed to her bathroom. When—a half hour later and he was smelling strongly of iodine and witch hazel—she stood beside his bed and waited, he abandoned the idea of a taxi accident.

"All right," he said. "I guess you're entitled to it. I

42

had quite a scrap with Collier."

"So I suppose. I hope you killed him."

"I did my feeble best. He'll wake up sooner or later, and he won't feel too good."

He did not go to the office Thursday morning. As a matter of fact he did not go anywhere. He lay in bed with a piece of expensive sirloin steak on his eye, and took a considerable amount of aspirin. But after a lunch he had difficulty in eating, and in spite of Margery's protests, he got up and dressed, trying not to see his face while he shaved.

To his fury his dinner jacket and the piece of wire were missing, and he shouted with rage.

"Where's my coat?" he bellowed down the stairs.

"It's gone to the tailor's," Margery's voice came back. "What did you expect?"

"Where's the piece of wire I had in the pocket?"

"Oh, that? I threw it out. Was it worth anything?"

He did not say. He was practically beyond speech, and his temper was not improved by the necessity of searching the big cans in the areaway. A group of small boys watched him attentively from above while he dug, evincing extreme interest.

"Do that for a dime, mister," one offered. "What you looking for?"

The face he turned up to them was so horrifying that they disappeared. The wire, of course, was at the very bottom of the can, but finally he found it. He rolled it up in a pocket and stopped a passing cab.

"Know where Police headquarters is?" he said. "On Centre Street?"

The cabby gave him a long look.

"What's the use of scaring them to death down there?" he said. "Better stop at a drugstore and get an eye patch."

He did so, and it was in this semidisguise that at

Centre Street he asked for a detective on Homicide he had known vaguely in the Marine Corps. His name was Close, and Forsythe found him in a small bare office with only a desk and a couple of chairs in it. Close got up as he entered.

"Afternoon," he said. "Anything I can do for you?" Then he stared. "Good God, it's Forsythe, isn't it? What the hell happened to you? Lost an eye?"

"That's what I came to talk about," Forsythe said, and sat down rather carefully. "The eye doesn't matter. I've still got it. I've been in a fight, that's all. But I've a story to tell, if you have the time."

Close eyed him.

"I'm Homicide," he said. "Is this murder you're going to talk about?"

"As near as can be. It's about a man who intends to kill his wife, if that interests you."

"Not exactly my pigeon," Close said, and took the cigarette he was offered. "I wait until the job's done as a rule. How do you know he wants to kill her? Banged her up some, eh? why don't you go to your precinct fellows? That's their stuff."

For an answer Forsythe hauled the strip of wire out of his pocket and laid it on the desk. Close picked it up and examined it.

"That was fastened across the top of a pretty steep flight of stairs last night," Forsythe said. "He'd gone out, the husband, but he knew she was going to mail some letters as soon as he left. She fell over it and almost broke her neck."

"I see," Close said thoughtfully. "Just why does he want her out of the way?"

"Because she's worth a good bit of money, and she doesn't want him to have it. It was to go in trust for her son, and I was about to draw a will to that effect when this happened."

44

Close was definitely interested now. He sat back smoking while Forsythe told the story. His interest increased when he learned about the radio program.

"I know it," he said. "Any time I get some hours off to sleep my wife's listening to the damn thing. So the girl who writes it is the one you're talking about!"

"Yes, although she uses a pen name. Her husband is Wilfred Collier. He sells secondhand cars, I believe."

"Collier, eh?" He picked up the telephone and asked for the Automobile Squad room. "Look," he said, and when someone answered, "put Joe Ellis on, will you, if he's there."

Ellis was there, and Close settled back in his chair.

"Remember Fred Collier, Joe?" he said. "Well, what have you got on him lately? Yeah, I know he's slippery. But what's new, if anything?"

When he hung up he grinned at Forsythe.

"Nothing new," he said. "Collier's been skating on thin ice for years. They're pretty sure he's mixed up with the stolen car racket. You know, get the car, use a paint sprayer, put some license tags on it and get it out of town. They know a lot about him, but they can't prove anything. Bad actor, too. Beat up one of his drivers and almost killed him. They'd have had him then, but the guy wouldn't talk."

But it was when Forsythe told him the amount at stake in the Gotham Trust that he really sat up and took notice.

"Great Scott," he said. "Is that the way they pay for that stuff? While I go out and risk my neck for a pittance, if that? It makes you wonder."

Nevertheless, he promised to keep an eye on the situation. Maybe the Automobile Squad could pick up Collier and hold him for a while. He suggested, too, that Forsythe get Anne to Connecticut as soon as

45

she could get about, and Forsythe felt distinctly better as he left. Better only mentally, that is. For he had been having a sharp pain in his side since he hit the table the night before, and to his horror it turned out to be a broken rib.

Saturday morning, strapped with adhesives, he dressed and went down to breakfast. There had been no word from Anne, but the day before he had talked to Hellinger, who said that she was all right and that Collier had disappeared the morning after the trouble and not come back.

As Margery always breakfasted in bed, he was alone in the basement dining-room, except for Thomas Carlyle who apparently had a hang-over and ignored his breakfast. Over his crisp bacon and eggs, and with a coffee cup in his hand, he glanced at the headlines in the paper. So far as he could see, the world was in a mess and getting messier, so he turned it over and looked idly down the page. Then he stiffened.

Anne Collier had shot and killed her husband the night before, and had tried to kill herself.

4

He read it twice before it really registered. The story was short. According to the paper, a man named Jamison in the apartment above had heard Fred Collier shouting at his wife, and a moment later had heard two shots. Jamison, however, had been badly crippled by a fall a day or so before, and it was thus some time before he managed to get down the stairs and notify the superintendent, Michael Hellinger.

It was Hellinger who discovered the tradegy. A doctor, called immediately, said that Collier had been shot in the back of the head and died immediately. The attempt at suicide on the part of the wife, however, had failed. She had been taken to a hospital, where she was under police guard. She was still unconscious and had made no statement.

Forsythe was stunned. Not Anne. Not Bill Blake's little sister. Not the girl who had kissed him only a few days before because he was going to help her. It wasn't possible. The police were crazy. Collier had tried to kill her, and then had killed himself. He got up furiously and hurried out of the house.

Being a Saturday his office was closed, so by nine o'clock that morning he was at the hospital. There he met the usual obstruction, but a ten-dollar bill and a friendly orderly got him at last to the floor where Anne had been taken. There were two men outside the door of her room. A weary-looking officer in

47

uniform was sitting in a chair, and a middle-aged detective was standing beside him. It was a moment before he recognized Close.

In his anger he was about to confront the detective, but as he approached, a doctor in a long white coat came out, closing the door behind him, and Close halted him.

"How about it, doc?" he said. "Going to live?"

The doctor yawned. He also looked as though he had been up all night.

"She's still in shock," he said. "If it means anything to you, she's got a pentrating wound in the left shoulder above the clavicle, but she missed both the subclavian artery and vein."

"Put in plain language, that means she's going to live?"

"Probably. Who knows?"

Then Close saw Forsythe and grinned.

"If this is your girl friend you sort of got it in reverse, didn't you?" he said. "She killed him, all right. Open-and-shut case. Maybe she can prove self-defense, but I doubt it. It looks pretty deliberate. Not that he's any loss," he added.

"What do you mean, open and shut?" Forsythe said indignantly. "Anybody see her do it?"

"Nothing to it. Gun beside her on the floor, and her husband dead ten feet away!"

"No chance he did it, then?"

"Not with a bullet from a thirty-eight in the back of his head, son. He never knew what hit him."

The doctor, looking interested, was standing by. Forsythe appealed to him.

"Just what are her chances?" he asked. "She's a friend of mine and if there's anything I can do—"

"We've operated. That's about all I can tell you. We got the bullet out. The rest is up to her. But apparently she struck her head on an iron doorstop when she fell. Seems to have considerable concussion."

He moved away, stethoscope trailing from the pocket of his coat, and the officer in uniform got up stiffly, said he was going to the men's room, and left. Forsythe found himself alone with Close, who seemed rather amused.

"Never know what a woman will do, do you?" he observed. "Looks like a nice girl, too. If she lives she can probably plead self-defense. Get off with a dozen years or so."

Forsythe's hands shook as he took a cigarette and lit it.

"I don't believe it," he said stubbornly. "She would never do a thing like this. Never. Is she conscious?"

"You heard the doc. She's had a concussion, she's had an anesthetic, and she's probably full of dope. Also she's a mighty sick girl, Forsythe. And maybe that's not a bad thing."

Forsythe knew what he meant. He felt a cold anger sweep over him.

"Just remember something, Close," he said. "I came to you with this story two or three days ago. Maybe if you'd been interested all this wouldn't have happened."

"What does that mean?" Close said shortly. "It wasn't my case then. It is now. As a matter of fact the Automobile Squad tried to pick up Collier that day, but he'd disappeared."

"He came home, didn't he?"

"All right. All right. Somebody slipped, but his wife didn't."

"I want to see her."

"The hell you do. Nobody's seeing her."

"I want to be sure it's Anne Collier in there," Forsythe said stubbornly. "How do you know it is? I advised her to go to her aunt in Connecticut. Possibly she's there now."

"She's been identified by Hellinger, the superintendent." But seeing Forsythe's face he moved aside. "All right," he said, "I'll give you thirty seconds."

It took less than that. It was Anne, a slim flat unconscious figure on the high hospital bed, with a nurse beside her taking her pulse, and the edge of a surgical bandage on her left shoulder showing above the blanket. Neither man spoke until they were in the hall again, Forsythe because he could not. Close eyed him.

"It's pretty early, but you need a drink, fellah," he said, not unkindly. "My car's outside. I'll buy you one."

Not until Forsythe had downed a straight Scotch at a near-by bar did Close say anything more to him. Then: "Just what's your interest in this case, Forsythe? You're taking it pretty hard, aren't you?"

"She's my client, and her brother was a friend of mine. Killed in the war."

"You said she came to you about a will?"

Forsythe nodded. "She knew she was in danger if he learned about the bank account."

"So you think he did learn?"

"Hell, I don't know and I don't care. Suppose she did kill him? Maybe a girl can be driven to desperation and do a thing like that. But look, Close, she had a kid she's crazy about. Why try to kill herself?"

"When she realized what she'd done—"

"Don't give me that! If he threatened her with a gun, she had a clear out, didn't she? He was a bad actor and she knew it."

"Did she know about the wire on the stairs?"

"I didn't tell her. It's possible Hellinger did. It's not likely it was Jamison. He doesn't know her."

"Jamison? The fellow who raised the alarm?"

"Yes. He lives on the floor above. The night Anne fell he ran down and got caught on the wire himself. He was pretty well banged up. I gather he still is."

But they were getting nowhere. Close looked at his watch.

"Got to go," he said. "The lab should have compared both bullets by now. Not that there's any doubt about them. Both from the same gun, a thirty-eight automatic. It belonged to him. The woman who comes in to clean has seen it in a drawer there."

"What about prints on it?" Forsythe asked.

"Don't get prints on these checkered wood grips," Close said. "Trigger smeared, but the laboratory has it. May get something. Don't really need it, of course."

Quite suddenly Forsythe was angry again. His face reddened and he had difficulty in keeping his hands off the detective with his complacent assurance.

"The fellow was a bastard," he said furiously. "And it might interest you to know that this woman you're so damned ready to railroad to the chair is a lady, and I'd like to bet she's never fired a gun in her life."

Close eyed him warily.

"I'm railroading nobody," he said. "This is my job. But even the best families slip up now and then. And keep your fists down. I'm wearing a new suit."

Forsythe felt foolish. It was silly to antagonize this man, and also it occurred to him that there was something he ought to do.

"Sorry," he said apologetically. "I guess I'm excited! There's another thing, too. She has this aunt

51

somewhere in Connecticut. Someone ought to see her. Only I don't know where she lives. I think it's back in the country, so she may not know what's happened."

"Know any way to reach her?"

"Maybe, in the apartment itself. She would write, I suppose."

Close grunted, then without further words he put Forsythe in his car and drove to the apartment. As in the hospital, there was a patrolman on guard outside the Collier door, and to his evident relief Close let him go.

"I'll give the key to the superintendent, O'Hara," he said. "We're finished here. Nothing doing, I suppose?"

O'Hara grinned.

"Not since the reporters left," he said. "One of them left a telephone message for you. Said to call some place in Connecticut."

Close took it and read it aloud.

" 'Old dame called up from this number. Didn't tell her anything, as not responsible for heart attacks in the aged.' "

"Know who left his, O'Hara?"

"*Daily News* man, I think. Don't know his name."

Inside, the apartment was spotlessly neat, except for the living-room, where bloodstains had turned brown on the carpet, where print powder was dusted here and there, and used flash bulbs from the camerman littered the floor.

Forsythe felt sickened, but Close had no such scruples.

"Not a bad place," he said. "Kept it nice, didn't she?"

"I said she was a lady," Forsythe said gruffly. "She lived like one."

But everything bore out Close's statement, even the chalk marks indicating the location of the ejected shells where Anne Collier's body had lain. Forsythe stared about him, remembering the last time he had seen her. Despite the evidence in front of him, it was impossible to believe that she had killed her husband and shot herself. It was impossible to believe the frightened girl of only a few days before had turned into a desperate woman who was willing to leave her young son alone in the world. It was wrong. All wrong. Fred Collier might have killed her, but she had never killed him.

"It works out like this," Close said. "They were quarreling, or he was. Maybe he had a gun. We don't know. Maybe he threatened her. We don't know that, either. But perhaps he put it down and turned his back, and she got hold of it. Anyhow the safety was off, so somebody meant trouble. You can be sure the defense will use that."

Forsythe tried to control himself, and for fear of the adrenalin which was making him shake with fury he stalked to the kitchen. He was still standing there when the detective followed him.

"You wanted to come here," he said. "It's your idea. For God's sake, what's the matter?"

Forsythe was staring at the kitchen table.

"Perhaps you'll tell me," he said, "why a woman prepares to fix herself a glass of hot milk to make her sleep and then leaves it to murder her husband? Look at this!"

There was an empty glass on the table, and on the stove a small pan with the remnants of what had been boiled milk. Close looked slightly shaken.

"How do you know when she did all this?" he asked. "It was eleven o'clock when the shots were fired."

53

"Look around you," Forsythe said impatiently. "Dinner was over. The place was cleaned up. And would she sit quietly by and let that milk pan boil dry? Don't be a fool, Close. Look where she was found, by the door there. It's my guess she was in the kitchen when it happened, and she came running in, to be shot herself."

"And so what?" Close said. "It's a guess. That's all."

"Was the hall door locked?"

"I wouldn't know. The squad car got here first. Maybe the super let them in."

"And maybe not. Let's get him."

Hellinger, when he arrived, said he had not had to admit police to the Collier apartment. The door had been closed but not locked. He had taken the officers up himself. And the little pan of milk had been boiling at the time. He had shut off the gas himself. Had to watch those stoves. They could raise hell. But he seemed uneasy while he was talking, and Forsythe had a strong feeling that he was not telling all he knew. He was not the same man who had shown him the wire only a couple of days before.

He said nothing, however, and it was clear Close had lost some of his assurance when Hellinger left. He eyed Forsythe soberly.

"Maybe you got something, at that," he said. "But who the devil stood to gain by shooting both of them? Let's go over that story of yours again, about the will and so on. Maybe there's a hole in it."

There seemed to be no hole, however. Forsythe wearily repeated what he knew, Anne's fear of her husband, the radio scripts, the accumulation of the money—to be left to her son—and the way it had been deposited. Close looked skeptical at this last.

"Damn-fool way to do business," he said. "Doesn't

54

help her any, though, that I can see. Never trust a woman when it comes to money. Well, I guess that's all, isn't it?"

"If you'll agree there's a reasonable doubt about her guilt, yes."

"Didn't by any chance do it yourself, did you, Forsythe?"

Sheer shock kept Forsythe still. Then: "Why would I?" he asked. "And her? Do you think I would try to kill her?"

"Suppose you're shooting at Collier and she gets in the way?" Close said nonchalantly. "Looks to me as if you knew her better than you claim. That's all. Not in love with her, were you?"

"I told you—" Forsythe began violently, but Close put up a protesting hand.

"All right, all right," he said. "I'm not accusing you. I keep forgetting that you need another hundred thousand about as much as I need an extra leg. Somebody killed Collier, that's all. If she didn't, who did?" He jerked at his hat. "Sorry to upset you. Apologies and all that. But you've laid yourself wide open, old man. What's the girl to you, if you've only seen her twice?"

"She's my client," Forsythe said, and felt himself flushing. "Also I think you're off on the wrong foot about this case. That's as good a reason as any. Mind if I stay? I'd like to be here if the aunt calls again."

Close nodded and jammed his hat down on his head. "Be seeing you," he said, "and give Hellinger the key when you leave."

Forsythe closed the door behind him, and stood still. All along he had hoped the apartment would tell him something, but outside of the milk pan he found nothing. The place was beautifully neat and well kept, but Anne's room was bare of the usual fripperies with which most women surround themselves. A bottle of cologne on the dresser, a silver comb, brush and mirror, and a jar of inexpensive face cream were her sole concessions to the amenities of living.

Life had been hard, he thought, for the seventeen-year-old girl he remembered, with her wide eyes and tender young mouth, and in an odd way he felt that her battle was now his. It was a long time since he had felt the tender pity which almost shook him. Poor brave little Anne, he thought, and touched the jar of cream gently.

Unconsciously he had been putting off the call to Connecticut, uncertain what to do. Now the shrill bell in that quiet place startled him.

"Is this Murray Hill 3-3861?" the operator asked.

"Yes."

"Danbury calling. Hold on, please."

A moment later a thin elderly voice was on the wire.

"Is that you, Anne?" it said.

"Anne's not here just now. Can I take the message?"

The voice stiffened slightly.

"This is Anne's aunt, Eliza Warrington," it said. "I've been trying to get her for hours. Will you have her call me?"

"Can't I give her the message?"

"Who are you?"

"Just a friend."

"Well, I—I really suppose there's no hurry. I'll call her later."

She hung up, leaving Forsythe with a sense of frustration. There had been urgency in her voice, controlled as it was, and he still had no address for her, except that she was near Danbury. But at least so far she did not know of the tragedy.

He left the apartment reluctantly. Downstairs Hellinger was waiting for the key. There was still something evasive about him, and Forsythe was convinced he knew more than he had told.

"What's wrong with you?" he asked menacingly. "Don't think you fooled me upstairs. Did you shoot those people?"

Hellinger gasped and went pale.

"No. For God's sake, Mr. Forsythe! Why should I? Collier was a nuisance but I liked the missus. What makes you say a thing like that?"

"Where were you when it happened?"

"I'd been out. I was just coming in when the third floor hobbled down the stairs. Scared to death, he was."

"Did you go up and look?"

"Not me, Mr. Forsythe. It wasn't my business, not with a gun loose in that apartment. I called the police."

"What about the Kerrs on the first floor?"

"They'd had a crowd in the night before. They said they were both asleep. Went to bed early."

"The shots didn't waken them?"

"They said something did. They didn't know what it was until they heard the police siren. They showed up then, all right."

Forsythe inspected the man. Whatever he was hiding, Forsythe thought it had nothing to do with the shootings. But he was still not satisfied.

"I'll check your story with Mr. Jamison," he said, and to Hellinger's obvious relief went up the stairs again.

On the third floor he rang the bell two or three times before it was answered. Then Jamison in pajamas opened the door a few inches. It was evidently on a chain.

"What the hell is it?" he demanded. "If you're police, I've told you all I know."

"I'm not police, Mr. Jamison. Don't you remember me?"

"Ah, Mr. Wade, aren't you? I'm not well, so I can't ask you in. What is it you want?"

He looked like a man who had had a shock. His color was bad, and Forsythe felt sorry for him.

"I don't want to bother you," he said. "You heard the shots, didn't you? Were they close together?"

"I guess so. Why?"

"I'm Mrs. Collier's lawyer. Naturally I'm interested. I imagine a suicide might wait a bit before—well, finishing the job."

Jamison attempted a pallid smile.

"I wouldn't know," he said. "I've never tried it."

He attempted to close the door, but Forsythe held it firmly.

"Just a moment," he said. "What happened when you finally got downstairs to raise the alarm?"

"I found Mike Hellinger coming in. He lives in the basement, and he was starting for it when I caught him. Now if you'll excuse me—"

Forsythe had released his hold on the door. Now it was closed, politely but firmly, and Forsythe made his way to the street. There was apparently nothing he could do for the time being. The thought of his own house, however, was revolting. He did not want to talk to Margery. He needed to think, to get out somewhere and try to arrange what few facts he had. He realized, too, that he was not conditioned to murder. He had never had a criminal case in his life. Like many young lawyers today, he found his practice largely a matter of taxes.

Yet he had certain data which might be important.

For one thing, he felt sure Anne's determination to make a will was involved, but how? The only beneficiary was to be her small son, unless there was something in her contract he did not know about. He found a phone book and called Martha Simmons, but no one answered, and at last he hung up in disgust. She had probably seen the morning paper, and was at home suffering from shock. Her home number, however, was not in the book.

Out on the pavement again he stood in a sort of desperation. It was useless to go back to the hospital, although the thought of Anne lying there hurt and defenseless was almost more than he could bear. Then he remembered the aunt. Eliza Warrington would have been in her confidence. She might know something. And obviously, when she called she had not heard the news.

He looked at his watch. It was still only eleven o'clock and Danbury was not too far away. Also it was not New York. It would not be hard to find her.

But Margery would worry. She read the morning paper carefully. He called her from the garage, and her voice sounded strained.

"Did she do it, Wade?"

"The police think she did."

"Is she—is she badly hurt?"

"She has a fair chance. That's all I know. Listen, Margery, there's something I don't understand about this. Hell, I don't understand any of it. Anyhow, I'm taking the car and going to the aunt in Danbury."

"Where the boy is?"

"Where the boy is," he said grimly. "Her name's Eliza Warrington, and she has a phone. Call me if anything turns up."

He never remembered the details of that trip. He liked to drive, although he seldom used the con-

59

vertible except for country week-ends or a golf game. That day, however, he drove with his foot hard down on the gas and an increasing sense of urgency he could not explain.

It was not until he turned off the Merritt Parkway that he realized he was being followed. A small black sedan kept behind him, always at a discreet distance, but try as he would he could not shake it off. Either Close really suspected him, after all, or he had finally thought of Eliza Warrington's telephone call and was sending a man to talk to her. In an attempt to see who was in the car he reached a curve and turned off onto a side road.

The sedan shot by, and to his utter amazement a woman was driving it. Not only that. The woman was Martha Simmons. As she passed him he saw she was driving with a set white face, and pushing the car to its limit.

In Danbury he lost her, however. Either he was luckier than she, or she had stopped for some purpose. In any event there was no sign of her when he located Eliza Warrington. She lived in a comfortable white frame house on the edge of town, and she herself answered the door. She was a smallish gray-haired woman with a pleasant tranquil face, although she looked puzzled when she saw him.

"Good morning," she said. "Or is it afternoon? I lose my sense of time when Billy's not here."

He stared at her blankly.

"The boy's not here?"

"Why no," she said, surprised. "Is there anything wrong? He's not sick, is he?"

"Do you know where he is?"

She made a small unhappy gesture.

"Perhaps you'd better come inside. I've been a little worried, but what could I do?"

She led him into a neat sitting-room with a wood fire, with a row of tin soldiers on the window sill and a blue-gray Persian cat on the hearth. She sat down in a rocking chair while he took a straight one, conscious of her keen eyes appraising him. He was relieved to see the morning paper still folded on a table, as though she had not yet read it.

"Just what *is* all this about Billy?" she said. "Why do you want to know about him?"

"I'm a lawyer, Miss Warrington. My name's Forsythe, and Mrs. Collier consulted me recently about a will. I'm afraid I am bringing you bad news. You see, she's in a hospital, rather badly hurt."

She stared at him, her small body rigid.

"Are you trying to tell me she's dying?"

"No," he said. "She has a very good chance, they tell me."

"Did that devil hurt her?"

"It's rather worse than that, Miss Warrington. Fred Collier is dead. I hoped you might be able to tell me something about him. Perhaps Anne has talked to you."

She did not speak. She merely stared at him with blank, incredulous eyes.

"Dead?" she said. "And you say Anne is in a hospital? Then where is Billy?"

5

She was badly shocked, and it took some time to get the story from her. Sometime after five o'clock on Thursday Fred Collier had driven to the house and demanded to see the boy. Billy was eating his supper, and Collier had gone to the dining-room to talk to him.

"He wasn't fond of his father," she said. "He was polite enough. He has very good manners. But when Fred said his mother wanted him to get him some new clothes he was willing enough. I tried to keep him until I called Anne, but while I was at the telephone Fred simply picked him up and carried him out to the car. When I finally got Anne she was upset. She hadn't sent for him at all. But she was glad she was going to see him. She's missed him dreadfully."

"I don't think he took him to her at all, Miss Warrington. There was no child there when the police—"

"The police! What about the police?"

He was obliged to tell her the story, the two shots, Collier dead on the floor, Anne badly hurt and suspected of the murder. She listened with dazed eyes.

"But what did he do with Billy?" she managed at last. "He must have hidden him somewhere to threaten her. It's the sort of thing he would do. Only, for heaven's sake, Mr. Forsythe, where is he? He's only six. He can't look after himself. If he's shut away somewhere—"

"Do you know about the radio program, Miss Warrington?"

"Yes. I listen to it sometimes."

"And that it's made your niece a great deal of money?"

She shook her head. Money evidently seemed unimportant to her just then.

"I wouldn't know about that," she said dully.

"The point is," he went on, trying to rouse her from what amounted to stupefaction, "she meant to make a will, leaving what amounts to a considerable sum to the boy, leaving her husband only what is legally necessary. It's possible he suspected that, and meant to use the boy as a lever; to hide him until he could get his hands on the money."

But he realized as he spoke that the police, if they learned about the child, might see in it the strongest possible motive for Anne's murdering her husband. If only he could prove a struggle, with Collier first shooting her and then Anne getting the gun and killing him—But there had been no struggle, no overturned chairs or upset tables. Even with his ears agog for whatever went on below, Mr. Jamison had not said there had been anything of the sort. Only Collier's loud, unpleasant voice.

Miss Warrington lay back in her chair and closed her eyes.

"If he told her about Billy, she killed him," she said drearily. "I don't believe in taking human life, but she had a right to."

"Why would she? Think a minute. He was probably the only one who knew where he'd taken the boy."

"Maybe she didn't stop to consider that. I guess I'd

63

better go to her." She got up slowly. She seemed to have aged in the last few minutes. "Would you mind taking me with you? I haven't a car."

He did not want her in New York where the police could get at her; not with her conviction that Anne had killed Collier because he had stolen the boy. He recognized a certain stubbornness in her. The murder was justified, she considered. Yet to leave her in Danbury was merely to postpone what would inevitably happen.

"Of course," he said, and lit a cigarette while she went to get ready. He realized his state of mind when he remembered it was his first cigarette since breakfast.

The boy was a problem, he thought. It was not a case of kidnaping; a father could not kidnap his own son. But with a man like Collier, who almost certainly had affiliations with the underworld, he might be hidden anywhere. Also Eliza Warrington was not going to sit back and wait for him to be found. Her first move, he considered, would be to the police. Somehow that had to be avoided.

She was not long. She called a neighbor, a tall gangling woman, who agreed to close the house and take the cat—whose name turned out to be Mehitabel—and who eyed Forsythe curiously, and shortly after she appeared with a small old-fashioned bag and got into the car.

There was no sign of Martha Simmons on the way back. What had she wanted in Danbury, he wondered. Had she, like himself, hoped Eliza Warrington could tell her something? And seeing his car had waited to see her until he was gone? It looked as though she was as puzzled as he was. In her offhand way, he had thought, she liked Anne, or at least admired her. Also the loss of the program would be a grave matter to her.

He drove back to town at a more deliberate pace. Both of them were largely silent. Eliza was sitting staring ahead, her jaw set and her eyes cold. In her plain black hat and ancient cloth coat she looked like the New Englander she was, intelligent, shrewd, and determined.

"Have you any plans when we reach town?" he asked.

"I can go to Anne's apartment, can't I?"

"I'm afraid not. The police have closed and locked it." For the first time she looked uncertain, and he pressed his advantage. "I live with my sister," he said. "We still have the family house. I'm sure she would like to have you."

She agreed rather unwillingly.

"I guess it would be all right if she'll let me pay my board," she said and she fell silent again until they were almost in Manhattan. Then out of a clear sky she asked, "Where was he shot? What part of him?"

"In the back of the head," he said uneasily.

She nodded.

"Anne never handled a gun, to my knowledge, but she sure as all get-out hit a bull's-eye that time."

"Now listen, Miss Warrington," he protested, "if you go to the police with that idea in your mind you may send her to the chair. And don't worry—they're smart. They'll get it out of you sooner or later."

Suddenly and to his surprise he saw she was crying. Tears were rolling down her soft elderly cheeks, and she fumbled in her bag for a handkerchief.

"Billy's such a baby," she moaned. "He was fixing those soldiers on the window sill only day before yesterday, before his father came. Now where is he? *How* is he?" Along with the handkerchief she had pulled a snapshot from her purse. She held it out to him. "Look at him," she said. "Think—if he was your own boy!"

He slowed the car and took the picture. It showed a blond youngster with feet apart and confident long-lashed eyes staring into the camera, and a wave of sympathy and understanding fairly shook him. So far his worry had been for Anne Collier. Now here was her son, and who was to say which was in more perilous straits?

"I'm sorry, believe me," he said grimly. "So far he's been only a name to me. Now, of course— We'll find him, Miss Warrington. Just remember, with Collier dead, nobody gains by hurting the boy."

"Then you'll tell the police?"

"I don't know what else I can do."

He was quiet after that, staring ahead through the windshield and driving by pure automatism. He knew what Anne's choice would be between herself and her boy. Nevertheless, he had a hideous feeling that he was somehow selling her out by providing the one motive Close lacked. If Collier had stolen and hidden the boy, she might easily have killed him.

At her insistence he took Eliza Warrington to the hospital as soon as they reached town. He had small hope she could see Anne, but he miscalculated that lady's indomitability. A half hour later she marched out, her head high and her face set, and crawled into the car.

"She's asleep," she said briefly. "She looks dreadful."

"You mean you saw her?" he asked, his voice incredulous.

"Do you think any policeman in the world was going to keep me out of that room?" she demanded furiously. "I just told him to get the hell out of my way, and he did."

He found himself smiling. The language—which he realized must be unusual—and the ferocity of her expression were totally unlike the tranquil little woman of a few hours before.

"I saw the doctor, too," she went on. "She's got a fair chance. But she's a mighty sick girl, Mr. Forsythe. I raised her. She's like one of my own and, God help me, to see a policeman outside her door—"

Her voice broke, but she did not cry again. She was tragically calm and competent when he took her home. And Margery, after a glance at his face, made her warmly welcome.

"Miss Warrington is Mrs. Collier's aunt," he explained. "I didn't think she'd want to go to a hotel."

"I should think not," Margery said briskly. "All those reporters and cameramen! You just stay quietly here and nobody will bother you."

Later on, with Eliza tucked in bed and a light tray supper beside her, he told Margery the story of the missing child. She was appalled.

"You need the FBI," she said. "After all, he probably took him over the state line."

"The boy was his own son, Margery."

"Then the police?"

"And give them a real motive for her killing him?"

It was an impasse, and they both knew it. Neither of them ate much dinner, and afterward he tried to marshal the facts as he knew them.

"It may not have anything to do with the money and the will at all," he said. "After all, a man like Collier makes enemies all over the lot. It may be a gang murder, with Anne seeing who did it and having to be put out of the way."

"You don't believe that, do you?"

"Certainly the police won't. There was the element

67

of trouble already there, Anne threatening a will and cutting out Collier, and Collier learning about the bank account. Because I think he did. From the agent, the Simmons woman, perhaps."

"Anne may have told him herself. Have you thought of that? Perhaps he found something, a script maybe. He could follow it up and find out what she'd been doing."

"It wouldn't lead to a double shooting. Why should it? Oh, god!" he exploded. "If I could only talk to her! Learn what really happened."

And then to his surprise the telephone rang, and Close was on the wire.

"Forsythe?" he said. "Glad you're in. Want to come to the hospital? The girl's conscious. We've got her in a private room. You can have ten minutes, the doc says. She won't talk to me. She wants you."

He never forgot that night—the frantic drive to the hospital, Close waiting to take him upstairs, and the group of men standing outside the door, an inspector of the Homicide Squad, an assistant district attorney and to his surprise the commissioner of police. The same doctor he had seen before was there, too, looking disapproving. Nobody greeted Forsythe. They eyed him curiously and, he thought, with some resentment. It was the doctor who spoke, and then to the group.

"I have told you gentlemen," he said, "that you cannot all go into the room. She's a sick girl, and I can't permit any excitement."

"Hell, doc," the commissioner said. "This is a murder case. If she's going to make a deposition, we want to take it down."

The doctor stiffened.

"Nobody's going to tell her she's about to die," he said firmly. "You'd have to tell her that, wouldn't you, before she makes a statement? Well, I won't have it. She isn't dying."

"So Forsythe goes in alone?"

"He can take one man. Fix it up among yourselves. You can have ten minutes. That's all."

There was no argument. Close followed Forsythe into the room, but remained in the background while Forsythe went to the bed. At first he thought she was asleep. She was lying flat in the bed, with no pillow under her head, and her eyes were closed. When he reached her, however, she opened them. She did not speak, but she put out a hand and he held it as he sat down beside her.

"I'm sorry, my dear," he said awkwardly. "You'll be all right, you know. This is the worst day."

She did not seem to listen. She was watching him however.

"Billy," she said feebly. "Little Bill. Is he all right?"

He was caught off base with the question, afraid his face would betray him, but he managed to smile.

"Of course he's all right," he said with affected heartiness. "What did you expect? Your aunt's here."

He could see her visibly relax. She closed her eyes again, but she left her hand in his. It was then that Close took over. He moved to the other side of the bed and stood looking down at her.

"Tell me, Mrs. Collier," he said quietly, "you knew your husband had a gun?"

She nodded weakly.

"Where did he keep it? Do you know?"

"On a shelf in his closet, so the boy couldn't get it."

"But you knew it was there. Now, when did you see it again?"

"I hadn't seen it for a long time. I don't know exactly."

"What about the wire on the stairs? Do you think your husband put it there?"

She frowned.

"Wire? What wire?"

"Don't you know why you fell that night?"

"I stumbled. I must have."

Close looked impatient. Time was running out and he was getting nowhere. His voice was cold now.

"I'll tell you how I see it," he said. "You hated Collier. I'll grant you he wasn't much, but he'd made life a particular hell for you. Last night he may have threatened you. He did something, anyhow, so you got the gun and shot him. Then you realized what you'd done, so you tried to kill yourself."

"No," she gasped. "Never. I didn't shoot him. I didn't shoot myself. You must believe me. You must."

Forsythe shot to his feet, overturning his chair.

"Stop it!" he said violently. "Do you want to finish her? Nobody agreed to a third degree in here. You can't bully her while I'm here."

"All right," Close said, with surprising mildness. "Keep your shirt on."

He sat down, and Forsythe bent over the bed.

"Listen, darling," he said. "Just tell what you remember. I know you didn't do any of those things. Take it easy and try."

She nodded and closed her eyes.

"I don't really know what happened," she said in a low voice. "I never saw anybody. I was in the kitchen heating some milk when I heard a shot. I ran back to the sitting-room and Fred was on the floor. I didn't hear the other shot at all, the one that hit me. Is he—is Fred dead?"

"I'm sorry, darling. I'm afraid he is."

That was all. The doctor came in and sent them

out, to face a disgusted group in the hall.

"So that's her story!" Close said sourly. "She didn't do it! Nobody did it! a boy with a twenty-two was out after pigeons, I suppose."

"Why don't you try believing what you hear?" Forsythe demanded hotly. "Maybe you didn't get it, but the first thing she asked was about her boy. She's crazy about him. Would she try to kill herself and leave him? And get this, you cold-blooded bastards," he added recklessly, "she doesn't know it, but her boy's missing. Fred Collier abducted him Thursday and hid him somewhere. Only God knows where he is."

"How did you learn that?"

"Come to my house and see the aunt he was staying with in Danbury. She'll tell you. And if you fellows don't find him soon, I'll get the FBI on it. Maybe a man can't kidnap his own son, but he can't take him from his proper custodian, and Eliza Warrington was that."

"So that's why Collier's wife killed him!" Close said. "What do you know. A real motive, after all."

At eight o'clock that night two police cars stopped in front of the Forsythe house and a group of bewildered officials got out, headed by Forsythe himself. Margery was in the living-room and it was typical of her that she watched them file in without surprise.

"I'm afraid Miss Warrington is asleep," she said. "She was very tired, and not very young."

"We'll have to wake her," Forsythe said. "I'd better do it, Margery. I'll have to explain what they want."

Eliza, however, was not asleep. When she heard him she called to him to come in. She was sitting up in bed in a long-sleeved high-necked nightgown, with her Bible in her hands. To his amazement

Thomas Carlyle was curled up on the bed beside her. He did not move and she gave Forsythe her dry smile.

"A cat's company," she said. "A cat and a Bible, and nobody needs to be lonely."

A few minutes later, an august company was gathered about her bed, listening to her story. At the end, however, she said what Forsythe had been afraid she would.

"He stole Billy and hid him," she said. "And Anne wasn't one to take a thing like that lying down."

"So you think she shot him?" Close asked.

"I know I would myself, if I'd been in her place," Eliza said defiantly.

6

It was ten o'clock that night when a police car with a uniformed driver stopped in front of the apartment house and two detectives, with Close and Forsythe, got out.

No one answered the superintendent's bell, but the Kerrs' lights were on, and Close rang for them. Mrs. Kerr came to the door, with her hair in curlers and looking apologetic.

"I'm sorry," she said. "I just washed my hair." She eyed the group with interest. "Police, aren't you?"

"Yes," Close said as they stepped inside. "We'd like to ask you a few questions, Mrs. Kerr. May we come in?"

"Of course," she said pleasantly. "Not that we know anything. We don't. We were both asleep."

Inside the apartment Kerr had been playing solitaire in the living-room. He looked annoyed at the intrusion, although he was civil enough.

"What's it about now?" he asked. "Just because we happen to live here is no reason why you fellows are on our heels."

Close ignored this. He got out his notebook and glanced at it.

"Name's Joseph H. Kerr," he said. "Occupation—teller in the Enterprise Bank. That right?"

"Sure," Kerr said nastily. "Age thirty-eight, white, weight one fifty-five."

"All right, Mr. Kerr. No need to be unpleasant. Do you know the Colliers' boy?"

"Billy? Sure I know him. Nice kid."

"When did you see him last?"

Kerr was thoughtful.

"A couple of months ago, I guess." He looked at his wife. "That correct?"

"About that," she corroborated. "Collier beat him with a strap one night, and his wife took the boy away the next day. At least that's what Hellinger says."

"Where is Hellinger? He doesn't answer his bell."

They laughed.

"He's out more often than he's in," Mrs. Kerr said. "I haven't seen him all day. Joe went down a while ago and put some coal on the furnace. We were freezing. But that's not unusual."

They got an equally indifferent result from the third floor. Mr. Jamison, dressed but still limping, had never seen Billy and didn't even know the Colliers had a child. As the group gathered on the pavement before dispersing, it was increasingly clear that Collier had hidden the boy somewhere, and Close stuck to the belief that it was the reason Anne had killed him.

"Why?" Forsythe demanded. "With him dead he couldn't tell her where Billy was."

"How do you know he didn't tell her?"

"Oh, for God's sweet sake! Of all the addlepated remarks I ever heard! If she knew he'd disappeared she'd have been wild to get the boy back. You saw her. She wasn't worried about him."

Nevertheless, the boy was missing, and the vast resources of the city were set in motion that Saturday night. Armed with the snapshot from Eliza's purse, they sent out a description of him by Teletype, to

State Police, to city precinct station houses, to squad cars on the prowl. It was too late to make the Sunday papers, but Monday's would have the picture. The press would make the most of it, the police knew. Murders were a dime a dozen in New York, but a missing child was news.

To Forsythe that Sunday was endless. Anne Collier had developed a temperature, so no one was allowed to see her, and Eliza Warrington had gone to church, to pray on her knees for the boy's safe return. Pacing the floor of the long living-room Forsythe tried to solve the puzzle.

Why had Collier taken the boy and hidden him? What had he to gain? As a lever against Anne, to force her to do something? To make her draw out the money in the bank, or some part of it? That would imply he knew about it, not only that it existed but possibly the amount.

The bank would not give out information of that sort, but the Simmons woman might. Under duress, perhaps, or because there was an unholy alliance between them. He did not think this last was possible. She had been too outspoken about Collier. She might, however, have known about the boy. He remembered the day before, when her small car had trailed him to Danbury.

Suppose Collier had threatened to steal Billy, and told her about it? What would be her first step when she learned Collier had been killed? To learn if the boy was all right, he thought, and he wondered if she had been in the neighborhood when he and Eliza left without the child. She would know then, he thought. She might have been pretty desperate as she drove back to the city.

He needed to see her, he realized, but only her office was listed in the telephone book, and it did not answer when he called.

There was no news whatever from the police. Close was not in his office, and at noon Forsythe took a cab and went to Centre Street. There was a sort of Sunday calm there after the usual Saturday night activities, but Missing Persons was apparently busy. When at last he contacted a tired-looking officer behind a desk there he got less than no satisfaction. On the contrary.

"The Collier boy?" he said. "Well, we're on it, of course. But this is Sunday. People hole up today. Even the kids aren't out much; no school, of course. Then, too, you have to remember he may never have reached town. According to the Auto Squad people, Collier may have had connections any place from here to Danbury, or elsewhere in the state. He may have left him anywhere. Provided, of course, he didn't do away with him entirely."

"But it was his own son, man!"

The tired man shrugged.

"It happens," he said. "And remember it took something pretty bad to make Collier's wife kill him. From what we hear about him, I'd say it's more than possible. It's probable."

Needless to say, he did not repeat that conversation to Eliza Warrington, or to Margery. But it left him with a haunting dread that made food impossible and even the house a prison. Late in the afternoon he went out, walking without purpose until he found himself near the Collier apartment. He was totally unaware that he was being followed by a small inconspicuous man who lost himself when necessary in the Sunday crowds but never lost sight of him.

As for Forsythe himself, it had become increasingly important to locate Martha Simmons and learn what she knew. Surely Anne would have had her home address. Not where Collier could find it, but she would have had it. She had to arrange those extraordinary meetings in the park, for one thing. Also, although he knew nothing about the radio business, there might have been last-minute changes, emergencies of all sorts. It was a hope, at least.

No one answered the superintendent's bell, however, and he was standing uncertainly in the foyer when Mrs. Kerr arrived. She was dressed for Sunday, looking quite pretty. She was startled when she saw him.

"Don't tell me!" she said. "Police again."

"I'm not a policeman, Mrs. Kerr. I'm Mrs. Collier's lawyer. I'd like to get something from her apartment."

"All right by me." She smiled at him. "Only my key won't fit. I suppose Mike's out as usual?"

"He doesn't answer his bell. I can at least go up and try," he said doubtfully. "If not, I can use the fire escape."

This seemed to amuse her, but she sobered quickly.

"Any news about Billy?" she asked. "It doesn't seem possible, does it?"

"No. I don't think he's been located yet. I hope to God they find him."

She watched him partway up the stairs, then disappeared into her own apartment. Forsythe had not much hope as he reached the second-floor landing. To his amazement, however, the door was slightly open, and although the apartment was dark, there was a faint sound coming from one of the bedrooms.

His first thought, like Mrs. Kerr's, was of the police. The movements, however, were stealthy, like someone moving cloth for some purpose, and he reached over and switched on a ceiling light. He heard a muttered exclamation, and a man appeared in the doorway.

He did not recognize him at once, without the usual old gray sweater and nondescript pants. But it was Hellinger, a Hellinger almost collapsing with terror when he saw him, and then ready for a fight. Forsythe eyed him warily.

"I'd advise against it, Mike," he said. "That's the boy's room, isn't it? What were you doing there?"

Hellinger had recovered somewhat. He unclenched his fists.

"Locking the windows," he said. "That one opens on the fire escape. Been some thieves around the neighborhood lately."

"Not taking anything yourself, for instance?"

"What's there to take in a kid's room?" He blustered. "Expect me to go round beating a drum?"

But he was still worried, his color still bad.

"I've been thinking quite a lot about you, Mike," Forsythe said easily. "You may like to know that Mrs. Collier is conscious. She didn't shoot her husband, and so far as she knows it might have been you."

Hellinger was plainly staggered.

"She can't say that. I swear, Mr. Forsythe, I don't even own a gun."

"It was Collier's gun. You have a key to the flat, so maybe you just stepped in there one day and took it."

All the fight was gone out of Hellinger by that time. He gave Forsythe a sickly grin.

"Joshing me, aren't you?" he muttered. "She couldn't have seen me because I wasn't here. Ask Jamison upstairs. He knows. He saw me come in that night."

Forsythe let him go then. He more or less slunk out of the apartment, while down on the street the anonymous gentleman took up his post across the way and watched with interest the light on the second floor.

The place was much as Forsythe had last seen it. Through the door into the kitchen he could see the pan on the stove and the glass still on the table. As he expected, Anne's neatly tidy desk offered only a list carefully typed of grocer, butcher, druggist, and so on.

Nor did the two bedrooms offer anything, although he searched them thoroughly. It was in the third one that he found Martha's home address.

The room had evidently been the boy's, and it was there Hellinger had been. There was no sign of any disturbance, however, and, as the superintendent claimed, the fire escape was outside the window.

Forsythe had not noticed it before. In fact he knew little about the apartment. The room itself was quite small, and in the closet on a shelf was Anne's typewriter, hidden along with stacks of yellow and white paper, behind a row of toys. Beside it was a notebook filled with seemingly unimportant data. But the address was there. The only items given were the initials M.S. and a street near Washington Square. Oddly enough, there was no telephone number.

About to put the lights out, he noticed the bed. It had been hastily thrown together, as though someone had searched it and only carelessly straightened the covers. He wondered if Hellinger had done it, but when he went downstairs again the superintendent was gone.

In any event the important thing now, of course, was to see Martha Simmons. The very fact that she had followed him to Danbury connected her with the case. But how? He had seen the bank's deposit receipts. They were clearly genuine enough. Was

79

there, he wondered, any other way she could get her hands on the money? He thought not; certainly not by killing both Anne and Fred Collier. Nevertheless, he had to see Martha, and see her soon.

It was seven o'clock when he took a taxi to her address. It proved to be a respectable-looking boardinghouse, and it was the landlady herself who answered the bell. She seemed anxious when he asked for Martha Simmons.

"She's not in," she said suspiciously. "Anything I can do for you?"

"Have you any idea where I can reach her?" he inquired.

She looked about her. There was a nondescript-looking man on the pavement who had stopped to light a cigarette, and she lowered her voice.

"Do you mind coming in?" she said. "I'm Mrs. Hicks, and some of my ladies are playing cards in the parlor. If you don't mind the dining-room—"

He said the dining-room was fine, and found himself in a long room, with the table already laid for breakfast, and Mrs. Hicks sitting across from him. He gave her his card, which she inspected carefully.

"A lawyer?" she said. "She isn't in any sort of trouble, is she?"

"Not so far as I know. Just when did she go out?"

"This morning," she said worriedly. "And you'd have to know Martha to understand. She's not one to gad about. Always home for dinner like clockwork. Especially on Sunday."

"She's been out all day?"

"She left about eleven this morning. I thought maybe she'd taken her car and gone somewhere, but the garage says it's still there."

"I'm sure she's all right, Mrs. Hicks."

"You never know, these days, the way taxis shoot

along the streets— Or maybe she's sick somewhere. I notice she's been kind of upset lately. Maybe she had a quarrel with her gentleman friend. I wouldn't know. But she'd been crying this morning while she packed for her vacation. It was no way to feel about a holiday."

"She expected to leave soon?"

"Tomorrow. Maybe she was going to be married. I don't know. She was no talker. All she said was she wouldn't be coming back."

"This—gentleman friend," Forsythe said. "Do you know him? I might need to get in touch with him."

"I understand he was a broker, but I never saw him," she said tartly. "Mighty careful about that, she was. I asked her once if he had a wooden leg, and she nearly slapped me. The way it was, she'd pick him up in her car, and drop him before she came home."

"Maybe that's what she's done today."

"I told you her car isn't out."

Forsythe got up.

"You don't think she's at her office?" he asked.

"On a Sunday? I wouldn't think so," Mrs. Hicks said doubtfully. "There's no program on the radio today. That's her job, you know. She's an agent."

"So I understand. But I might drop by her office," Forsythe said. "It's not likely, but if she's there and all right, I'll let you know."

She seemed grateful as he said good night and left, but he himself was highly suspicious. Martha Simmons had said nothing to him about leaving town. What had happened, then, to change her plans? Was she afraid? he wondered. Or was she so deeply involved in the Collier case that she was obliged to escape? In other words, had she meant to kill Collier and only accidentally shot Anne?

81

He stopped on the pavement to consider that. He had not liked the woman, but it was hard to think of her as a deliberate killer. What had she to gain by it? And what about the boy? Department of utter confusion, he thought, with some amusement.

At the corner he found a cab and drove without much expectation to the building where she had her office. Rather to his surprise the watchman let him in without protest. Evidently there was a radio or television program going on in the building, and people were crowding in. But when he reached Martha Simmons's office it was dark, and there was no movement inside when he rapped. He felt rather silly as a cleaning woman passing him in the hall stopped and eyed him.

"She won't be there," she said. "Never comes at night. Especially Sunday. Not like the rest of the radio crowd. You'd think I'd get a night off now and then."

She went on, carrying her pail and mop, and Forsythe stood outside the door. Just what impulse made him turn the knob he did not know, but the door swung open onto the darkness beyond, and he stepped inside.

When he found the light switch and turned it on, the small anteroom was dark and empty, with the unused look he had noticed before. The private office was dark, also, but now that he was there he meant if possible to see the files. He found the switch inside the door and went in.

It took only a moment to realize that someone had been there before him. Both the safe and the drawers of the steel cases were standing open, and one of the folders lay empty on the desk.

That was when he saw Martha Simmons. She was lying on the floor partly behind the desk, and she was dead.

7

He did not hear the cleaning woman behind him as he stooped over the body. He did not know she was there until she ran out screaming, her eyes wild, her mouth wide open. When he looked up he was dimly aware of other cleaning women crowding in the doorway, and of someone behind them yelling for police.

He was still stunned. She had been very recently killed. He was no judge of such matters, but her body was warm, and as he picked up her hand to try to find a pulse the arm was limp. That she had been strangled was clear, however, the protruding eyes and tongue, the still cyanotic face told their own story. And it took only a moment to feel the thin steel wire around her neck.

The men from the squad car were highly suspicious when they came. They shooed away the crowd, closed the door, and stood over Forsythe, making him tell his story over and over: that he had wanted to see the dead woman on a client's business, that her landlady had sent him there, and so on. Nor were things improved when the Homicide crowd arrived. They brought in the cleaning woman, who pointed a finger at Forsythe and wailed hysterically.

"He did it," she cried. "I was suspicious of him right away. He had time, too. I cleaned next door, then I thought I'd better see what he was up to."

But Forsythe's fighting blood was up by that time.

"I want Lieutenant Close, and I want him fast," he demanded furiously. "He would know why I'm here. I never touched her, of course. And for God's sake will somebody look in the files over there for some bank deposit receipts or anything under the name of Blake? Jessica Blake?"

Someone did. There was no file of bank deposit receipts made out to one Jessica Blake. Nor to Anne Collier, either. They eyed him coldly, and the anonymous man who had followed him all day spoke quietly to the officer in charge.

"Hold him," he said. "It's the break Lieutenant Close has been waiting for. He's in this up to his neck."

Close had not appeared when they took Forsythe to the precinct station house. For a time they kept him there, under guard in a small room. He was seething with fury, but he had ceased protesting by that time, and when he ran out of cigarettes the uniformed man even gave him one. He was apparently not under arrest. He was merely being detained for questioning. But it was two o'clock in the morning before Close appeared, dismissed the guard, and sat down behind the desk.

He looked tired to the point of exhaustion, and he was coldly angry.

"First of all," he said, "why didn't you tell me the boy had been in the Collier apartment?"

Forsythe stared.

"I don't get it. When was he there?"

"Don't give me that. I've had a man tailing you. You went to the place today, and up to the Collier apartment. Don't bother to deny it, Forsythe. We've had the lab men up there tonight. Your prints are all over the boy's room."

"I was there. I'm not denying it."

"All right. Now get this. One of the men is allergic to cats. He started sneezing in the boy's room, and what do you think we picked up with the vacuum? Hairs from a cat. A blue-gray Persian cat. The Colliers didn't have a cat, but the kid's aunt did. So he was there, and you knew it. See here, Forsythe, I don't get any of this unless you killed Collier yourself, and after the Simmons woman tonight I think maybe you did. You had a fight with him. Remember?"

"What's that got to do with it?"

Close did not answer. He leaned on the desk and drew a long breath.

"Let me tell you how this thing shapes up," he said. "You're in love with Anne Collier. That sticks out a mile, and Collier is a louse. So you shoot him, and by accident you get her, too. But something happens you didn't expect. The boy's there and sees you. He has to be taken away. What's more, you have to be sure he's left nothing behind to show he'd been there. That's why you went back today, to smooth up his bed. She'd turned it down for him."

Forsythe managed a wry grin.

"Why don't you ask Hellinger about that?" he said. "And aren't you forgetting something? I put a piece of wire on the stairs so Anne would fall and break her neck. I suppose that's love!"

"Maybe it was meant for Collier. Where's that wire now, Forsythe?"

"You mean it was around Martha Simmons's neck, I suppose."

"Where is it? That's what I asked."

"In a pocket of one of my coats. I'd be doubtful about it, but my sister doesn't send my clothes to be pressed until Tuesday. I suppose you realize, Close, that everything you've said about me can apply to

85

someone else. What you don't want to admit is that there's a killer loose, and you have no idea who it is. For my choice it's Hellinger."

"What about Mike Hellinger?" Close asked sharply.

"I found him in the boy's room when I went there. He was scared. He made some excuse about being there, but I didn't believe him. He was after something."

"So were you, weren't you?"

Forsythe grinned wryly.

"Sure I was," he said. "I was after Martha Simmons's address. She'd trailed me to Danbury, for one thing. And in the expression one of your men used about me, she was in this up to her neck." He shrugged. "That's an unfortunate phrase just now, but remember all this happened after I told her Anne Collier was going to make a will. I don't think Anne was shot by accident. There was a deliberate attempt to murder her. If there was any hanky-panky about the money, she had to be killed."

"What sort of hanky-panky?"

"I wish I knew. But there was. That's why Martha Simmons is dead. She wasn't in it alone. It was— well, it stinks of an accomplice. If you want the facts, I thought so when I went to the apartment tonight. It's Sunday, and she's not in the telephone book. In my bumbling way I had an idea Anne Collier would have an address for her. That's what I was looking for. And I found it in a notebook on a shelf in the boy's closet."

Close got up and paced up and down the room, his head bent. When he stopped it was to fire a question at Forsythe.

"What do you know about Mike Hellinger?"

"Nothing, except his job. Why?"

86

"Mike's smarter than he makes out," Close said, and sat down on the edge of the desk. "He's a leftover from the war. Couldn't settle down to a real job. Took this one five years ago. It suits him. It's easy. He lives in the basement and does as little as he can. He had a wife once but she left him. The point is, he and Collier used to be pretty thick."

"Mike mixed up in the used-car business?"

"I don't know. But he's not a bad-looking fellow when he cleans up. Now all along you've been talking about Anne Collier's money, and tonight you had the boys looking for her files in the Simmons woman's office. If Mike knew her and there was some trickery going on, it might make some sort of sense. Suppose he didn't know the kid was there, and the boy saw him? He could have shut him up in that basement apartment of his until he got rid of him."

What with the excitement, his own exhaustion, and even the fact he had eaten very little since breakfast the day before, Forsythe felt physically sick.

"Get rid of him! How, for God's sake?"

"What do you think? Don't be a fool, Forsythe. We have two murders already. Do you think a third one will stop anybody? And let's get some coffee in here. We both need it."

He ordered the coffee, and over it Forsythe mulled the problem.

"Why?" he said. "Why kill anybody? What had Hellinger to gain?"

"Money, if the Simmons woman was cheating. Might have been quite a bit in her safe. Anyway, could she get her hands on this bank account of Anne Collier's?"

"I don't see how. I'd have gone to the trust company, but they're closed yesterday and today, of course."

It was about dawn when at last Forsythe got home. Careful as he was, Margery heard him and came out, dragging a dressing-gown around her. She motioned him not to speak and followed him into his room.

"I've had a time with Eliza," she said, closing the door. "The police called up tonight to know if she had a cat. At first she thought the cat was dead, but it seems all they had was some hair from it. She says Billy's clothes were always covered with cat hairs. Then she broke down. She's sure Collier killed him."

"Someone may have," Forsythe said morosely. "He's still missing."

He did not tell her about Martha Simmons. He went to bed and fell into an exhausted sleep. When she wakened him at ten o'clock it was to say that Close was downstairs and wanted him to go to the hospital with him. He shaved and dressed quickly, to find Close waiting impatiently in the hall and a police car at the door.

"She's not worse, is she?"

"She's all right. Why not ask about me? I had two hours' sleep in my office chair. I've had a doughnut and a cup of coffee since noon yesterday, and my wife's threatening to divorce me. See here, Forsythe, we've got to tell Mrs. Collier about the boy. Maybe she knows something, and God knows we need everything we can get."

"It will about kill her."

They found Anne distinctly better. She was propped up in bed, her hair loose and brushed, her eyes clear. She was disappointed, however, when only the two of them came in.

"I thought you might bring Billy," she said. "I'm well enough to see him, and he won't understand if I don't."

"Time enough for that later," Close said, to

Forsythe's relief. "Just now I want the details of that night, Mrs. Collier. Just why did your husband get the boy and bring him home?"

She hesitated.

"I suppose it's all right to tell it now." She had grown pale. "Somehow he'd learned about what I was doing. I think Mr. Jamison upstairs complained to the superintendent about my typing. The floors are very thin. Then he may have followed Martha Simmons the last time I met her in Central Park. I don't think she told him about me, but he knew she was an agent. It was on her office door."

"I see. Then what?"

"I had no idea he was going for Billy. I almost fell over when he brought him in. But Billy was excited. He kissed me and then ran into his room to see if his toys were still there. That was when Fred told me what he wanted."

She almost broke down, and Forsythe sat down beside her and took her hand.

"It's all right, my dear," he said. "They know you didn't shoot him."

"He was in trouble," she went on in a half-whisper. "He'd been selling stolen cars—hot cars, he called them—and the Automobile Squad or something was after him. They hadn't got him yet, but in a day or two he'd have to leave town. What I was to do was to draw the money out of the bank and give it to him. If I didn't he'd take little Billy with him and shoot it out if he had to. I knew what that meant. They'd both be killed."

"You've made a pretty good case against yourself," Close said wryly. "What about the gun, Mrs. Collier? Did he threaten you with it?"

"No. He looked for it but he couldn't find it. I told him I hadn't seen it for several days, and he was frantic. That's when he began yelling at me. I'd turned down Billy's bed and gone to the kitchen to get some hot milk for him. He'd had a long cold drive. But it wasn't ready. I was coming back when I heard the shot."

"Where was the boy?"

"He was still in his room, I suppose. I had no time to look around."

"Wouldn't it be possible the boy saw who fired the shots?"

"What does he say? He'll tell you if he knows. He's completely honest."

There it was. Forsythe took a tighter grip on her hand, and Close looked unhappy.

"I'm afraid I have to tell you something," he said. "I don't want to, but it's vital. You see, we haven't located Billy. There was no boy there when we got there that night."

She lay back on her pillows and closed her eyes. Forsythe felt her trembling.

"Where is he?" she said faintly. "He must be somewhere."

"Well, it's probably not as bad as it sounds." Close spoke encouragingly. "He is six, and I understand he is a pretty intelligent lad. Personally I think he was scared and beat it. Have you any idea where he would go? It was his neighborhood. He must have known plenty of kids there."

She brightened somewhat, and proceeded to name a half dozen families. Close soberly wrote them down, although they had already been questioned without result. He put his notebook away and got up.

"I'll look him up," he said as he picked up his hat. "You see, we didn't know about him until kind of late. Don't you worry. We'll locate him, all right."

Forsythe did not leave when Close did. He sat beside the bed, watching the color come back into her face and the trembling stop. She even smiled at him.

"Of course that's what happened," she said. "With Fred gone and me here, they would just keep him. Mike Hellinger might know. Have they talked to him?"

"I don't know. It was some little time after the shots when Jamison got up his courage and notified him. Plenty of time for Billy to run, probably."

On the whole, Close had managed it better than Forsythe had expected. The story she had told, however, left him coldly angry. Fred Collier had not changed. He was still the sergeant he had known in the service, crooked and unscrupulous and narrowly escaping court-martial. That this girl had ever married him seemed impossible. It must have been seven years of hell, but she made no complaint. She had done it, and she had taken her medicine. Only no longer, he thought. She was free now, and some day—

"You've been very kind to me, Wade," she said. "How can I ever thank you?"

"We'll talk about it when you get well."

"I never made a will, after all, did I?"

"You don't need it now, my dear."

She was free now, he thought. Free as air. Free to love, even to marry. How little he knew of her, and yet how much! And Close had accused him of being crazy about her. Perhaps he was. Close was a smart detective, in some ways.

He left soon after. But he carried with him the picture of her smiling at him as he left her, and for the first time a bit of hope which he did not formulate, even to himself.

8

It was well after eleven that morning when he presented himself at the Gotham Trust Company's big bronze doors and asked to see Mr. Stone, the president. It took his card and his insistence on urgent business to admit him to this august presence, but once in he lost no time.

"I am here about two murders," he said flatly. "Also about a woman who has been shot and is in the hospital. Does the name Jessica Blake mean anything to you?"

Mr. Stone looked startled.

"Murders!" he said. "We bankers are accused of a good many things, but scarcely that."

Forsythe sat down. He had not been asked to do so.

"I'd better explain all this," he said. "Jessica Blake is the pen name of a young woman who writes radio scripts. They pay her a lot of money. And according to her agent's files that money is here. It has been accumulating here for several years. I want to know about it."

The change from murder to banking was an obvious relief, especially as Forsythe offered his card. He looked up from it with a frown.

"My dear fellow," he said. "You're a lawyer. You know we don't give out information of that sort."

"You can tell me if she has an account or a safe-deposit box here. I'd rather not bring the police in, but if I have to I will."

The word "police," like murder, stirred Mr. Stone to the depths of his soul. He recovered enough to press a button, which resulted in the appearance, rather like a jack-in-the-box, of an elegant young man, obviously a secretary.

"Find out if a Jessica Blake has an account or a safe-deposit box here and let me know at once," he instructed. "I don't want figures. Just the facts."

The elegant young gentleman left smartly, and Mr. Stone lit a cigar and inspected Forsythe, who was not looking his best.

"This Blake woman a friend of yours?"

"I never saw her but once until a few days ago."

"And she's been murdered?"

"No. She's been accused herself of murder. She's innocent, of course. The police realize that now."

"I see. Most unpleasant. Who did she—who was she supposed to have killed?"

"Her husband," Forsythe said stiffly. "A man named Collier."

This seemed rather to stun Mr. Stone, who observed he had seen something about it in the papers. There was rather an unhappy silence, during which Mr. Stone smoked nervously and Forsythe lit a cigarette. It was only broken by the return of the secretary.

"Sorry to have been so long, sir," he said, "but the bookkeeping department is pretty well demoralized. Flu, of course. As to the Blake account, there is none. No box, and nothing on the books at all, sir. Never has been, apparently."

Immediately all was well with Mr. Stone's world. He got up and clapped Forsythe jovially on the shoulder.

"So you see we haven't murdered anybody," he

said. "There's a mistake somewhere, of course. Sorry not to be more helpful."

"I don't see how it's possible," Forsythe said slowly. "I've seen the deposit receipts, on your own slips."

"My dear boy! For fifty years we have borne an unbelmished reputation. If there is no Jessica Blake account on our books there is no such account."

There was no suavity in Mr. Stone now, in spite of the "dear boy." He glared at Forsythe.

"That's a dangerous statement you've just made, and I hope you realize it, Mr. Forsythe."

"All right," Forsythe said stiffly. "I'll ask you another. Have you an account or a safe-deposit box either for Anne Collier or a Martha Simmons?"

The secretary stiffened. Evidently he read the papers, but he did not move. He eyed his chief, who was looking apoplectic.

"Will you tell me by what authority you come in and investigate the affairs of this bank?" he demanded.

But Forsythe was tired as well as bewildered. He was irritated, too.

"As I said before, I thought you'd prefer me to the police."

There was a moment when Mr. Stone apparently contemplated an ink bottle with the intention of throwing it. Then: "Very well," he said resignedly. "Get those names, Harold? And don't upset the whole staff. Just make a casual inquiry. It's not a matter of life and death."

"It's been a matter of two deaths already, and possibly a third," Forsythe said dryly.

A startled Harold scuttled from the room, and Mr. Stone took out a cigar and bit off the end of it savagely.

This time the silence was not pleasant. The banker pretended to examine some papers on his desk, while Forsythe got up and, ignoring the banker's indignant looks, paced the floor. What was the trick? How had it been done? It would have been easy to fool Anne, but the deposit receipts had not only looked genuine, they had been genuine. There was something about the neat figures, the red stamp, the whole setup, which was unmistakable.

He was not surprised, when Harold returned, to learn Anne Collier had no account whatever, but that Martha Simmons had three hundred and forty dollars in a checking account.

"I suppose it's too much to ask the names of your bookkeeping staff," he said stiffly. "The police can get that, and you may be sure they will."

He left both men staring after him and stalked out of the office. One thing was clear to him. The Jessica Blake checks had either been cashed as they came in or else deposited under another name. In either case Martha Simmons was guilty, but also in either case she had had an accomplice who forged the deposit receipts.

How had it been done? Her landlady had said her "gentleman friend" was a broker, but was that necessarily true?

At his office he called Close, but he was out and nobody knew where. When Miss Potter came in he realized there were a number of people in the outer office. She closed the door carefully behind her, and he looked up in surprise.

"What's going on out there?" he demanded.

"The gentlemen of the press," she said. "What did you expect? Or haven't you seen the morning papers?"

"I haven't had time. What about them?"

"They say you found a Martha Simmons's body last night, and were taken to a precinct station house for questioning. It made quite a story, especially the wire you used. Want to see these boys? I'm afraid you'll have to, and I must say I've seen you look beter. And, for heaven's sake, be polite. They can ruin you."

"Give me five minutes, Potter. I dressed in a hurry this morning."

She went out, and in the lavatory mirror Forsythe surveyed himself. His eye was only faintly discolored, but he looked haggard, his tie was crooked and his hair showed the haste with which he had dressed. He made such repairs as he could, and was the young member of the bar and of an old New York family when at last Potter opened the door.

There were six reporters and two cameramen in the crowd which surged in, and he eyed them with alarm.

"No pictures, please," he said. "Not if you want me to talk. That's final."

Under protest the photographers went out, and the others stood around the desk.

"Sorry to bother you, counselor," one of them said, "but we understand you found this murdered woman last night."

"I did indeed," he agreed soberly. "I was on a tax case, and Miss Simmons's landlady sent me to her office. She said it was unusual for her to be away on Sunday, so she was worried."

"How did she look when you found her?" This was from one of the tabloids, and Forsythe ignored it. In the main they accepted what he told them. He had not been detained for questioning, Lieutenant Close was a friend of his, and they had discussed the situation together. However, one astute young man had been watching him.

"Does this tie up with the Collier case, counselor?" he inquired. "I understand you're acquainted with Mrs. Collier."

"I knew Mrs. Collier's brother at college," Forsythe said shortly. "As for tying the two cases together, that's for the police. I'm only a lawyer."

"And how about that eye you've got?"

"Oh, that," Forsythe said blandly. "I ran into a door."

They laughed and finally went away. He found himself mopping his face after they had gone. It had been a strain, but he thought he had carried it off pretty well.

He tried to work that morning, but he accomplished very little. Also matters were not helped by a call from Margery, who seemed almost hysterical.

"I've just seen the papers, Wade. I can't believe it."

"Not pleasant, Margery, but not too bad for me. I wasn't arrested."

"But the wire, Wade. Was it—was it like the piece you were hunting the other day?" Forsythe lost such patience as he had left.

"Oh, for God's sake! Do you think I strangled her?" he said angrily. "You've got the wire there, haven't you? I brought it back in a coat pocket."

"That's what I called about," Margery said in a half-whisper. "As soon as I read the paper I took it out to one of the docks and threw it in the river. Now the police want it."

"Fine! Wonderful!" he said. "Nothing like a sister to help me out. Thanks, Margery. If you don't hear from me, I'll probably be in jail."

He hung up and sat still, wondering what to do next. So Close was still suspicious of him. Probably they had tried the paraffin test on Anne's hands, and knew she had not fired the gun which killed Collier.

He had to admit his own situation did not look too promising now, with the wire on the bottom of the East River—

He was somewhat relieved when Close called him an hour or so later. He even sounded pleased, which was unusual.

"We've got something," he said. "Not much, but something. We've found the cabby who drove a man and a small boy up to the Bronx that night. The boy seemed all right. Driver thought he'd been crying at first, but he cheered up. He let them out on Fordham Road, near the Botanical Gardens."

"Any description of the man?"

"Might possibly be Hellinger from what we've got. Medium size, which lets you out. The driver picked them up about four a.m. on Lexington Avenue. Was on his way home or he wouldn't have taken them. He lives up there."

"Four o'clock! Where was the boy all that time?"

"What do you expect for a nickel? The kid saw something so he had to be got rid of, for a time anyhow."

"Or for good," Forsythe said bitterly. "You'd better know this. The money's gone. Either it never went to the bank, or it's there under another name."

But Close was a Homicide man. He dismissed the matter of Anne's savings with what amounted to a shrug. Something, however, was amusing him.

"That's a nice sister you have," he said, in an apparent *non sequitur*. "Fond of you, isn't she?"

"Don't go cryptic on me," Forsythe said shortly, but Close laughed.

"I never went to college, son," he said. "Just plain English is all I know. But you'll be glad to know your sister didn't do so good with that piece of wire. It caught on an old piling, and the river police got it

98

for us."

"So we've got the river police now, have we?"

"You ought to be damned thankful we have," Close said dryly. "It rather lets you out, unless you've got a bale of it cached away somewhere."

Forsythe sat back at his desk and thought desperately. Some things were clear enough. Anne's threat to make a will with the necessary identification at the bank, had made the situation impossible for Martha Simmons, since discovery would be inevitable. But it was clear she had not been working alone. Wherever the money had been, it looked to him as though she had withdrawn it, probably in cash, and locked it in her safe. Then, preparing to escape with it, her accomplice had killed her.

With a sense of futility he called the bank again, asking for a list of its bookkeepers. None of the names was familiar, however. There were about a dozen of them, and except for two, one in a hospital and the other vacationing in Florida after the flu, they were all present and working.

He worked frantically the rest of the afternoon. His calendar showed him only a few days until what he called the Ides of March. The red-bound book beside him he worked on "spin-off" reorganization, on capital gains and losses (new amendment), and so on until his head ached and his very soul rebelled.

At six o'clock he went back to the hospital. He dreaded meeting Anne's eyes and what he had to tell her. Not only about her son. She had to know about the fund she had been so carefully saving for him. One or two things, however, he must try to learn. Had Martha talked about herself at all, for instance, or mentioned the name of the man whom Mrs. Hicks referred to as her "gentleman friend"?

Anne was sitting up in bed when he arrived. He

was glad to see the guard had been removed from her door, but she was showing strain and the nurse warned him not to excite her. Her first words were about the boy.

"Have they found him?" she asked eagerly.

"They've traced him to the neighborhood of the Botanical Gardens. That narrows the search. They'll find him, my dear. Don't worry. About eighteen thousand cops are on the job. Not to mention the State Police."

"The Botanical Gardens!" she gasped. "He could never go there alone."

"I'm afraid he didn't, Anne. We think someone took him and is hiding him. You have to know, my dear. It must have been someone he knew, for apparently he went willingly. How long had he been in Connecticut?"

"Only a couple of months."

"And before that. Who did he know?"

She was trying to be calm, but he hated seeing the look in her eyes.

"I don't know," she said vaguely. "Just children, mostly. I kept him with me as much as I could, but I did let him out to play on the pavement now and then."

"And in the building?"

"He liked Mike Hellinger. The couple on the first floor both work. He seldom saw them, and the man above us—his name's Jamison, I think—hadn't been there long. He never saw Billy."

It was Hellinger, of course. The lad would have gone with Hellinger. A scared little boy, not really knowing what had happened. Running desperately down the stairs, finding the superintendent there and going into his arms. He got up and went to the window, away from Anne's tragic face.

100

Close had said Hellinger was smart, a cut above his job. He was muscular too, strong and able to strangle a woman like Martha Simmons. Yet the puzzle still remained. Could he have forged the bank deposit receipts? Had he in his drifting career since the war once worked at the Gotham Trust? But even then—

He went back to Anne and smiled down at her.

"Try to trust us all, darling," he said. "The boy's all right. I'm sure of it. Why not? He's no danger to anyone."

"He could have seen who fired those shots."

"You said he was in his own room. Remember? He was probably just scared, poor kid, and ran out."

She took a little comfort from that, he thought. On the other subject, Martha Simmons's affairs, however, he drew a complete blank.

"She never talked about herself," she said. "I'm afraid she'll be worrying. About the program, you know."

He straightened and looked down at her, making an effort to smile.

"I've seen her, Anne. She's—not worrying."

He left her then. He was a poor actor and he knew it. He hated lying to her, even by indirection. But he was perfectly aware, as he hunted a pay telephone downstairs in the hospital, that he had left something of himself behind him in her small room above. And that something was what was euphemistically called his heart.

He could not locate Close, and his first impulse was to go to the big dirty building on Centre Street, with its pigeons strutting about outside and its dusty halls within. But time was important. If Hellinger had taken the boy, the whole aspect of the case changed. He would only have done so if the boy had seen him with the gun, and if Billy had he was not only in danger. He might already be beyond help.

That it was at least possible was borne out by the situation when he reached the apartment house. Repeated ringing brought no response until Mrs. Kerr came in from the street, fumbling in her bag for a key. She smiled at him pleasantly.

"Nobody in, I'm afraid," she said. "Not even Mike."

"He's the one I wanted to see."

She laughed.

"My husband and I would like it, too," she said. "Mike always took his job pretty lightly, but now he's disappeared entirely. My husband's been keeping up the furnace, or we'd have frozen."

"How long since Mike has been gone?"

"Well, we've had a dripping faucet for the last week, but he only really vamoosed yesterday. We've taken about all we can. I'm looking for another apartment. so's the third floor, I believe. You need service in an old building like this. Anyhow, the place is ghastly. I want to get out."

Forsythe hesitated. If Hellinger had hidden the boy, there might be some sign of it in his rooms. He needed badly to see them.

"There's not much use waiting for him, then," he said. "Perhaps if I could leave him a note—"

She smiled again.

"I don't think it will do much good," she said, "but he has a couple of rooms in the basement. Down the stairs there. I don't think he locks them. Nothing valuable, I imagine."

But they were locked. Forsythe groped his way down in the dark, and striking a match to discover a light switch, found himself in a long bare hall, with the furnace room and coalbin toward the street, and Hellinger's quarters behind them.

He tried the doors without result. They were sturdy enough to resist any pressure he exerted and at last he hauled off and gave one of them a resounding kick. Nothing happened, except that a male voice from the hall above called down.

"Is that you, Mike?" it said sharply.

"I'm sorry." Forsythe felt embarrassed and uncomfortable. "I knocked over something. He's not here."

"Well, he'd better get here and attend to the furnace," said the angry voice. "This place is like an icehouse." The speaker came down the stairs and stopped, peering at him nearsightedly. It was Jamison.

"Why, it's Mr. Wade, isn't it?" he said. "I'm afraid Hellinger's out. He often is. Anything I can do for you?"

Forsythe thought fast.

"Mrs. Collier wants some things to use in the hospital. I need to get into her apartment."

"Too bad. I'm afraid I can't help you there. Care to have a drink with me?"

"Thanks. I need to get home and clean up. Been out all day. Got all over your fall on the stairs?"

"Practically. I'm still very lame. That was a trap, Mr. Wade," he said somberly. "And I have reason to believe it was meant for me."

He did not explain, and limped back to the stairs again. Forsythe was thoughtful. Just why did Jamison think someone wanted to kill him? It seemed unlikely. He impressed Forsythe as a harmless little man, and he promptly forgot him in what followed.

Yet it was not much, merely a kitchen chair in the front cellar. It was a curious place for a chair, however. It was not in the furnace room, where a man might conceivably sit down to rest. It was beside the coalbin, and Forsythe stood staring down at it.

Had the boy been hidden here the night of the murders, until the police had gone? He had been somewhere until four in the morning. And the chair had not been there long. It was dusty, but not from the coal. Forsythe was convinced Hellinger had kept the boy here, either warned not to move or possibly gagged and tied. A six-year-old youngster in a place like this! So sure was he that if he had laid his hands on Hellinger at that moment he would have killed him.

As he was going out he met Joe Kerr at the front door. Kerr gave one look at his stormy face and would have passed him, but Forsythe caught him by the arm.

"Just a minute," he said. "I want to ask you something. The night Collier was shot, did you hear a child crying?"

"A child?"

"That's what I said."

"How could we hear anything, with police all over the place?"

Forsythe's furious anger was slowly cooling. Kerr's detached attitude annoyed him, however.

"I wonder," he said. "Those floors are thin. How come you and your wife didn't hear those shots, Kerr?"

"I've told the police. If we heard anything it probably would have sounded like a backfire. But we were asleep. Not," he added, "that I think it's any of your business."

He left Forsythe and put his key into the door of his apartment. Over his shoulder he said, "A lot of cars backfire around here. It's hard to tell the difference."

"They don't backfire over your head, do they?"

Kerr did not deign to answer. He opened the door and slammed it behind him.

9

He stopped at a pay phone on his way home and called Close.

"I think I've found where Billy Collier was hidden until four that morning," he said. "In the coal cellar of the apartment, probably tied to a chair."

Close had been yawning, but he was instantly wide awake.

"The hell you say!" he said. "So it was Mike Hellinger, after all."

"I think Hellinger took the boy, yes," Forsythe said dubiously. "But what about the rest of it? If he forged those bank deposit receipts, I'll eat them."

"Forget them," Close said, sounding cross. "He's our man, and I'll bet we'll find some of that wire around the place when we search it. Used it for repairs probably."

"You've got young Kerr in the building. He works in a bank. Ever thought of him?"

"What's your beef?" Close was definitely angry. "We've got our killer, hands down, or we will get him. Wait a minute. The other phone's ringing. Hold on."

It was not easy. A stout woman laden with bundles kept rapping on the door of the pay booth. Also Forsythe began to run out of small change. He was fishing desperately for another coin when Close came back on the wire.

"Sorry," he said. "Only the commissioner raising hell as usual. I'll tell you this much, Forsythe. One of our fellows in the Bronx thinks he saw Hellinger on the street there this morning. He followed him for a while, but he got wise and our man lost him. Don't worry. We'll get him yet. We've covered the airports, the bus stations, and the railroads. State Police are watching the roads, too. But if he saw our man he'll try to escape. Probably tonight."

"Taking the boy with him?"

"Why would he? The whole country's watching for the kid. We went over those rooms of his after the report came in, Forsythe. He's packed to go, and get this. He has five thousand dollars in new bills in a cigar box, hidden on a rafter in the furnace room. Better go home and get a good night's sleep, fella. This is our business. We're all set to grab him, and don't believe we won't."

Forsythe hung up, letting the stout woman pass him. "And about time," she said grumpily. But he did not go home. Instead he got a cup of coffee at a near-by restaurant and tried to work out the puzzle. He had a strong sense of impending tragedy as he sat there. With Hellinger ready to escape, what about the boy? He couldn't mean to take him with him. Was he already safely out of the way, in some forgotten corner of the Botanical Gardens? The very thought turned him cold.

He knew he was not at his best. He had had an exhausting twenty-four hours. He had, in effect, been accused of murder, he had had very little sleep and practically no food, and he realized that the full extent of the story depended on a thread so thin as to be almost nonexistent.

For somewhere the picture was wrong. Why had Hellinger held the boy—if he had held him—for

106

almost a week before trying to escape? So far as Forsythe could see, no one had been in any hurry to escape. It was as though what was over was over, and why not take it easy? It was ridiculous, preposterous, on any other theory than that something was not finished. Was it possible part of Anne's money was still missing, had not been in Martha's safe after all?

It was a thin thread on which to hang a case, but it was all he had. What about the locked bags in her room Mrs. Hicks had mentioned? Had anyone tried to get at them? Was Hellinger the anonymous lover Mrs. Hicks had never seen? It was possible, he thought. He would have been attractive to women. But even if he was, he did not believe Mrs. Hicks would turn the bags over to him easily, without some positive identification.

He got up wearily and took a taxi to Washington Square, where he found Mrs. Hicks at home and in a state of suppressed excitement. As before, her ladies were in the parlor, and somewhat unwillingly she led him back to the dining-room.

"The paper says you found her," she said, not too pleasantly. "But if you want to talk about her, I've told the police all I know. It's bad for my business, Mr. Forsythe, having cops in and out all day, going over her room, opening her bags, and everything. And to make things worse an attempt at burglary last night! I don't know what the world's coming to."

"Someone tried to break in?"

"Someone *got* in," she said. "He was on the stairs when one of my ladies got up to—to go to the bathroom. She screamed and he ran. Believe me, I sat up the rest of the night, with all the lights on and my dead husband's gun in my hand."

He had been right so far, Forsythe considered. The money had not all been in the safe. Martha Simmons had not trusted her accomplice and had tried to protect herself. But the police had opened the bags. If the money had been in them—

"What did they find in her luggage?" he asked. "Anything important?"

"Nothing but her clothes. I stood over them while they did it, Mr. Forsythe. I didn't like the idea. Her poor bits and pieces, and their big clumsy hands! And her crying the way she did before she left on Sunday morning."

"Why was she crying? Did she say?"

"Just that she was worried about something, and to forget it."

"And that's all she left? Just the suitcases?"

Mrs. Hicks hesitated.

"Well, no," she admitted. "Before she went she gave me her dressing case to keep for her. I didn't show it to them. I didn't see they had any business with her brushes and combs, and maybe a nightgown and fresh underwear. It was hardly decent."

Forsythe drew a long breath.

"I see," he said. "It would be a good idea to keep it locked away somewhere, Mrs. Hicks. I have a feeling it will help to solve her murder. And it's just possible your burglar may come back for it."

"Let him try," she said firmly. "Just let him try."

As he got up to leave, however, she remembered something.

"There was a small snapshot of her and some man," she said. "I found it when I was straightening her room after the police left. It was on the floor under the edge of her rug. I suppose it's her friend. Maybe you'd like to see it."

"Thank you, I would," Forsythe said without expression, and lit a cigarette with unsteady hands when she left the room. If this was the break in the case it might explain everything, his own apparently unfounded suspicions of the last few hours, the boy's kidnaping, and Hellinger's strange and almost purposeless activities.

It was the break. When she returned he stared at the picture with complete unbelief, and without so much as a good-by to an astonished landlady rushed out of the house. He was still running when he hit the pavement, and no cab being in sight, kept right on until he picked one up a few blocks farther on Fifty Avenue.

He had left his hat, and the driver looked at him suspiciously as he jerked the door open and climbed in.

"What's the rush?" he said. "Police after you?"

"No, but it's ten dollars if you drive like hell to Lexington and Fifty-Fourth Street."

The driver let in the clutch with a jerk, but he was still curious.

"Not having a baby, are you?" he said dryly.

Forsythe did not hear him. He leaned forward and changed the order. "Stop first at my house on Thirty-Sixth Street. I have to get something there."

"The ten still stands?"

"Sure. Here it is."

He passed over the money and sat back, deep in thought. It was seven o'clock, and at almost any time now Hellinger might try for his money and his luggage. In that case—

It had commenced to snow, a thin March snow which lay on the streets only briefly and then melted. The cab skidded here and there, but he paid no attention to it. At his own house, however, he had a bit of luck. Both Margery and Eliza were in the basement dining-room. Not eating much, he thought, but at least they and Tillie were out of the way. Only Thomas Carlyle was in the hall, making a mute appeal to be let out.

His gun was where he kept it. It was a heavy one, a .45-Colt, and it sagged his overcoat pocket. Fortunately the cabby did not notice it when he went out, but now they had had to leave First Avenue and were on Lexington.

"Can't do so good here," the driver said. "Too much light."

"Do the best you can," Forsythe said impatiently. "If a cop tries to stop you, go on. I'll fix it for you later."

"Sez you!" the man grumbled, but they made good time, and Forsythe stopped the cab a block from the apartment house, leaving the cabby staring after him. But Forsythe realized suddenly as he walked on that he had no way of entering the place. The Kerrs' windows were dark, which relieved him somewhat, and he moved on to the service entrance at the side. This was a narrow alleyway leading back to the rear of the building, and he turned in and walked back, ignorant of the fact that a young sergeant in a doorway across the street, with a walkie-talkie hung from his shoulder, had pushed up his six-foot aerial and was speaking softly.

"Man just went in service alley," he said. "Heavy coat, no hat. May be fellow you're after."

A squad car which had been standing around the corner slowly moved up and stopped, but there was no other activity. Forsythe had reached the rear door by that time. To his surprise it was unlocked, and he stepped in cautiously, his hand on his gun. At the head of the back stairs to the basement he stood for a moment, listening. There were muffled sounds from below, the dragging of what might have been a heavy suitcase along the floor, and once the striking of a

110

match, as though someone had lit a cigarette.

Evidently Hellinger had beaten him to it.

Forsythe looked around him. The bare hall was empty, but there was a door under the stairs and he opened it cautiously. It was the usual space allotted for a baby carriage or two, or a boy's bicycle. All it contained now, however, was a small, probably outgrown tricycle, and, careful not to touch it, Forsythe slid inside. He left the door open an inch or two, and waited, his gun in his hand.

Nothing happened. Below he heard Hellinger snap off a light and begin slowly and with extreme caution to climb the stairs. There was no other sound whatever. Hellinger was at the top now, and Forsythe could see him. In the dim light he was little more than a shadow. Then, with no warning whatever, a shot was fired from the front of the hall, followed by two others, and Hellinger dropped where he stood.

Forsythe came out of his closet shooting, or so he remembered it later. He fired four times, while outside men converged on the building from every direction, and someone threw open the front door. All at once the hall was crowded, with Close staring down at the man lying just inside, and from there to Forsythe. His voice was frozen.

"So it was you, after all!" he said. "Don't move if you want to live."

"Don't be more of a fool than God made you," Forsythe said. "He just killed Mike Hellinger. He's back there, if you care to look. And there went your chance for finding Billy Collier. A lot of good you've been tonight."

All at once he felt dizzy. It was a long time since he had killed anyone. Not since the war, and then it had been remote, impersonal. He sat down on the bottom stair and tried to light a cigarette.

111

"Hellinger fooled you," he said. "He's been hiding out here ever since he was spotted this morning. In the Collier apartment, probably. Poor devil!"

Close stared at him, but he made no comment, and Forsythe only roused again when he heard him order an ambulance as well as the morgue car. He looked up and Close gave him a sickly grin.

"You didn't shoot so good," he said. "Fellow here's still alive."

Strangely, it was only ten o'clock when Forsythe found himself in a small room at the local precinct station house, with Close behind a desk and a sergeant taking shorthand notes at a table. Close was still not too friendly. He looked rather as though he had been flying a kite, only to have the string jerked out of his hands.

"All right," he said gruffly. "Let's have it, Forsythe. What did you know, and how did you know it?"

"I didn't actually know anything until tonight, when Martha Simmons's landlady showed me a picture. Then I knew who her accomplice was. But from the start I'd seen those bank deposit receipts. You hadn't. They were genuine, as far as they went, but Anne's money was gone just the same. That meant a bank connection, and it let Hellinger out.

"I think the stealing had been going on ever since the radio program was a hit, but two things happened to scare them. One was Collier's suspicion, beginning maybe a month or so ago. The other was Anne's intention of making a will. Just when Collier's gun was stolen I don't know, but it was meant to use in case of emergency, and it was. Only Anne wasn't killed. That was a blow.

"The other, of course, was the boy. It convinced me Collier was murdered by someone in the building. If

112

not, if the boy saw someone and was in danger, why not shoot him, too? Or take him along, dump him into the river, get rid of him somehow?

"But the way I saw it, the murderer was still in the building when he heard the boy crying and running down to Hellinger. Up to that time nobody knew he was there, but he'd spilled the beans pretty badly. Maybe he saw the killer, maybe he didn't. But he'd got to be put out of the way, for a time anyhow, and Hellinger was no fool. To him Collier was a louse, as well dead as not, and five thousand dollars was a lot of money. So he hid the boy in the cellar before he called the police.

"I'd got that far up to tonight, when the whole setup began to seem queer to me. So far as I could see, nobody except Hellinger was trying to escape, and I didn't think he was smart enough to fake those receipts. Outside of him, everybody was sitting pretty. It looked as though whoever killed Collier and shot Anne was waiting for something, and I could only guess that all the money hadn't been in Martha's safe the night she was killed. I knew this— she'd been planning to go away. She was all packed by Sunday when she left the house. We'll probably never know where she spent most of that day. Personally I think she was trying to find out what had happened to the boy. She had known him since he was a baby. Very likely she was fond of him. The landlady said she was crying that morning when she left."

"If she did find out, it might have been one reason she was killed," Close suggested. He was less gruff now, his eyes alert and interested.

"That and the money," Forsythe agreed. "She was a bad actor, but Collier's murder and the attempt on Anne must have been terrific blows. She hadn't

113

counted on any killing. Then the kidnaping of the boy—"

"She didn't know that when she followed you to Danbury."

"I'm not sure she did follow me. I think she wanted to see Eliza Warrington. To find out if she knew about Anne's radio program. If she didn't, with Anne badly hurt, Martha was still safe until she could get away."

"What about you? *You* knew."

"Maybe I was next on the list," Forsythe said grimly. "Anyhow, she had no chance to talk to Eliza, and she saw her leave the house alone with me. So where was the boy? Very likely she asked the neighbors, and they told her his father had taken him several days ago.

"Well, there it was. Nobody had killed the boy, at least the night Collier was killed. I was pretty sure he'd been hidden in the coal cellar until Hellinger could get him away. That meant there were three men in the building who might be involved—Kerr, Jamison, and Hellinger. Kerr worked in a bank but not the Gotham Trust. Of the lot Jamison could hardly have put the wire on the stairs, since he fell over it himself and was pretty badly knocked out. That left Kerr and Hellinger, and I didn't believe Hellinger was smart enough. So there I was, until I found the snapshot tonight. Then I knew."

It was after midnight when he got home. Close drove him there on his way to Centre Street, and rather to his surprise accepted his offer of a drink. He had been visibly more cheerful since he received a telephone call an hour or so before. Now he seemed quietly amused. To Forsythe's surprise a wide-eyed and smiling Tillie opened the door to them, and he saw Margery beckoning from the top of the stairs.

Both men went up and she led them to the guest room Eliza was occupying. It was brightly lighted, and sitting in the center of the bed, with a resentful Thomas Carlyle in his arms, was a freshly scrubbed and smiling boy. Forsythe stared.

"Who found him?" he asked hoarsely.

"Apparently he found himself," Close said. "Walked up to a cop near the Bronx River Parkway and said he was lost and wanted to go home. Only the address he gave was in Manhattan, which didn't check with where he was found. The cop was going off duty, so he took the kid home and fed him. I guess his wife cleaned him up some."

Billy laughed.

"I got awful dirty getting out the window," he said. "That cop was nice. I liked him."

"Right-o, son," Close said, grinning. "Only I'll have a few words to say to your friend some day. It took his wife and a washcloth to identify you. Better let that cat go. I think he has other things on his mind."

Billy relinquished Thomas Carlyle, who shot out of the room, and Forsythe dropped heavily into a chair. He saw Eliza then. She had been on her knees beside the bed, as though she had been praying. He rather thought she had.

"I got tired in that room," Billy said. "I waited and waited, and Mike didn't come back. So I climbed out the window onto a shed. I tore my pants," he added regretfully. "My best pants, too."

Forsythe looked around the room, at Close, now cheerful and a bit smug, at Eliza's dedicated face and Margery's happy one. It seemed impossible to have come from injury and violent death to this quiet room.

"Was Mike good to you?" he asked.

115

"Sure. He's not much of a cook," said Billy judicially, "but he got my pajamas for me, and a clean shirt."

So that was why the man had been in the boy's room the day Forsythe found him there. To smooth up the turned-down bed, too. Bit by bit the story was becoming clear. And then he thought of Anne.

"His mother?" he asked Close. "Does she know?"

"Doctor said better wait until morning. He'd given her a sedative by the time young Bill was brought in."

Only later, over a hasty drink before Close left to make his final report on the case, did Forsythe learn any further details. So far as they had been able to find out, the boy had not seen who did the shooting. All he remembered was the noise, and of seeing a gun thrown into the room. He was too frightened to move at once. Then he ran downstairs to Hellinger, and Hellinger put him in his bed before he called the police.

"Just when he was bribed to hide him we'll probably never know," Close said. "Hellinger wasn't all bad, but he was a realist. Only as time went on he knew he'd got a tiger by the tail and couldn't let go. When the boy escaped, he knew the game was up. He came back to get his bags and his money—and a bullet in his head."

He yawned as he got up to go.

"Even for me it's been a long evening," he said. "There used to be a sign in the old saloons, 'Take a dozen fried oysters home to your wife.' Only my wife doesn't like oysters."

10

After long strain the human body either breaks down or sets about to make its own repairs. So it was that Forsythe slept that night, slept without even dreaming. When he wakened early his head was clear, and he lay still for some time, thinking about Anne Collier. It was just a week since she had come into his office. It was ten years since the night Bill had collared him and led him to the shy little sister in a badly fitting white dress and he had danced with her.

One dance, but she had remembered it.

What did she feel about him now? Was it fair, in her weakened condition, to ask her? He was unsure, not of himself but of her. He thought he had probably fallen in love with her that first day, when she put her head on his desk and wept.

He was roused by the opening of his door, and a small figure in pajamas which came over and stood by his bed.

"I hope I didn't wake you," Billy said politely. "Nobody else is up yet."

"Of course not. How did *you* sleep?"

"I always sleep. Mike says I'm the best sleeper he ever knew."

Forsythe stirred uneasily, thinking of the body lying motionless in the hall the night before.

"Why don't you get into bed here?" he said. "The room's pretty cold. I'll move over."

Billy crawled in, and he tucked the blankets around him. He was touched by the child's confidence, and he liked the feeling of the small body next to him.

"Are you sure I'm not crowding you?" Billy inquired.

"Of course not. You see, I like boys. I was one myself once."

He had to explain that. In fact he was still explaining when he realized Billy was asleep again. He put an arm over him and drew him close, and it was there a frightened Margery found them both a half hour later and scolded him roundly.

"We thought he was gone again," she said. "Eliza's about to have hysterics."

It was ten o'clock that morning before Forsythe reached the hospital, and Anne already had been told. He found her with the head of her bed raised, and sheer happiness written all over her. Her eyes were shining, and she held out her one useful hand to him.

"I don't know what to say, or how to thank you," she said. "The police say you never gave up."

"Billy found himself, Anne. He's—he's a fine boy. He came into my room this morning and got into my bed. It was the most flattering thing ever happened to me."

"He must have liked you. He wouldn't do that with everybody."

But the unspoken question was still between them. She looked at him searchingly.

"Why did it happen, Wade?" she asked. "Why on earth would Mike steal him? I've been lying here trying to understand. All they told me this morning was that he was back, and at your house."

"Why not let it wait until you're stronger, my dear?

118

It's a long story. I can tell you this. Mike never meant to hurt Billy. He was being kept out of the way for fear he had seen who shot you.''

"And who did that?" she said. "I'm not a child, Wade. I'm entitled to know."

She was right. Sooner or later she would have to know, so still holding her hand he told her, of the plot about her money, of the faked bank deposit receipts in Martha Simmons's files, of his discovery at the bank that she had no money there, and the threat to the conspirators of her making a will.

"Remember," he said, "we were to go to the Gotham Trust and transfer the account to your own name. It would have blown things wide open."

Her eyes were wide with astonishment.

"I trusted Martha," she said. "It's hard to believe she would do a thing like that. Maybe she can explain it. I hope so."

He could not tell her Martha Simmons was dead. She had endured too much.

"I don't think she can, my dear," he said quietly. "Apparently she and the man who worked with her split about even. The police found sixty-five thousand dollars in new bank money in her dressing case, and the rest was recovered tonight, in a locked suitcase. It's all yours now, yours and Billy's."

She brushed the money aside, as though it was of no importance.

"But who *was* the man?" she insisted. "Don't you want to tell me? Or do you know?"

He would have told her. She could have taken it, he knew. Her eyes were brave and steady. But at that moment Close rapped on the door and came in. A new Close, carefully shaved and dressed, and mildly triumphant.

He smiled when he saw Forsythe.

119

"Some day," he said, "when you're an old married man, try a bottle of perfume instead of fried oysters. It works like a charm. But maybe you like fried oysters, Mrs. Collier."

Anne blushed.

"I do," she said valiantly. "You look as though you're off for a holiday."

"I'd hardly call it that." Close grinned again. "I'm on my way to be kissed by the commissioner. I hope he shaved this morning." He glanced at the roses. I see you got ahead of me, Forsythe."

Forsythe looked guilty.

"I wish I'd thought of them," he said. "They're not mine."

Anne smiled at them. Happiness had made her very lovely.

"I'm sure you've both been too busy," she said. "These came yesterday from that nice Mr. Jamison who lives above us. Such a kind card, too. He wants to see me when I'm ready to have visitors."

To her complete surprise Close went abruptly to the table and jerked up the vase. His face was flushed with anger.

"So he hopes to see you again!" he said furiously. "So he could put another piece of wire on the stairs to make you fall and break your neck, and when you didn't, he could pretend to fall over it himself? So he could kill Fred Collier and try to kill you? So he could plot to rob you, and have your boy kidnaped? So he could strangle Martha Simmons, who had worked and plotted with him, and last night kill that poor fool, Mike Hellinger! That's your nice kind Mr. Jamison. Only that's not his name."

He glanced at Forsythe.

"*He's* the fellow the commissioner ought to kiss," he said. "Not me. Only he's a rotten shot. The fellow's going to live to go to the chair."

"Mr. Jamison!" Anne said faintly. "But we hardly knew him. Why should he do all that?"

"Money," Close said, with disgust. "Your money. Let Forsythe tell you the story. I'm taking those roses out in the hall and tearing them to bits." He went toward the door and stopped. "That was a damned good guess of yours last night, Forsythe," he said. "At two a.m. this morning the boys hauled a gent named Stone out of his bed and over roars of fury took him to look at Jamison. He's their absent bookkeeper, all right. Name of Jenkins and supposed to be in Florida. Last I heard of him Stone was on his knees before a crowd of reporters, begging them to respect the sacred name of the Gotham Trust."

He went out then, flowers and all, and Forsythe watched Anne anxiously. She had lain back on her pillows, but her eyes were still clear.

"He seemed such a harmless little man," she said. "And he sent me roses! It's hard to believe."

"Try not to think too much about it," Forsythe said worriedly. "You have Billy, and if it means anything, darling, you have me."

She smiled up into his anxious face.

"It means everything," she said. "And—I know I'm not the commissioner, but if you don't mind—"

"Mind!" he said. He bent down to her, and Close, receiving a stiff and formal accolade from his superior officer, would certainly have approved and probably envied what followed.

"You've done a mighty fine job, lieutenant," the commissioner said, when the formalities were over. "As I said before, the Department is proud of you, Close."

"I had some help, sir. I want you to know that. Without Wade Forsythe I might be patrolling Staten Island."

"Forsythe? Who is he? One of our fellows?"

"No, sir. He's a lawyer. As a matter of fact he specializes in taxes."

Which left the commissioner practically speechless.

If Only
it were
Yesterday

1

Amy had run all the way back from the party but when she reached the corner she knew she was too late. The big red house was brightly lighted, a car she recognized as the doctor's was in the drive, and a police siren was shrieking and coming closer.

She was gasping for breath as she stood there, her knees shaking under her, and her face, had anyone seen it, showing complete despair. There was no one near, however. It was the dinner hour for the unfashionable neighborhood, which ate between six and seven. The bitter cold had driven even the dogwalkers inside, and the police car had not yet appeared, although the siren sounded closer.

She tried to think, standing there in her mink coat and with the wind blowing the feathers of her party hat in every direction. She looked precisely what she was, a stoutish handsome woman in her thirties, with a square jaw and a rather bitter mouth, who had obviously been to a smart reception and was on her way home. Only she was not going home; not to face the police, or the doctor, or—

Her mind stopped there, as if it could not go on. But she dared not stay where she was. She turned and gasped her way around the corner, walking stiffly, not noticing where she was going. After a few blocks she found herself in front of an apartment house, and stood there staring at it. She and Jessie had quarreled over it, she remembered. She had wanted to give up the big unwieldy house and go there, and Jessie had objected.

"I love it, Amy," she said. "It's the only house I've ever known. I was born here, you know. Even if you weren't I should think the fact that Mother—"

"It was only Mother's by her second marriage," Amy said sharply. "I have no sentiment about that."

"You never liked my father, did you?" Jessie inquired. "Why not, Amy? He was kind to you."

"I was only his stepchild. When you came along I was fourteen. It wasn't easy."

That had been only a few months ago. But then there had been the accident and there was no question of moving Jessie, even after she came home from the hospital. Her back had been hurt, so she had to spend her time in bed or on her chaise longue.

Amy moved toward the wall out of the wind. She was breathing easier, but she still could not decide what to do. Her head was aching viciously again, as it had the day of the accident. Jessie had suggested a drive in the fresh air to help it, and in spite of Jessie's protests Amy had taken the wheel. Then, somewhere out in the country, Jessie had said casually, "Ranny Mason has asked me to the concert next Saturday. I hope you don't mind, Amy."

"Mind! Why should I mind?" Amy had said stolidly. And somehow the car had left the road and crashed into a tree. She had never known, she did not know now as she stood there, whether it had been deliberate or not.

She had never hated Jessie, she thought. When her widowed mother died and left her with a nine-year-old half sister to raise she had accepted it as a duty. She might have married at that time, but no man wanted to adopt an orphan, and for long years she

126

had done her best, sat along the wall at dancing school, while Jessie's curls bobbed and her short white skirts fluttered; saw to her education; her clothes. And watched the boys who always seemed to surround her.

Then, as time went on, there had been four years of wonderful peace. Jessie had gone to college, and had spent her vacations with friends. For the first time Amy was living a life of her own. She felt younger, gayer, even more attractive, for beside Jessie she always seemed faded and old. And it was during that period that Randolph Mason began to pay her some attention.

Not as a lover. She knew that now, but at least he liked her; and she bloomed under his interest. It was new and wonderful to have a big handsome man to take her out to dinner or the theater, or to send the occasional flowers. She was still blooming when Jessie finished college and came home to stay.

In all fairness, probably Jessie did not realize that he was Amy's property. But Amy was no fool. She had seen his face when Jessie came into the old-fashioned parlor on her way out to something or other. He had fairly gasped.

"Is this the little sister?" he said. "And not so little at that."

She knew then it was all over. Not at once, of course. He still took her out occasionally, and Jessie still had all sorts of men around her. Little by little, however, the balance shifted, especially after the accident. When Jessie was brought home she was quite definitely the one he came to see. Not that he ignored Amy. He would ring the doorbell, and when Susan, the parlormaid, admitted him, he would stop in the door of the parlor and greet her.

"Hi! How's our invalid today?"

"Expecting you, I daresay," she would say dryly.

She could not break herself of that habit, of waiting in the old-fashioned room so he had to speak to her. Once or twice she was tempted to tell him of the fancy pillows and bed jackets with which Jessie prepared for his visits.

"All fixed up for you," she wanted to say. "Lipstick, too, and a new manicure." She never did, however. He did not wait, for one thing. She would hear him climbing the stairs, carrying a book or a box of flowers. And Susan going back to the service quarters probably to whisper that he was back again, and wasn't Amy's nose out of joint!

Whatever Jessie thought, she had never blamed her for the accident, even when she was at her worst.

"The road was slippery," she said. "The car simply skidded off the road. It was my bad luck to get hurt. That's all."

But one day after they brought her home Amy spoke to her about it.

"You know that crash was my fault, Jessie," she said. "I don't need protecting, if that's what you're doing."

Jessie had looked rather odd.

"It's all over, Amy," she said. "Anyhow you're my half sister. You've always been good to me. I owe you a lot for that." And she added, "I wish we were better friends, Amy."

"I only did my duty," Amy said, and walked out of the room. Neither of them had mentioned Ranny, but there he was between them, and they both knew it.

Amy had been frightened after the accident. It seemed to her, too, that her headaches were coming oftener, headaches which drove her almost crazy with pain and made her do strange and impulsive things.

One day she went to a psychiatrist, giving another name and wearing her oldest clothes. But he had been quite useless. He wanted to talk about her childhood, and when she said she had reared a half sister he had almost gloated.

"I see," he said. "How old is she now?"

"Twenty-two."

She could not see him, but she felt he was looking at her.

"Get along pretty well, I suppose," he said. "No trouble about that, of course?"

She assured him there was not, but he could not let Jessie alone. He kept on about her, and at last Amy got up, flushing angrily.

"Why should I resent her?" she demanded. "After I've devoted most of my life to her!"

"That in itself might be a reason," he said, smiling. "Women who have to care for old mothers often hate them without realizing it."

She had never gone back to him after that, and her headaches were, if anything, worse.

She had been having one that day. She leaned against the wall of the apartment house and tried to think about what had happened. In a way it had started innocently enough. As she had to be out, she had put the two sleeping tablets in Jessie's sherry so she would be asleep when Ranny came. She had not meant anything more than that. But later when she went into the room it had looked so easy—Jessie asleep and the gas fire burning.

Suddenly she felt very cold. The wind was blowing her coat, and she wrapped it around her and walked on. She could no longer hear the siren, but she knew the police were there at the house. For the first time the instinct for self-preservation asserted itself. So far she had not thought about herself. Now she realized that she must do so, must have an alibi for the last few hours. Perhaps if she went back to the party it would help.

After all, why not? It was her brother John's daughter Brenda who was making her debut. And it might not be over. Certainly they had seen her there before. John and Emily, his wife, and Brenda. Even her own two maids, Susan and Hilda, whom she had loaned Emily for the cloakroom. That had left only old Nora, the cook, in the house with Jessie, and Amy had told her not to go upstairs until Jessie rang her bell.

She knew now that had been a mistake. Or had it? Wasn't it natural to let Jessie sleep? Even if Nora talked, what could the police do about it?

As she walked on she went back over the afternoon, shivering as she did so. When she had arrived at the party Susan and Hilda had been busy in the cloakroom, and although she was almost blind with headache she saw that Susan had had her hair done at the hairdresser's and was wearing a pair of ridiculous high-heeled shoes. But they were there and she knew they would be there for hours.

She stopped suddenly when she remembered that. If they were still at the party, who had rung Jessie's bell? Certainly not Jessie. Then who? Her heart began to beat fast until she remembered that Nora had probably been worried, after all, and gone upstairs. But almost certainly it had been too late, or else why the police.

When she reached John's house she stopped under a street lamp and looked at her watch. It was after seven but evidently the reception was still going on. Cars were lined up along the curb, and she could hear faintly the strains of the orchestra from the drawing-room above.

Apparently they had heard nothing yet, and she turned and went up the steps. The door was open, and a chattering group of young people was just leaving. John's butler, Saunders, was in the hall, and the caterer's men were still moving about with trays of drinks. The noise upstairs was rather less, however.

Saunders seemed surprised to see her again as she stopped by the mirror to straighten her hat.

"I dropped a handkerchief," she said. "One of my best. Is—is my brother still here?"

He looked even more surprised, and she realized it had been an error.

"I thought I saw him going out," she said hurriedly. "It's been a nice party, Saunders."

"Yes, madam."

But perhaps he knew something, after all. He was gazing at her suspiciously. Maybe she looked queer. Maybe she looked as if she had just murdered her half sister. But when she glanced again at the mirror she seemed much as usual. She stiffened her shaking knees and slowly climbed the stairs.

At the end of the big drawing-room Emily was sitting, looking exhausted after the long hours on her feet, but Brenda was still standing, in her pale-blue dress, apparently as fresh as ever. She would probably go out and dance all night, Amy thought. Or no. Of course she wouldn't. Not tonight.

The room was hot in spite of the open windows, and Emily was having the heat turned off. She raised her eyebrows when she saw Amy.

"You must be a glutton for punishment," she said. "I thought you'd gone long ago."

"I just went out for a little air, I have a headache."

But Emily was watching her shrewdly, and unexpectedly Amy's legs gave way beneath her. She

131

sat down abruptly in the nearest chair.

"I dropped a handkerchief," she said. "One of my nicest ones." Then, when Emily said nothing, she drew a long breath and looked around the room. "I didn't see the flowers before. They're very nice, aren't they?"

Emily smiled.

"Yes," she said. "There are a lot of them. John said we looked like a first-class funeral."

Amy jerked at the word, and her handbag slid from her lap to the floor. Its contents were dumped out, and of course there was her handkerchief for everyone to see. No one mentioned it, however. Brenda dropped to her knees and began gathering up the contents. She picked up a small bottle and looked at it. Then she stared at Amy.

"What in the world are you doing with sleeping pills?" she inquired. "I thought you objected to them."

Amy was startled. She stared at the bottle. She recovered quickly, however.

"I don't take them," she said. "They're Jessie's." Then all at once she saw a way out. She lowered her voice. "I don't like to leave them around where she can get at them."

Brenda stared up at her.

"What on earth do you mean by that?" she asked.

"She has despondent spells," Amy said darkly. "When she thinks she'll never get better. She has frightened me more than once."

Even Emily wasn't smiling now. She looked hard at Amy.

"I thought she'd been exceptionally cheerful lately," she said. "She was gay enough yesterday when I saw her. Look here, Amy, don't you feel well?"

"I'm all right," Amy said, her lips stiff. "Just one of my headaches. I guess I'm tired, too."

She closed her eyes, feeling dizzy and sick with the heavy scent of flowers. Like a funeral, John had said. Like a funeral!

The last callers were about to leave, and Emily groaned and got up. She forced a smile, and as they departed she motioned to the orchestra to stop. All at once there was a welcome quiet. The men picked up their instruments and left, and Emily sat down again and kicked off her slippers. Brenda, having repacked Amy's bag, gave it back to her.

"Do you really mean that you're afraid Aunt Jessie would take an overdose of those things?" she asked. "It seems so silly. Why would she kill herself? She's getting better all the time."

"I just think it's wiser to be safe," Amy said, and got up. "Well, I'll have to be going. You must be exhausted. It's been a nice party, Brenda. Thanks for asking me."

She straightened her hat again and moved toward the hall and the stairs. Her knees were steadier now, but she felt she had to get out of the house. And she did not like the way Emily was still watching her.

"Good night," she said. "It's getting late. They'll wonder at home what's happened to me."

Brenda was looking at her, too.

"Can't I get you something for the headache?" she asked.

"Don't bother. Nothing helps it except a night's sleep."

She had started for the hall when Emily stopped her.

"Aren't you going to look for your handkerchief?" she said. "Or is that it in your bag?"

"I had another one," Amy said, and turning back

133

went rather hastily into the library. There, and in the long dining-room behind, she made a perfunctory search in case someone was watching. And as a matter of fact someone was. Emily, soundless in her stocking feet, had come in and was taking a small sandwich from the table.

"I'm starved," she said. "John and I will have a tray later on. No use cooking dinner. I wonder where he is, anyhow. Of course he hates parties. Want something to eat?"

But Amy did not want anything to eat. All she wanted was to get away. She shook her head.

"I don't see my handkerchief," she said. "If you come across it just keep it for me."

"All right." Emily sounded faintly skeptical. "Oh, I knew there was something. Thanks for sending your maids over. The cloakroom downstairs must have been a riot."

She took another sandwich and Amy eyed her with distaste. The woman must be hollow all the way down. But Emily ate it calmly.

"You ought to try these," she said. "They're paté. By the way, Ranny Mason came after you'd gone, but he didn't stay. He hurried off. Maybe he took John with him. John's very fond of him, you know."

Amy stared at her.

"Fond of him!" she said. "John's almost twice his age. It's ridiculous."

"I can think of a reason." Emily smiled and lit a cigarette. "And, incidentally, we may drop in tonight," she said. "That is, if John ever gets back, and I'm able to stand on my feet. I know John wants to talk to you and Jessie."

Jessie! But he wouldn't talk to Jessie. Not ever again. And with Emily's eyes on her she was back in Jessie's room, her head thumping and Jessie asleep with the window open and the gas heater burning. She had gone beside the bed to speak to her, but Jessie had not answered. So she had closed the window, turned out the flame in the heater and then turned on the gas again. It had been an impulse, dark and deadly, like the crash. Only this was different. This was death.

She turned so pale that Emily got up quickly.

"Sit down," she said imperatively. "Put your head down between your knees while I get you a drink."

The whisky helped somewhat. Amy was able to sit up, even to look at the clock.

"I don't know what came over me," she said. "I suppose I was overtired." And when Emily said nothing she got up. "It's half past seven. I'd better take the maids home. They must be through now."

Because she was determined not to go home alone to face what was waiting there. Emily, however, only took another sandwich.

"They're probably having supper downstairs," she said placidly. "They can walk over later. It's not far. Or we can take them when we come over. Unless you need them."

"We can manage," Amy said, and went out into the hall. There was a different sort of activity there now. The caterer's men were carrying out the small gilt chairs, and in the drawing-room someone was pushing furniture about. From the kitchen below came sounds of excited laughter and the smell of fresh-made coffee. The noise and activity made her feel dizzy, and she clutched the rail tightly as she went down the stairs.

For the first time she wondered why John and Emily were coming over that night, after a day like this. It must be important, she thought numbly. But she did not want to see Emily again. Not after the way she had looked at her, as though she was acting strangely, as though she was not normal.

The hall and cloakroom below were deserted save for men carrying out the long coat racks to a waiting truck. Not even Saunders was in sight, and with relief she found herself outside on the pavement. The fresh air cleared her head, and she could think more clearly.

She did not go directly home, however. She had to prepare herself for what was to come. But, oddly enough, she was not able to do so. Instead her mind was filled with pictures—of Jessie doing her homework, her little face puckered over the library desk; of Jessie graduating from college in cap and gown—and voted the prettiest girl in the class; and of Jessie only a few hours ago, quietly asleep in her bed, asleep and trusting.

She stopped and sat down on an empty doorstep. She had to get ready for the police, put up a reasonable front. But to her horror she found she was crying, hopelessly and drearily. If only it were yesterday, she thought, if only it were yesterday!

It was after eight when she finally reached the corner again. The doctor and police cars were still there, but as she drew nearer she saw something she had not expected. The big white city emergency truck was in front of the house, the thing they carried the Pulmotor in.

She stopped abruptly and gazed at it. Then she realized that its presence was probably only a part of the usual routine; and her entrance was all she had planned it to be, her hat on one side, her chest heaving, her eyes dilated with fear.

There was a group of men in the hall. John was there, and two others she did not know. And to her shocked astonishment Ranny was with them, looking white and strange. It was John who took her arm and put her gently into a chair.

"It's all right, Amy," he said. "It's over. Jessie is coming out of it."

She looked at him blankly. Coming out of it! Jessie was going to live, after all. O God! After all she had been through! John leaned down and patted her.

"Out of what?" she managed.

"There was an accident," he said. "It might have been a bad one only she was found in time. Don't look like that, my dear. You've got plenty of courage. Bring her some brandy, Ranny. She's had a bad shock."

Shock! What did he know about shock? But the two men were watching her. She realized they were detectives, and braced herself.

"What went wrong?" she asked. "She was fine when I left. I thought she was asleep."

"It was the gas stove," John said. "It got turned on somehow, and her window was closed."

Ranny brought her the brandy, but she thought he avoided her eyes. And the strange men waited until she drank it before they spoke. Then one of them came forward.

"How had she been all day?" he asked. "Cheerful? Normal? Or had you any idea she might try to take her own life?"

She glanced at Ranny and moistened her dry lips. This was it, after all. They suspected her. But what could they do to her? Jessie was alive, was going to live. Nevertheless, she was wary.

"I can't imagine why she would," she said. "Although now and then she's had spells of being despondent. Not when people were around, of course," she added. "She was gay enough then. But sometimes she was afraid her back would never get

137

better." And she went on: "As a matter of fact, I took her bottle of sleeping pills with me this afternoon."

"For fear she would take an overdose?"

"Well, partly that. She was pretty careless about how she used them. I have them here now."

She opened her bag and fumbled for the bottle. The detective took it and examined it.

"I see," he said. "Not many in it, are there? Did she have any today?"

"Not that I know of."

Her headache was suddenly gone. And her mind was clear again. She was doing pretty well, she thought, although John was looking bewildered. Good old John, he never had any brains. He simply bumbled his way through life. But she did not like the way Ranny was avoiding looking at her. He acted as if he was—well, hostile.

The detective slid the bottle into his pocket and changed the subject abruptly.

"According to the cook, you took your sister a glass of sherry every day after her lunch. Did you do that today?"

"Of course. She had it every afternoon. It helped her to sleep."

"There is no glass in her room."

"Naturally not. I rinsed it out and left it on the upper hall table. After I dressed for the party I carried it downstairs to the dining-room."

"I see. You smelled no gas before you left?"

"What are you trying to do?" she said indignantly. "Do you think I would have left the house if I smelled gas anywhere?"

Still Ranny had not spoken. He had hardly moved since he brought the brandy. Now, however, he did speak. Hoarsely, as though he could hardly control his voice.

"Suicide is out," he said definitely. "She was not depressed. I saw her yesterday. She was perfectly cheerful and happy."

"Then it was an accident," she said. "They happen with gas stoves. Perhaps she got up half asleep and stumbled against it."

"I'm sure that was it," John said sturdily. "My sister here was devoted to Jessie. She has cared for her since she was a child. It's ridiculous to question her like this. It's no time to worry her. I'm sure these men will let you go up to your room and rest." He added with his kindly smile, "You do that, and I'll have Nora fix you a tray."

But she did not want to see Nora, Nora who must certainly suspect her. That order not to go to Jessie's room—she must have been insane to put herself in the woman's hands like that.

"I don't want any food," she said sharply. "All I want is to be let alone. I don't understand all this questioning. I've had a terrible headache all day. If you'll only let me go to bed—"

She attempted to get up, but the detective motioned her back.

"In a moment," he said. "Now about this sherry glass? Where did you rinse it, Miss Lawrence?"

"At the washstand in the bathroom."

"Your sister's bathroom?"

"My half sister's. Yes."

He turned to the other officer.

"Might have Kerrigan look there," he said. "At the trap underneath. Something might show up."

John looked puzzled, but the detective did not explain, and Amy herself was growing confused. What about the glass? She had rinsed it, but she had not used much water. Just a little. If they opened the trap— She knew there was a police laboratory, and that they could do all sorts of things there. Her head felt as though it was spinning around, and she put up a hand to steady it.

Ranny had still not spoken to her. The other detective had disappeared, and now John was talking to her. It appeared that Susan had turned her ankle on those high heels of hers, and Hilda had had to bring her home early in a taxi. It had been Hilda who smelled the gas and opened Jessie's door.

"Just in time," John said, in his tired voice. "She opened the window and then called the doctor. He worked over Jessie for a while before he got the police."

"But why the police?" Her own voice sounded strange in her ears.

"They're always called in a case like this," he said. "It's a God's blessing they were, Amy. She's been through enough, and always been brave about it."

But now she was realizing the full extent of her peril. Jessie would be able to talk before long, to deny she had closed the window or turned on the stove or even taken anything to make her sleep. They would believe her, too. Everybody believed Jessie.

The doctor came down the stairs. He looked worn but cheerful.

"All over," he said. "She's asleep now. It's a real sleep, too, thank heaven. I'll have to go home, but I'll be back. The nurses are taking over while I'm gone." He turned to the detective. "Your men are packing up. They'll be down soon. I'm damned grateful to them."

"It's our job," said the detective calmly. "Will you look at this bottle, doctor? Would you know how many pills there should be in it?"

The doctor took out his glasses and reached for the bottle. "Let's see," he said. "There were a dozen this

140

morning." He poured them out into his palm. "Only nine now. That's curious."

"Did she take them whenever she wanted to?"

"Great Scott, no! One in the evening, and another if she was awake at midnight."

"You are sure about this morning?"

"Absolutely. I looked to see if I needed to renew the prescription."

Nobody spoke. John had vanished, to the telephone to call Emily, she thought, and Ranny had not moved. Several men came down from above, bringing their apparatus with them, and she was vaguely aware that the doctor was seeing them out. The other detective appeared, said the laboratory was sending Kerrigan over, and went up the stairs again. And the doctor had come back and was eyeing her.

"Didn't take any of these pills yourself, did you, Amy?"

"No," she said dully. "I dropped the bottle at Emily's. Maybe I spilled some."

He seemed relieved.

"That's probably what happened," he said, and picking up his bag went out to his waiting car. To her relief Ranny followed him, so now it was only the detective and herself. He put the pills back into the bottle and the bottle into his pocket before he spoke.

"If you have anything to say, I'd advise you to say it now, miss."

"Say? What can I say?"

"You might know if someone tried to murder your sister."

Her heart almost stopped.

"Murder?" she said thickly. "What do you mean, murder?"

"I'll tell you," he said. "I don't think she tried to kill herself. I think she was doped this afternoon so

141

she would sleep. Probably in the sherry. I think after she was asleep someone went into that room, closed the window, and turned on the gas. And there were only two people in the house at that time, the cook—and you."

That roused her. She got to her feet, her face pale with terror.

"How dare you?" she demanded. "You heard my brother. I've nursed her for weeks. I've had to look after her for years, since my mother died. And I was out of the house while all this happened. Ask my sister-in-law. Ask anybody."

"I'm sure," he said politely, "that your alibi is perfect. It would be. Only as it happens I always suspect things like that."

She did not have to answer him, for both Ranny and John came back. But as she stood she caught a glimpse of herself in the hall mirror. Her face shocked her. It looked old and incredibly ravaged, and on top of it the gay party hat looked almost obscene. She jerked it off and threw it on the floor. Then without speaking she turned and went with a certain stiff dignity up the stairs.

The bell rang as she reached the landing, and looking down she saw Emily and Brenda come in, Emily grave and Brenda frightened and excited. It was John who greeted them. Ranny merely nodded, as though he hardly saw them.

But Ranny no longer mattered. Nor did Emily, nor anyone else. She went drearily into her room and closed the door.

She did not turn on the light. She sat down on the side of her bed in the dark, and after a time she became aware of sounds in Jessie's bathroom next door. She knew what they were. They would find traces of the pills in the trap, and Jessie would look incredulous when they told her and would deny having taken them herself.

"I thought the sherry tasted slightly bitter," she would say. "I told Amy that, but she said I imagined it."

She had said that, Amy remembered. She had asked if it was a new sort of sherry. And then they would ask her about the gas, and she would deny that. She would lie there among her pretty pillows—or maybe they were not pretty now—and say she could not understand it; that she never turned on the heater. It still hurt her back to stoop.

"Not even if I was half asleep," she would say. "I couldn't possibly have done it."

So there were only Amy herself and Nora, and Nora had not come upstairs. She would moan and cry and tell them what Amy's orders had been. And how she loved Jessie, and would crawl on her stomach for her.

There was only one comfort. Amy knew there were no fingerprints on the key to the gas heater. She had used her white-gloved hands to turn it. They might suspect her, but they could never prove anything.

After a while her tight corset began to hurt her. She got up and took off her clothes, slipping a nightgown over her head. She did it automatically, her mind busy with other things. Suppose Jessie had died, for instance. She could not have told them what she was sure to tell them. But of course she was glad Jessie had not died. The hours since she left her there had been dreadful. But they would all know what she had done, and perhaps why she had done it. Only she was not sure of that herself. It had been like the car wreck, as though some deadly impulse had forced her to act.

When she finished undressing, the sounds from

143

the bathroom had ceased. She crawled into bed and lay there, staring into the dark. Pretty soon they would come for her; as soon as Jessie could talk. They would all know then, even if they couldn't prove it. Even Ranny would know. Perhaps he already suspected. He had been strange, down in the hall.

She was roused by a faint knock on the door, followed by Brenda's entrance. She came over and took one of Amy's inert hands.

"You poor thing," Brenda said. "What a blow you've had! And with a headache, too. But Aunt Jessie's coming around all right. The nurses say she's fine." And when Amy said nothing she perched herself on the side of the bed. "You mustn't mind the police, you know. They're only doing their job. We all know it was an accident."

Amy forced herself to speak.

"I think she tried to kill herself," she said. "She may deny it, but she's been afraid she'd never be really well again."

"You really do think that, don't you?" Brenda sounded astonished. "Then Mother didn't tell you, after all."

"Tell me what?"

"Jessie and Ranny are engaged to be married, Aunt Amy. He told us this afternoon, and they were coming over tonight to discuss it."

Amy did not move. Her last prop was gone, but even Ranny was not important now. She closed her eyes, and Brenda got up.

"I'll let you rest," she said. "I just thought you'd be glad to know. You always liked Ranny, didn't you? You've been friends for years."

Like him! How foolish it sounded. When you had tried to commit murder for a man— Because she knew now that was it. She smiled faintly, there in

144

the dark.

"Yes, I always liked him," she said steadily.

Brenda went toward the door. She felt uncomfortable, without knowing why.

"I'll send you some hot milk," she said. "Maybe it will help you sleep."

Yes, Amy thought, she intended to sleep. That was all she could do now. She waited until Brenda had closed the door behind her. Then she got up and took a small bottle from where she had hidden it behind a picture frame. She had swallowed most of its contents when Nora tapped and brought in a Thermos jug.

"Here's your milk, Miss Amy," she said, with the repressed excitement of all servants in a family crisis. "Mr. John said you didn't want any dinner."

But there was something else in her voice. It was as though she and Nora shared a secret, and a deadly one. She was at the mercy of this creature, she thought. Then she remembered that it did not matter, and closed her eyes.

"No," she said. "And tell them downstairs I don't want to be disturbed. I'm going to try to sleep."

Nora, however, was not to be robbed of her moment of importance.

"It's a good thing Hilda's got a sharp nose, isn't it?" she said. "If she hadn't smelled that gas there'd have been a lot of trouble. That stove didn't turn itself on, and you'd told me not to go upstairs."

For a moment Amy wanted to throttle the skinny neck beside the bed. It was too much trouble, however, and already she was feeling relaxed as she had not felt for months. Not indeed since Jessie came home from college.

"Yes," she said drowsily. "I'm sorry I told you that, Nora. But it's all right now. Everything's all right."

145

Nora went out, and Amy turned comfortably in her bed. She lifted her right hand and let it drop. The hand was all right. It had not killed Jessie. She felt relieved, as though she had been reprieved from something horrible.

Shortly afterward John stood outside her door and listened. She seemed to be asleep, but of course she had to know what Jessie had said when she became conscious. He hesitated, however, for his simple mind was still confused. Why, for instance, had the detective left Jessie's room after he heard her statement and slammed in rage out the front door? Why had Ranny Mason listened in astonishment and then leaned over and kissed Jessie? And why had Emily said abruptly that she had to go home, and taken Brenda and the car with her, refusing to talk and leaving him more or less high and dry?

He rapped at the door, and on receiving no answer opened it carefully. Amy did not move, so he went to the side of the bed and cleared his throat.

"I hate to waken you, Amy," he said, "but I have some news for you." In the faint light he saw her eyes opening, so he went on. "It's all right, my dear. Jessie has told us about it. It seems she got up, half asleep, and stumbled against the stove. That's how it must have been turned on."

She did not move, but he thought she was smiling faintly.

"So like Jessie," she said thickly and closed her eyes again.

He went away and left her, to sleep.

The
Scandal

1

Steve Wallace waited uneasily in the bleak small parlor. He did not like his errand. He did not like the story behind it, and he was prepared not to like the girl. But when he heard her coming he stood up and braced himself to shake hands.

He did not shake hands, however. The girl did not come near him. She stood just inside the door and looked at him.

"Yes?" she said.

"I've brought the check," he explained. "Mr. Davies is laid up with an attack of arthritis."

She did not say she was sorry. She did not say anything. He fumbled with his wallet, feeling awkward.

"I'm his junior partner," he said. "Name's Wallace. Steve Wallace. Oh, here it is."

"Thanks." Her voice was indifferent, but looking at her he realized she had been crying. Otherwise she was quite a pretty girl, but he had heard that love children often were. The thought embarrassed him.

"About your mother," he said. "Mr. Davies feels you should have some help there. He thinks the estate would stand for a nurse."

This was not precisely true. What old Davies had said was that if the heirs didn't fork up he would damned well do it himself. But the girl's expression did not change.

"Thanks. I can manage all right," she said. "We don't need a nurse."

"Even a part-time one?"

"We want no one prying around. I am perfectly capable."

She annoyed him, her set young face, her complete indifference to him, her obvious desire to get rid of him.

"What about the woman who let me in?" he inquired. "She's here, isn't she?"

"She minds her own business. She's only here once in a while. And it won't be long." She hesitated. "I suppose you know. My mother is dying."

She was refusing sympathy. He saw that. His perfunctory "Sorry" met with no response, and he was picking up his hat when the doorbell rang. Perhaps the woman had gone, for no one answered it. When it rang again the girl went to the window and looked out. Whatever she saw there seemed to startled her. She went out and opened the door herself, and he heard another voice.

"I'm Mrs. Jenkins," it said. "I heard your mother was sick, so I brought over some chicken broth. I—"

Her voice faded out, as though she hesitated to go on, and he heard the girl's perfectly civil reply.

"Thank you, Mrs. Jenkins," she said. "You're very kind, but I'm afraid it's too late."

"Too late!" the woman gasped. "Is your mother—"

"About four years too late," the girl said politely, and Wallace heard the door quietly but firmly close. From the window he saw the woman hurrying away, clutching a napkin-covered bowl and crimson with indignation. When the girl came in she met his cold eyes squarely.

"And where did that get you?" he asked. "She

150

meant well. Do you have to make enemies like that?"

She sat down suddenly, as though the brief scene had unnerved her. The set look had gone out of her face. She looked pale and shaken. But she did not cry.

"You heard me," she said. "It's taken four years for that bowl of soup to get across the street. Only across the street. Do you know what that means? Of course you don't. You're Steve Wallace. People call you that, don't they? But they don't know what to call me, or Mother. So they don't call us anything. They just—let us alone."

She got up abruptly.

"I'm not sorry for myself," she said defiantly. "I'm sorry for Mother. That's all. Now, if you've finished, I'll go up to her."

She left him standing there, and he heard a door upstairs open and close. He was divided between resentment and a sense of failure as he left the small brick house. He had had no reason to attack her. If he had been friendly—God knows she needed friends, he thought—or just given her the check and gone, it would have been better. When he finally got into his car he did not go back to the office. Instead he drove past the old Coleman place, huge but now empty and falling into disrepair, the grounds overgrown with weeds, the windows closely shuttered, and an air of death and decay everywhere.

It was more than twenty years since Caroline Coleman had closed it and gone elsewhere to live. He could still remember her, however, the great lady of the town, the donor of the Coleman Library, the builder of the vast mausoleum which dominated the cemetery on the hill. As a boy he had watched her in her pew at St. James, sitting aloof and haughty before her God, while the rest of the congregation knelt in humility. She never knelt, did old Caroline, not even when her young son was killed at the end of the First World War.

But he had only a vague memory of her daughter Jennifer, the quiet subdued young woman who trailed her mother like the insignificant tail of a blazing comet. Jennie, they called her. And it was Jennie who lay dying in the shabby house he had just left.

He found Mr. Davies in his library, his leg bandaged and on a hassock, but his eyes full of curiosity.

"I see you escaped unscathed, Steve," he said, smiling.

"I bear a few scars," Steve told him. "I don't think she liked me much. Or the check, either."

"The check is her monthly cross. She has to have it, the way things are, but she hates taking it. She's a nice girl, really. What about the nurse for her mother?"

"It's out. I gathered she wanted nobody prying around. That's what she said. Why on earth did they come here? It's the last thing I would have expected."

Davies leaned back in his chair and eased his leg.

"You didn't know old Caroline very well, did you?" he inquired. "You were only a youngster. But she never forgave Jennifer for insisting on having the child. Never saw either of them again. It's a queer story, Steve. Jennifer Coleman was the last person in the world to go off the rails like that. I've never understood it."

"But she came back here four years ago. I still wonder why."

"She came because she had to. She was never very strong. I'd managed by threats to get a small allowance for her from her mother. After all, it was her father's money. The girl was born in England,

and they stayed there until old Caroline died. I've often wondered how she dared face the heavenly gates after the wicked will she left. I think I'll have a drink, Steve. I need one when I think about it."

He looked thoughtful over his highball when it came.

"By the will," he said, "Jennie was to have the house you saw today. Caroline owned it. But she was to come back here and live in it. Otherwise no allowance, no anything. That's vengeance beyond the grave, Steve. As though Caroline had reached out of that mausoleum of hers on the hill here and shaken her fat old fist at her daughter and her child."

"What about the man in the case?" Steve inquired. "He died, didn't he?"

"He was killed. He and Jennie were to be married the next day. Even had the license. At least so Jennie told me. But that night the Coleman garage burned, and the smoke finished him. They got him out, but it was too late."

There was something odd in the elderly lawyer's voice, and Steve looked at him.

"Good God!" he said. "Don't tell me the old girl set fire to the place!"

"It wouldn't surprise me any," said Davies comfortably. "You see, young Burton had had to leave college after the crash of twenty-nine. Jobs were pretty hard to get and Caroline hired him as a chauffeur. He was a good-looking boy, Chris Burton. I always liked him. But of course it was inevitable. He and Jennie fell in love and all hell broke loose when they told Caroline. She fired him. He was to leave the next morning, but that night the garage burned."

"It looks like the hell of a coincidence."

"So it does. So it did at the time. But all I know is that Jennie left early the next day and collapsed in the

153

railroad station at Springfield. I was notified and got her to a hospital. Then I went back and saw her mother."

He looked complacent, and Steve laughed.

"That must have been something," he said.

"It was. I gave her her choice of a charge of arson, and maybe murder, or an allowance for Jennie. She denied it, of course, but I got the allowance. Not much. Just enough. I guess I scared her, for she closed the house and went to New York. Never came back, until she was brought here after she died. Left her money to some remote relatives who detested her."

"She'd have been a nice study in psychiatry," Steve said. "Sounds crazy to me."

"Got to remember people were pretty cruel about illegitimate children twenty years ago. Even worse than now." Mr. Davies finished his highball and put down the glass. "And there's this, too, Steve. Every now and then the good Lord makes someone like Caroline Coleman maybe as a lesson to the rest of us. Like Hitler. He leaves out the heart and just puts in a pump instead. That was Caroline."

Steve sat silent, nursing his drink. He felt profoundly shocked, and not a little indignant.

"What about the girl, this Edith?" he asked. "None of this was her fault."

"You can't hide an illegitimate child under a bushel, son. And we're a respectable lot in this town," he added dryly. "We may commit sins, but we don't flaunt them."

"But she knows, doesn't she?"

"Jennie had to tell her. When they came back here four years ago Edith started at the high school, but the kids there soon let her know. She left the school after that, but she's carried on her education since. I've helped her a bit. She's a smart girl and a pretty

154

fine one. Took it like a soldier. Crazy about her mother, of course."

Steve got up.

"I wish I'd known the story when I was there. I more or less made a fool of myself. Talked to her like a Dutch uncle."

He was still resentful when he left the Davies house, and as a gesture of apology he stopped at a florist's and bought a box of spring flowers: gay little tulips, hyacinths, and white lilacs, and a small bunch of wide-eyed pansies. Their faces looked appealing and gentle, he thought. But he found he was nervous when he got out of his car and, box in hand, rang the doorbell of the small house again.

He heard steps on the stairs, and was unhappily aware that he was being inspected from the parlor window. He felt rather silly, but he set his jaw as the door opened and the girl confronted him. She did not bother to greet him. She looked at the box and spoke with cold politeness.

"I'm very sorry," she said. "I'm sure you mean well. But I don't want any presents. Even flowers."

Suddenly the tension of the afternoon exploded, his resentment at her situation, his earlier mistake, and now this unnecessary rebuff. He felt his color rising, his collar tight.

"See here," he said, to his own amazement, "this isn't a bowl of soup. It hasn't been four years in coming either. About two hours, I imagine. And this is for your mother, not you. You can't speak for her. Not to me, anyhow."

He stepped past her into the hall and with his free hand closed the street door behind him.

"Get something to put them in," he said. "And I'm not taking any chances. I stay here until she gets them."

She turned away abruptly and went into the back of the house. He was shaking as he walked into the parlor and put the box on the table. When she came back with a couple of cheap vases he had the pansies in his hand, and a look of abject apology on his face.

"I guess I'm acting like an idiot," he said. "The plain truth is that I thought the pansies could speak for me. They're gentle little flowers, you know, and forgiving."

Quite suddenly she sat down and put her head on the table, and he realized she was crying. He felt awkward and uncomfortable. After a minute or two, manlike, he took a handkerchief from his pocket and slid it into her hand. He wanted to touch her, to comfort her, even to apologize again. But he did not move, and when she finally looked up she made a desperate attempt to smile.

"That's over," she said. "It was the pansies. She always loved them. Only it won't be long now. It's her heart." She got up, and gravely gave him back his handkerchief. "I'll fix them, if you'll wait. She'll love them."

"I don't need to wait," he said awkwardly. "I don't know what the hell got into me. I didn't come back here to attack you."

"I'd like you to see them," she told him. "And don't feel sorry. I understand."

He watched her as she deftly sorted them and put them in water. The crying had loosed her hair and given her face a needed softness. She looked young and brave and terribly alone. He wanted to say something, to tell her that she must be proud of her mother, since she had been willing to pay such a price for her. But, after all, it was the girl who was paying the price now. Jennifer Coleman was beyond it.

"The pansies are for you," he told her.

"Thank you," she said gravely, and picking up the vases started up the stairs. At the top she turned and looked down at him, but she did not smile or speak.

He let himself out and drove back to his sister's house, where he lived. Edna Wallace was alone when he got there, and she looked up from her knitting when he flung into the room.

"Now what have I done?" she said comfortably. "Has the laundry lost a shirt?"

"So far as I know," he said, "it's what you haven't done that I want to talk about. How is it that Jennifer Coleman and her daughter have been treated like pariahs ever since they came back here?"

Edna looked faintly exasperated.

"What in the world could anyone do?" she inquired. "You couldn't ask them out to dinner, could you? Or take them to the country club. For heaven's sake, Steve, show some sense. We stand for something in this town. Do you want me to be ostracized, to lose every friend I have?"

"It's like that, is it?"

"Of course it's like that. If you think that old scandal has ever died you're crazy. Jennifer Coleman insisted on having her baby, father or no father. The whole town knows it. If she chose to come back here to live it's up to her. The sins of the fathers, Steve."

He looked at her round contented elder-sister face with a fury he could hardly control.

"They came back," he said, "because they had to. Jennifer Coleman has been an invalid for years. She couldn't earn a living. The girl has had to look after her. As for coming here, the sainted Caroline put that in her will. No come, no house, no money. And now she's dying."

Edna put down her knitting and stared at him.

"Don't tell me you've fallen for that girl!" she said. "With a dozen of them here in town after you, and you only needing to reach out a hand. I don't believe it."

"For God's sake, Edna!" he shouted. "I'm talking to you about a rankling injustice and a dying woman, and you ask me if I'm falling in love! What's going to happen to this girl when she's left alone? We've got plenty of decent kindly people here. Where are they?"

"Don't shout at me," Edna said firmly. "I admit it's hard on the girl, but whose fault is it? The Colemans were always too good for this town. I remember I cried my eyes out when I wasn't invited to Jennie's coming-out party. I'm sorry if she's dying now, but she never knew I was alive twenty years ago."

He looked at her as if he had never seen her before.

"So that's it," he said. "How pleasant when the mighty fall! That's the idea, isn't it? Not an old sin, but an old jealousy. I thought better of you, Edna."

He slept rather badly that night. He could see no hope for the girl, and nothing that he himself could do. And for a day or so he did not go back to the house. Mr. Davies's absence from the office kept him busy, and also he felt that another call would be an intrusion. For now Jennie Coleman was close to the end, and the town knew it.

Then one night he took his car and drove out again past the old Coleman place. It was a warm spring night and downtown the streets were crowded with people, on the way to the movies or simply walking for sheer pleasure. But the Coleman place was deserted. Under the young moon he could see the debris where the garage had burned and carried a young life and much hope with it. He remembered climbing over it as a boy, looking for treasure.

Had Caroline actually burned it? Davies suspected it. It could never be proved, of course, but when he found himself by the near-by fire station he automatically stopped the car. The men in their shirt sleeves were sitting in a row along the pavement, their shining apparatus behind them, their cigarettes gleaming like fireflies in the dark. He nodded and asked for the chief.

"Gone home," someone told him. "Looked like a quiet night, so he left."

They were curious, but they asked no questions. He got the chief's home address and drove there, still with the odd feeling of urgency he had had all evening. The chief, also in his shirt sleeves, was alone on the front steps of his house. He knew Steve and nodded to him.

"Nice night," he said. "Came out for a last pipe. Anything I can do for you, Mr. Wallace?"

Steve sat down on the step below him.

"I'm not sure," he said. "It's a long time ago. Twenty years or more. I don't even know if you were at the fire I'm thinking of, or remember it."

The chief nodded.

"I was a rookie then," he said. "What fire was it?"

"The one that burned the Coleman garage."

The chief put down his pipe.

"You think I'd forget that baby?" he demanded. "Boy, I was the one who got that fellow out, the chauffeur. Damn near passed out of smoke poisoning myself, too. He was dead, of course." He eyed Steve. "What about it, son?"

"I just wondered," Steve said warily. "I was only a kid then, but Mr. Davies was telling me about it today."

"What did he have to say?" The chief sounded interested.

"Not a great deal. I gathered the man's death didn't bother Mrs. Coleman much. I guess you know the story."

"Who doesn't?" said the chief succinctly. And added: "She was a hard woman, Caroline Coleman. Mean as they come. Most times in a case like that they ask the men in for coffee after it's over. Not she! But I seen her on the terrace that night, and if I didn't know better I'd say she was looking mighty cheerful." He stopped and reloaded his pipe. "It was the girl we had trouble with. She carried on like crazy. I guess you couldn't blame her."

"No. I suppose it wasn't deliberate. The fire, I mean."

The chief did not answer at once.

"Well, it might have been at that," he said. "The thing was wood, and it went pretty fast. But don't you quote me on that. I never did think that place of hers in the cemetery would hold Caroline Coleman if she really wanted to get at somebody."

Steve drove home slowly, but as he passed the small brick house he saw a change in it. The light in the sickroom was low and the window was open, and as he stopped his car he saw one of the local doctors coming out. The doctor saw him and came to the curb.

"Nothing you can do, Steve," he said. "She's gone. About an hour ago. Edith asked me to call you. She said you'd been kind to them. God knows they needed kindness."

"How is she taking it? Edith, I mean."

"Well, she's had a long time to prepare for it, but it's always a shock when it comes. I've left her a

160

sedative, but I doubt if she takes it. I'm going to try to find someone to stay with her tonight. She shouldn't be alone."

"How about my staying downstairs until you locate somebody?" Steve suggested.

"It would help. I've left the front door unlocked, in case I'm lucky." He paused uncomfortably. "You know something?" he said. "She died with that dead boy's picture in her hands. After all this time!"

He hurried away, as if ashamed of any show of emotion, and left Steve standing on the pavement. After the car had gone, however, he turned and went into the house.

Except for a dim light in the hall, the lower floor was empty, and he went into the parlor and finding a chair sat down in the dark. It was quiet overhead, and after a time he wanted a cigarette badly. But he decided against it, and let his thoughts wander to the girl upstairs, and to what she faced in what to her was a cold and cruel world.

She did not know he was there. She was alone in her mother's room. She had been on her knees for some time. Then lifting herself stiffly she prepared for what she had to do. She brought in fresh linen for the bed, and slowly and carefully changed it. But she left the picture where it was. It had been a part of her life so long as she could remember, the faded yellowing snapshot of the smiling young man who was her father.

She wondered vaguely if somewhere he was still waiting. She hoped he was. But her thoughts were still chaotic as she moved mechanically about the room, taking the bottles from the bedside table, and at last with a comb arranging her mother's heavy dark hair. Then, with nothing more left to do, she closed the door behind her and went out into the hall.

161

It was at the top of the stairs that she fainted.

Steve heard the soft crumple as she went down, and found her there, a young slim figure, in a nightgown and bathrobe, and had the sense to leave her flat on the floor until her eyes opened. They looked blank at first. Then she stirred and tried to sit up.

"Don't move for a minute or two," he said quietly. "I'm here. There's nothing to worry about."

"What happened?"

"You're overtired. That's all. You fainted."

She seemed to think that over, the faint, not his presence. She seemed to take that for granted.

"I've never done that before," she said at last. "May I sit up now?"

"If you'll let me help you."

He put an arm under her shoulders and raised her, and she gave him her slight smile.

"Thanks," she said. "You're being very kind."

Kind! She had had little enough of kindness, he thought, and tightened his arm around her.

"How about getting you up to bed?" he asked, his voice slightly husky. "You needn't worry. I'm staying, at least until the doctor finds somebody."

"You know, then?"

"I know. Yes."

"I'd like you to see her."

"All right. After I get you settled."

"I think if you see her you'll understand. She was so good. She was a good woman always, Steve."

"I'm sure of it," he told her, and managed to get her to her feet. The light was on in her room, but even the bleakness of the house had not prepared him for its austerity. It looked stripped, as though she had denuded it of everything which made it livable. And later in Jennie Coleman's room he realized she had done exactly that, and why.

162

It was no time for prudery. He helped her out of the bathrobe, and waited until in her cheap cotton nightgown she was settled in her bed.

"Will you see her now?" she asked anxiously. "I want you to, because I'm going to ask you to do something for me, after you do."

"You ought to try to sleep."

"I can't. Not yet."

The light was low in Jennie's room, but the air was fresh and there was a hint of spring in it. He glanced around him. Whatever the poverty and ugliness of the little house, there was none of it here. There were fresh ruffled curtains at the windows, and bright covers on the chairs. The old wallpaper was covered with pictures, and the bed itself was immaculate. But it was the woman's face that caught and held his attention. It had suffered, but it was both peaceful and beautiful.

He had not remembered Jennie Coleman as beautiful, but he realized there is a beauty which comes from character and goodness, and looking at her he understood what the girl had said. Whatever her early sin—if sin it was—she had earned the peace that was hers now.

When he went back, Edith was watching for him. Apparently what she saw satisfied her, for she lay back in the bed.

"You saw what I meant, didn't you?"

"I did indeed," he said gravely.

But she still seemed to feel the need of making her case.

"She was wonderful," she said. "she was always wonderful. All through the war we stayed in London, and she worked day and night. She was never strong, but she did that, and never complained."

"I can believe that, too, my dear."

She eyed him carefully, waiting a moment as though to be sure of him. Then she sat up in bed, careless that the nightgown outlined her small breasts.

"Then you'll promise to do what I ask you?" she said.

He smiled down at her.

"I'm a lawyer. I don't commit myself in advance. But I'll go through hell and high water to try."

He meant it. He was surprised himself to realize how much he meant it. Or how he wanted to take the girl in his arms and comfort her. He had a brief and rather grim picture of Edna peering in if he did so, and dismissed her with a gesture.

"What is it I'm to do?" he asked.

She hesitated, as though she was rallying her courage.

"I don't want her buried in the Coleman mausoleum," she said, her voice low. "Don't ask me why. I just couldn't bear it. Nor could she."

Whatever he had expected it was not that. It rather set him back on his heels.

"Look," she said feverishly, "there will be nobody there. The people here didn't care for her, living. Why should they now? And I've saved a little. I can pay something. The estate won't have to do it."

He was puzzled, uneasy.

"But you must have a reason, my dear. After all she has a right to lie there."

"No, no." Her voice was choked. "Please, no. I promised her. I promised her." She burst into tears, and he sat down beside the bed and put an arm over her trembling body. He waited until she was quiet before he spoke again.

"Tell me about it," he said. "You can trust me. It's

164

just between the two of us, and I'll do what I can. You know that."

She made a small despairing gesture of surrender.

"Because my grandmother killed my father," she said. "They were going to Springfield the next morning to be married, and she knew it. She set fire to the garage and Mother saw her doing it."

He was appalled. Whatever he had suspected he had not realized that Jennie Coleman had been a witness. It accounted for her wild flight from home, her illness and desperation.

"How long have you known all this?" he asked gently.

"Only the last month or so. When she knew she couldn't live. Do you think I'd have taken that money all these years if I had? I'd have starved first."

"I wouldn't worry about the money," he told her. "Your mother had to have it. You see, she wanted you very badly, and she was willing to pay that price for you."

"She paid a good many prices."

But he saw he had given her something to think about. The defiance had died out of her face, even some of the bewilderment. She looked like a tired child, and on impulse he stooped and kissed her lightly.

"I think I can promise about the mausoleum," he said. "And I'll be downstairs until someone comes. Now go to sleep. You need it."

It was three o'clock when a nurse sent by the doctor arrived, and he got into his car and drove home. Edna was sleeping soundly, her door open against the warm night, and callously he walked in and turned on the big ceiling light. Edna stirred and blinked at him.

"What's the matter?" she asked sleepily. "Is it fire

or burglars?"

He went over beside the bed and stared down at her.

"I have a job for you," he said. "Jennie Coleman died last night, and the funeral will be tomorrow. That gives you a day to rouse the populace."

She sat up in bed, her mouth open with amazement.

"The populace! What does that mean? Or have you been drinking?"

"I'm completely sober. What I am telling you is that at her own request she will not be buried in her mother's mausoleum. I am also stating that the best people in this town are going to her funeral. What's more, they are sending flowers, beginning with you and me. I mean it, Edna."

There was no sleep in her now. She was both puzzled and indignant.

"I suppose you've fallen for the girl," she said furiously, "but even that's no reason for you to ask the impossible. How can I do a thing like that? It sounds crazy."

He smiled at her grimly.

"I told you before, I think there are decent kindly people here," he said. "If there aren't, then I'll break this town wide open with a scandal that will make it tear down Caroline Coleman's library stone by stone. And, for all I care her mausoleum, too. Is that clear? And for good measure," he added, "I *have* fallen for the girl."

He stalked out of the room, leaving Edna in what she would have called a state. But after a time she reached out for the pad and pencil beside her bed and began making a list of names. In spite of Steve, she knew she need make no threats. Just a mention of the Coleman benefactions would do, and the town liked a good funeral. It was quite a list when she finished.

166

Steve told the story to Mr. Davies in the morning, and was surprised to find that gentleman chuckling.

"Good for you, and good for Edith," he said. "We'll do what she wants. And when all this blows over, perhaps you'll have some other news for me."

Steve colored. "It's a little early for that, isn't it?"

"Never too early if you want the girl," said Mr. Davies. "Maybe that's not in the lawbooks, but it's sure as hell in the human heart."

It was Steve and Edna, the next day, who saw Edith Coleman through the impressive crowded service which laid Jennifer Coleman to her last rest. But it was Steve alone who took her home into the empty little house with all its memories. In the parlor there he put her into a chair and stood rather stiffly in front of her.

"Maybe I'm being a bit of a fool," he said. "However, I'm acting under my law partner's advice, and he's a wise old bird. What I want to tell you is that you aren't alone any more, my dear. And when the time comes, God willing, you need never be alone again."

He kissed her quickly and left her. But he knew he would be back, and she knew it, too. It was no time for words, or for doubt, either. He would be back, and when he came the door would be open for him.

Murder
and the
South Wind

1

The trouble was that no one knew just when the bridge game started that afternoon. That left none of us with an alibi—not even Mother—and at least two of us had a possible motive.

It was frightfully hot in Florida last winter. There had been a south wind for weeks, which meant mosquitoes, no fishing, and everybody's nerves in poor shape. I had coaxed Tom, my husband, down for a month's vacation from the Washington madhouse, but with no fishing he risked sunstroke by playing golf every day. Thank God, he was on the course that afternoon. At least he had an alibi.

Anyhow, there we were, the four of us, and the fifth who wasn't there in body was certainly there in spirit. He was Captain Hugh Gardiner, on a ten-day furlough, and he was there in spirit because one of our players, Fanny Raeburn, had divorced him and taken her maiden name, and because Pat Wilson was supposed to be going to marry him.

They had wandered in separately in search of a cool place, but even our patio was hot that day. Fanny was already there when Pat came in. Pat looked as though she was going to back out, but Fanny gave a queer little laugh.

"Come on, Pat," she said. "I hope we're civilized enough to behave ourselves. How about some bridge?"

Pat came in. She looked lovely in spite of the heat, and I saw Fanny staring at her. But Pat didn't look well. There were circles around her eyes, and Fanny leaned toward me as she put up her bicycle. We all used bicycles on the island. No gas.

"She and Hugh had a fight last night," she said. "Something about a girl at the hotel."

"How on earth do you know?"

"Our Mary Pearl," she said smugly. "The Negroes know everything that goes on. It gives me the creeps."

"Where's Roy?" I said, to change the subject. Roy was the brother she was visiting.

"Where do you think?"

Well, of course, I knew. Roy Raeburn was out after seashells. It was more than a mania with him. It was a science. He was an authority on shells of all sorts, and every beach on the island knew his stooped, near-sighted body and the collector's box he carried. Which, of course, put him in the picture later.

We played in the patio, but the game wasn't a success. For one thing, Pat played terribly. And there were five or six fighter planes out over the Gulf of Mexico shooting at a towed target and making a lot of noise. I remember Mother tucking away the two dollars she had won when it was over and looking up at them.

"I hope it's cool for those boys out there," she said. "When I think of what's ahead of them—"

Pat stared at the sky.

"I don't think it's safe," she said. "Those bullets travel a long way. If anyone is out there in a boat—"

Fanny grinned.

"Worried about Hugh?" she inquired, rather nastily. Pat flushed.

"Hugh?" I said, astonished. "Don't tell me he's fishing?"

"He heard the tarpon were in," Pat said defensively.

"That's ridiculous," I said. "With this wind? There isn't a tarpon within a hundred miles."

"They may be in, but they're not showing," Mother said idly.

I kept quiet. There is an old argument about the tarpon. One school of thought maintains that they are in the Pass all the year round but simply not interested. The other insists that they go somewhere—perhaps Mexico—for the winter and come back to spawn in the spring. Friendships have crashed over this. But this is only incidentally a tarpon story. Actually it is about a murder.

I remember that Fanny had gone into the house to get her sun hat when one of the guides came through the gate in the hedge. He seemed embarrassed when he saw us, and took off his cap.

"Could I speak to you, Mrs. Hull?" he said to Mother.

"Why, of course, Joe," Mother said. "What is it?"

I think now that he was pale, under his leathery tan. And just then a four-engined bomber came over the treetops and nobody could speak for a minute or so. Joe simply waited. I noticed that he had not looked at Pat.

"If you don't mind, I'd rather see you alone, ma'am," he said doggedly when the noise had subsided. "It's sort of a private matter."

Mother looked surprised. She got up, however, and took him into the house. Only Pat and I were left, and Pat had lost all her color under her make-up.

"Something's happened, Peg," she said. "Did you see Joe's face?"

"Probably just a row about something," I said.

She stood still, looking rather odd. A Navy dirigible had come sailing overhead, and as it was low the engines made a lot of noise. But Mother was still in the house and I was puzzled.

"Joe wouldn't look at me," she said, her lips stiff. "I think it's about Hugh."

"Don't be an idiot," I said sharply. "He's safe enough. Who's guiding him?"

She said it was Bill Smith, and I said Bill was a good guide and to stop worrying. Then Fanny came out of the house, with her hat on one side of her head and her eyes wide.

"Why on earth is your mother calling the sheriff?" she demanded. "What's wrong?"

"Didn't you hear?"

She let that pass. She was not above listening to things that didn't concern her, but now she was excited.

"Only the call," she said. "After that she shut the door."

I grinned. Then I saw Pat's face. "It's probably nothing," I said. "The whole village comes to Mother. Sit down, Pat. Fanny, your hat's crooked. What's all the excitement anyhow?"

But I knew something was wrong when Mother came out of the house, followed by Joe. She didn't look at Pat or Fanny. She glanced at me.

"I'm going down to the guide dock, Peggy," she said. "Joe's got his car here. You'd better come with me."

I got up, and so did Pat. She stared at Mother.

"It's Hugh, isn't it, Mrs. Hull?"

I think Mother had meant to lie, but there was something in Pat's face that warned her.

"There's been an accident," she said. "I wouldn't worry too much, Pat dear. Wait until we know."

"What sort of accident?" Pat's voice was frozen.

"Bill Smith says it was a bullet from one of the planes."

"Is he badly hurt?"

"I don't know yet. Better go home, Pat. I'll let you know at once."

But Pat was not going home nor, as it turned out, was Fanny. I suppose you can divorce a man and even hate him, but it must come as a shock to know something has happened to him. Anyhow we all got into Joe's ancient open car and headed for the guide dock. None of us said anything, but over our heads the dirigible had turned suddenly and headed for the Pass which leads between the islands to the Gulf, and from down at the mouth of the bayou I could hear a Coast Guard boat moving out. That's nothing unusual, of course. The guides have a conviction that the Coast Guard puts out merely to go fishing. But they were not going fishing that day.

At the guide house Bill Smith was sitting on the dilapidated steps, with his head in his hands and three or four guides around him, not talking. Just standing. Pat was the first out of the car.

"Where is he?" she said. "Maybe he's not—Why haven't you got a doctor, or somebody?"

Bill looked up. His face was agonized when he saw who it was.

"He ain't here, Miss Wilson," he said. "He went overboard and he never came up. I've been an hour in the Pass, looking."

It was Fanny who spoke then, her voice incredulous.

"You're crazy, Bill," she said. "He can swim like a fish."

"He was shot first," said Bill, and put his head down in his horny fisherman's hands again.

Pat didn't faint. She just stood there, and she made no protest when one of the guides offered to take her home. She even got into the car herself, but she looked completely dazed. I wanted to go with her. I

175

didn't like to think of her going back by herself, but she refused.

"Let me alone, Peg," she said. "I'm all right. It's just—"

She didn't finish. The car drove off, and after that Bill told his story.

"I been afraid of them planes right along," he said. "But Captain Gardiner was set to go." He got out a cigarette and tried to light it, but his hands shook too much. "I told him it was no good with this south wind, but you know how he was. And I was wrong at that. He struck a fish right off." He gulped. "Never anything like this happened to me before," he said dully. "If only I could have brought him in, but he was gone in a second. Must have caught in the line some way, and he never came up. I been looking for him like a crazy man for the last hour or more."

That was Bill's story, and the details did not change it. Hugh had struck a tarpon on the slack tide. It was a good one, a hundred pounds or more, Bill thought. It had been a fighter, and it had jumped seven times, trying to throw the hook. The boat had been all over the Pass, and it was near the lighthouse when it happened.

Hugh had been excited. He stood up when the fish stopped jumping, and began to pump it in.

"He's licked," he said. "Get ready, Bill."

Bill warned him to get in his chair again. There was a lot of fight still in the fish. "Those big boys don't know when they're whipped," he told him. However, Hugh only swore at him and kept on reeling. Then it happened. It looked as though something hit him in the head, for he put his hand there. Then he staggered, and the next minute he went overboard. He never came up.

"Only way I can figure it," Bill said, "is that the

176

fish was towing him. He may be out in the Gulf by now."

"You think it was a spent bullet from a plane?" I asked.

"What else? There was a pelican with a broken wing out there yesterday. I had to shoot it."

"I thought you weren't allowed to carry guns now," I said.

"What's a fellow to do if somebody he's guiding gets a shark?" Bill asked defensively. "I didn't shoot the captain, if that's what you mean."

But, of course, there it was. Bill didn't carry a watch, and he had no real idea when it happened. But he had had a gun in his boat, and Hugh was dead.

I got Mother home after that. She was looking shocked, for, if she hadn't liked Hugh Gardiner, she was fond of Bill. But she knew Bill's temper, too, and that Hugh was the cocksure type to rouse it. The one thing a guide knows is fishing, and if there is one thing he wants in that part of the world it is to bring in the year's first big tarpon. If Hugh had mishandled his fish, and the two men had quarreled—

But there was no body, and there was Bill's story about the pelican to account for the fact that his rifle had been recently fired. Anyhow, none of us was really thinking about murder then.

On my way home I stopped to see how Pat was. The Wilson house is beyond ours. After the lighthouse on the point at the Pass is Roy Raeburn's, and next to it the Wilsons'. Beyond that is the Drakes', who were not there this season, and then comes ours. The rest sprawl for a couple of miles along the beach, each fairly hidden in palms and tropical stuff, and with the village and the hotel behind them.

I walked in without ringing and went up the stairs. Pat's door was closed, but her mother's was open and she called to me from her bed. She had broken her hip the summer before and was still practically bed-ridden.

"Come in, Peggy," she said. "What's this about the Gardiner man? Lulie says he's dead. I can't get anything out of Pat. She's shut in her room."

Lulie was their colored maid, and as all our servants are Negroes our domestic grapevine just misses being the African drum sort of thing.

"I wonder how she heard about it," I said. "I'm afraid it's true, Mrs. Wilson. A spent bullet from a plane, probably."

I told her what I knew. In a way I felt sorry for her, cooped up as she was and all this drama going on around her. She was a little woman, and she looked pathetic lying there. She listened intently.

"I'm not pretending I'm grieving," she said. "I didn't like the fellow. He treated Fanny like dirt, and I hear he's flirting with some girl or other at the hotel. I told Pat so, but it didn't do any good," she added dryly.

Lulie carried in her supper tray just then. She looked sulky, as well she might, with one maid in a house that needed four, although Pat helped her all she could. Mrs. Wilson was what locally was called close with her money. I left them and went across the hall. Pat didn't answer my knock, so I opened the door and looked in. She was standing at the window, staring out at the water, and when she didn't turn I closed the door and went away.

Nevertheless, I didn't like to leave her alone. Our colored servants all make a break for their homes after they finish dinner in the evening, and I was afraid Pat's unnatural calm would break. I bribed Lulie to stay until eleven, when I would take over for the night, and I told her to say nothing about it.

178

When I got home Tom was already back from his golf game. He was having a Scotch and soda and listening to Mother, and I thought it was a pity to have his month's vacation from Washington disturbed. But when I said so he merely observed that when men were dying all over the world we couldn't expect not to have some troubles of our own. His detachment made me indignant.

"Don't tell me a spent bullet killed him," I said. "They're falling all over the island, and nobody's been hurt."

"He was standing in the boat. It could have knocked him out, and the fish did the rest."

"Bill said he was hit in the side of the head. Would a bullet from the air do that?"

"Possibly. How about some dinner?"

We ate in the patio, although the mosquitoes were pretty bad, and we had just reached the dessert when the sheriff appeared, having come by a boat from the mainland. He was a tall, gangling man with a battered soft hat and an equally soft voice. Mother knew him, of course, and he accepted a glass of iced coffee, putting his hat carefully on the tiles as he did so.

"Kind of a funny accident, Mrs. Hull," he said. "Don't know as I've ever heard of one like it before."

"I'm glad you realize it must have been an accident," Mother said. "I've known Bill Smith for thirty years. He's quite incapable of murder."

He sipped his coffee. "Don't know it's murder yet," he said dryly. "Trouble about Bill is his rifle's been fired lately."

"I understand he shot a wounded pelican."

"So he says. But until we find the body—Anybody else around here would want to shoot the captain? If he was shot, or course."

"Nobody," Mother said firmly. "His former wife is visiting her brother, but she is out of the question. For one thing, she was playing bridge here when it happened."

"Far as I can make out, nobody knows when it did happen," he drawled. "Anyhow, I guess divorce isn't a cause for murder any more. Time was when—" He let that go. "I've been to the hotel," he said. "Nothing in his room, except a lot of good-looking clothes. No letters, no anything." He put down his glass and got up. "Ate a hearty breakfast this morning, read the papers, went swimming and back to the hotel for lunch. Hotel says he was playing around with a Patricia Wilson. What about her?"

"She was engaged to him, or about to be," Mother said shortly. "Also she was here this afternoon. Why on earth do you think this is murder anyhow? The way those bullets are falling—"

"They're falling over most of the state," he said, and picked up his hat. "Nobody's been killed yet."

Tom went out to the street with him, but he had nothing to say when he came back, except to protest violently when I said I was staying with Pat that night. He may not always know when I am around, but he certainly raises the roof when I am not. In the end I simply walked out on him at eleven o'clock. Owing to the blackout I had practically to feel my way, and the temperature was still a good ninety degrees. Not a leaf or branch was moving, and I was drying the back of my neck with a handkerchief when someone grabbed me by the arm.

I had just opened my mouth to yell when Fanny spoke in a whisper.

"I was on my way to see you," she said.

"What's the idea, scaring me to death?"

"I thought you were the sheriff, so I hid in the

shrubbery. He thinks it's murder, doesn't he? That somebody shot Hugh from the beach?"

"How on earth did you get that?"

"How does anyone learn anything here?" she said dully. "Mary Pearl told me. She says he's looking for rifles, and I can't find Roy's."

"Doesn't Roy know where it is?"

"He's asleep. He was out shelling all day, and he went to bed early. Peg, I'm frightened. He and Hugh had a terrific row the other day. Hugh was behind in my alimony, and I'm about out of money. If anybody heard it—"

The idea of Roy shooting anybody because he hadn't paid his alimony made me smile. I reassured her as well as I could and went on to the Wilson's. But I was rather startled to find the sheriff at their back door, talking to a frightened Lulie.

"Now listen," he said. "I don't want any lies out of you. People have been trying to lie to me for years. They don't get away with it."

"I'm not lying," Lulie said shrilly. "There's no gun in this house. I been here every winter for five years. I ain't never seen no old gun."

He let her go then, and she scurried off like a small black beetle. He looked at me.

"Never know where you are with these people," he said. "Do you know if they have a rifle here? Or any sort of gun?"

"I'm pretty sure they haven't," I told him. "They had one, years ago, when we had a rifle range. But after the golf course was extended Mrs. Wilson gave hers to Bill Smith. I suppose that's the one he had in his boat."

Lulie had left the door open, and when he had gone I went in. Upstairs everything was quiet. Mrs. Wilson was asleep and Pat's door was locked, so I

181

turned out the lights and tried to find a breath of air on the porch. I couldn't see the Pass from where I sat, but out in the Gulf a number of boats were moving slowly about, their lights looked strange, since no boats had been allowed out after sunset since the war began. They were searching for the body, of course, and in spite of the heat I felt chilly.

I was still convinced, however, that Hugh's death had been an act of God, if not of Providence. Upstairs at one time I heard Pat moving about, but when I listened she was merely getting her mother a glass of water. I could hear Mrs. Wilson's querulous voice.

"You ought to thank heaven he's gone," she said. "He was no good. He never was any good."

"I'd rather not discuss it, Mother."

There was more, but I didn't listen. I was turning away when I had a surprise. Standing where I was I could see across to the Raeburn house, and someone was moving about in it and carrying a light. Not a flashlight—we couldn't buy batteries for them, of course—but what seemed to be a candle. It was going from room to room on the lower floor, and at first I thought it was Fanny, still looking for Roy's rifle.

I walked across, determined to send her to bed, but when I reached the window I saw it was not Fanny. It was Roy, Roy in his pajamas and bedroom slippers, moving furtively from the living-room to the library, and peering about through his spectacles. As I watched he set the candle on a table and began feeling behind some books on the shelves. He fumbled for a minute or two. Then to my horror he took out a row of books and set them on the floor. And the next thing he did was to haul out his missing rifle.

I was stunned; steady mild old Roy, with his spectacles and his stoop, and his shells. It didn't make sense. It didn't make any more sense when I saw the light next in the basement and was certain he was down there cleaning the gun.

I went home at daylight, confused and in what is called a state. Tom was still asleep, and I didn't tell him. For there had been something fumbling about Roy as he found the rifle. As though he wasn't sure where it was. In that case, had Fanny killed Hugh? She loathed him, of course, and she might have done it before the bridge game. But in that event why tell me she couldn't find the gun? Why not have thrown it into the sea? Or have cleaned it herself? Or—and this kept me awake a long time—was she merely being clever and involving Roy? Fanny was nobody's fool. Only—her own brother!

I overslept that morning and was late for the Red Cross. But I was not surprised when Fanny came into the workroom where we were about to make new kitbags for the Army. I was still puzzling how to put the stuff together when I saw her getting off her bicycle at the curb outside. She came directly to me, and she was looking cheerful and perfectly calm.

"I'm sorry I made an idiot of myself last night, Peggy," she said. "I suppose I was excited."

"Does that mean you've found the gun?"

"Of course. It was in the hall closet. In Roy's golf bag. I didn't see it, that's all. It hasn't been fired for ages."

I let it go at that. After all, we still had no body and so no murder, and I had always felt sorry for Fanny.

They had not found the body by the third day, and the sheriff left that morning. Then at noon Peter Randolph arrived. He was not Peter Randolph to me at that time. He was merely a nice-looking young man, getting off the train across from the Red Cross room along with a lot of other visitors, and armed with an old suitcase and a brand-new rod trunk. But he looked rather lost. He was still there when the train pulled out. Then to my astonishment I saw my own Tom loping across the platform and shaking hands with him; Tom, who should have been on the golf course and who never met a train for anybody.

He says I have a suspicious nature. Perhaps I have, but the whole thing looked phony to me. I put down my work and went across the street, and I saw that my beloved husband was longing to strangle me. He pulled himself together, however.

"Well, Pete," he said, "here's the whole family to meet you. Peg, this is Peter Randolph, an old friend of mine. My wife, Pete."

I looked at them. I didn't believe they were old friends. I knew all Tom's friends, and there wasn't a Pete among them. I didn't believe they had ever seen each other before. I even had an idea that a wilted red carnation in Pete's buttonhole was for identification purposes. And I certainly wasn't going to let them put anything over on me.

"How nice!" I said. "Any old friend of Tom's is mine, of course. We can't let you go to the hotel, can we, Tom? You'd probably have to sleep in a bathtub. Mother has loads of room. Where's the car, Tom? He'll want to clean up."

Tom looked furious and Pete slightly bewildered. But I won in the end. There wasn't much else they could do about it. I drove them both home in triumph, although Tom didn't speak to me until we reached the house. Then he caught me alone.

"I suppose you think you've pulled a fast one," he said sourly. "Why the hell bring him here?"

"Any old friend of yours, darling," I told him primly, "is welcome at my mother's house. And you're the one who's pulling a fast one, aren't you?"

Mother was faintly surprised but rather pleased

when she discovered Pete at lunch and learned he was staying with her. And he must have been delighted with Mother. She told him all about everybody, including Bill Smith and Hugh Gardiner's death. And when the meal was over and Ebenezer, the colored butler, had disappeared, she said something else which made him sit up rather sharply. She had been quiet for a minute or two, as though she was listening.

"I wonder what's wrong with the servants," she said. "They're too quiet."

"Maybe it's the heat," Tom said idly. Tom is, of course, an import. He doesn't know the Negroes as we do. But Mother shook her head.

"Usually the kitchen sounds like a Holy Roller meeting," she said. "Now, as Peggy would say, they've clammed up. That always means something."

As I say, Pete was watching her.

"What do you think it means?" he asked.

"It's a form of self-protection," Mother said. "They know something, and they don't intend to be mixed up in it. Of course, it may be only a knifing among themselves."

Pete lit a cigarette.

"How long has it been going on?" he inquired, conversationally.

"Just the last day or two," Mother said. "It isn't the heat. They like it. And it isn't only here. It's all over the island. Even my laundress acts as if she'd lost her tongue."

I saw he was interested, but he asked no more questions. He went fishing that afternoon, in an old pair of slacks and a sweater, and I was not surprised when I learned Bill Smith was taking him. I tried my best to get something out of Tom about him while he was gone. I even played a round of golf in the heat to do it. But, while Tom is the king of my particular world, the good old oyster has nothing on him when it comes to keeping his mouth shut, if that is what an oyster does.

"It's funny you never spoke about Peter Randolph before," I said. "When and how did you know him?"

"Oh, hither and yon," he said vaguely. "Look don't try to drive over the bayou and talk at the same time. We're almost out of balls."

"Well, I ought to know something about him. After all, he's our guest."

"Only because you acted like an idiot," he said. Which made me so furious that I drove straight into the water. There was no use asking any more about Pete after that. We were hardly on speaking terms until dinner.

Pete was gone all afternoon. He came home with a violent sunburn and said he had caught a ladyfish, which Bill had thrown away, and hooked onto a mackerel shark, which towed them all over the Pass. He showed his blisters with pride, but I didn't believe for a moment that he had only been fishing.

And then, of course, he met Pat Wilson. Perhaps I haven't said enough about Pat, how gay she has always been, and how lovely to look at, and—in a way—how lonely she was that season, with so few other young people around and a querulous mother to care for. But Pete saw it in a minute. He had come down, looking very nice in flannels and a tweed jacket, and Tom was mixing cocktails when she ran in, pale and scared to death.

"It's Mother," she gasped. "She's had a heart attack. Telephone for a doctor, somebody."

Of course, they had no telephone. It had been taken out, to send to Russia probably. But Mother had kept hers by threatening to sue the company for breaking and entering or something of the sort if they tried to get it. She went to it at once.

Tom grabbed a cocktail and offered it to Pat, but she shook her head. "I'm all right," she said. "I have to go back. It's Lulie's day out. Mother's alone."

She started out and Pete hurried after her. By the time I got to the house they were both upstairs, and he had broken an ammonia capsule under Mrs. Wilson's nose and was feeling her pulse and telling Pat everything was under control.

He came downstairs after the doctor arrived, and stood at a window looking out.

"Does that girl live with this old woman all the time?" he asked.

"She's her mother. What else can she do?"

"It must be the hell of a life," he said glumly. "She was engaged to Gardiner, wasn't she?"

"I think she was. She never said so."

"Anything to escape, eh?"

I had no time to speak. Pat herself came down, looking almost collapsed, and he put her on a sofa and offered to get Lulie for her. She only closed her eyes and nodded. I suppose he located Lulie—it was movie night on the island—and I heard him coming in very late.

We still had the south wind the next day. Mrs. Wilson was better, but I was nervous and irritable, and so was everybody else. They had stopped the search for Hugh's body, and in a way it was a relief. After all, death was all around us anyhow. Every now and then some poor lad would crash his plane into the Gulf and never be seen again. And it was time for the mackerel and kingfish to come in. All the boats were out loaded with visitors and with boxes and barrels for the catch, but the only people who got anything were the guides, who were being paid. We saw very little of Pete, although he turned up each night for dinner. He had hired a bicycle, but I didn't think he was using it for exercise, although he seemed to be all over the island.

Then, three days after his arrival, I decided to go out with Bill Smith to get a breeze, if nothing else, and that was when they found Hugh. I had just closed about four million pores when I saw Bill staring seaward with his sharp fisherman's eyes.

"Something going on out at that channel marker," he said. "Maybe we'd better run out and see."

It was a good thing we did. The people in the boat were guests from the hotel, and one woman had already fainted. There was something behind them in the water, and the guide was holding it with a gaff. We left him there, and took the others back to the guide dock in our boat. Then I telephoned Tom.

"You'd better come down," I said, "and bring Pete if you can. I think they've found Hugh."

I passed the two of them in the local taxi as I went home, but they didn't see me. And Tom had nothing to say when he came back, except that it was Hugh, all right, and that he was glad I hadn't seen him. Pete didn't turn up until the next morning, and then it was only to say grimly that Hugh had been shot in the head with a bullet from a rifle, and that they had the bullet.

"Not too hard a shot," he said. "Anybody on the beach near the Pass could have done it. Bill says they weren't far from the lighthouse when it happened."

Well, there we were. With all the tropical stuff around our houses, the beach was practically cut off, and as I said at the beginning none of us really had an alibi, except Tom. What with the shooting in the air and the bombers and even the blimp that were constantly overhead, the noise would never have been noticed. And the next day Fanny came in, looking like death and on the edge of hysteria.

Pete had taken Roy's rifle away.

She sat down as though her legs wouldn't hold her, and stared at me out of red-rimmed eyes.

"Maybe he did do it," she said. "I've tried not to believe it, but I lied to you before. That rifle wasn't in his golf bag. I looked. It wasn't there until the next morning." She tried to light a cigarette with shaking hands. "If you tell that, I'll deny it, but it's the truth."

"He couldn't have seen well enough to shoot anybody," I said. "His eyes are bad. I just don't believe it, Fanny."

But she only got up and put down her cigarette. "It had a telescopic sight," she said drearily, "and I'd like to bet Mary Pearl was out of the house the minute I left it that day."

She went back to the house, leaving me pretty thoughtful. It might be, I considered. Maybe that was what our colored servants knew, that Mary Pearl had been out, and that Roy's rifle had been missing that evening when Fanny looked for it. That wasn't all they knew, of course, but I didn't realize it then.

I didn't even realize it that same night when the Wilson garage was burned.

It was a terrific excitement. The fire siren got us all out of bed, and Pete was on his way before I was fully awake. The garage was dry and it burned with a tremendous noise and with sparks that flew all over the neighborhood. It was in full blast when I got there. The fire engine was useless, and for a while I thought the house would go, too. Even the palms were burning. Pete had carried Mrs. Wilson out and put her in a chair on the lawn, and Pat was standing beside her looking worried and bewildered.

"It's the car," she told Pete. "There was no time to get it out. Even if there had been, there was no gas in it."

She was pretty well shocked, and Pete wanted to get her a drink. She shook her head, however.

"It's queer," she said. "We haven't used the garage this year. I didn't even keep my bicycle there. What in the world set it on fire?"

Just then the roof crashed in, and the whole structure fell. I can still remember Pete's face as he stared at the ruins.

"Is there a cellar under it?" he asked.

"No. Why?"

"Because there's no car there," he said. "Not even the skeleton of one."

Well, anyone could see that. The onlookers seemed to realize it, too. They were muttering. As for Mrs. Wilson, she was not too feeble to be furious.

"Somebody took it out and wrecked it," she said shrilly. "That's why they burned the garage. To cover it up."

Nobody argued with her, even when she accused Pat of having done it herself. When it was all over, Pete and Tom carried her up to her bed, and we went home. Tom fixed some highballs and we sat around, but Pete seemed thoughtful. He spoke only once, and that was to say that Pat was an unusual sort of girl.

"Found her trying to carry the old lady downstairs herself," he said. "Me, I'd have let her burn!"

But before he went to bed he said something else.

"If I knew why and how that car got away I'd know the hell of a lot of things," was what he said.

It was still hotter than blazes the next morning. Pete stayed around the house. He seemed to be waiting for something, and it turned out finally to be a telephone call from the mainland. The next thing I

190

knew he and Roy Raeburn were on their way to the dock. I felt a little sick, but if Tom knew anything he wasn't talking.

"Does that mean the bullet came from Roy's gun?" I asked anxiously.

"How do I know?" he said stiffly. "This is the hell of a vacation anyhow. Look at that thermometer!"

I didn't look at the thermometer. I didn't need to. And I tried to see Fanny that morning, but Mary Pearl said she was shut in her room with the door locked. She looked excited, as all our servants do when anything happens to any of us, but she looked secretive, too. And when I went to the Wilsons' their Lulie looked the same. I lost patience finally.

"See here, Lulie," I said, "if you know anything about Mr. Gardiner's death you'd better talk, and talk soon. They put people in jail for suppressing evidence."

"I don't know nothing," she said sullenly. "Me, I mind my business and let other people mind theirs."

Which was, I thought, a not too delicate hint.

Pat looked rather better that day, although she was still bewildered about the fire. I wondered if she had really been in love with Hugh, after all, or if Pete wasn't right and he had been an escape from the life she had been living, dragged around after her mother for years, and without much prospect of anything else. But there was a difference in her. She looked worried.

"I never thought of Roy," she said. "He doesn't seem the sort, does he? I suppose—well, Hugh must have treated Fanny pretty badly, for this to happen."

"She thinks he did," I said, rather dryly.

That was as far as we got, for at that minute one of the clerks from the general store drove up in a car and we stared at him in astonishment. For the car he

191

brought was the Wilsons', and he was grinning cheerfully as he got out.

"Found it up the island," he said. "Went up for some pinfish, and there it was, on a back road. Looks all right, too."

He eyed us both with interest. The village likes the winter visitors, but it is always curious about them.

"Not very far from the railroad trestle," he said. "Looks like somebody stole it and then set fire to your garage. Unless you left it there yourself," he added.

"I haven't used it this winter," Pat said, bewildered. "There wasn't even any gas in the tank."

"Well, there's some there now," he said. "Came back under its own steam."

So there was a new mystery. Not that it seemed very important at the time, although, of course, it was. The heat still obsessed us. The mosquitoes had come out of the mangrove swamps and hung around in clouds. The hotel porch was crowded with irritated fishermen who watched the flag on its pole still defiantly pointing north when it pointed at all. Tom was, I presumed, playing golf and using language unbefitting a gentleman. Fanny was still incommunicado. And late in the afternoon Mrs. Wilson had another heart attack, and the doctor got a nurse from the mainland to look after her.

I was in the patio when Tom came home. He drove up in the village taxi, and he looked as if he wanted to bite me when he saw me. He got his clubs out of the car and then lifted out what was obviously a heavy suitcase.

"What's that?" I inquired. "And what's in it? Bricks?"

"It belongs to Pete."

"Good heavens! Is he planning to stay forever?"

He didn't answer that. He carried the thing in carefully and took it upstairs, leaving me to get his golf clubs, and when I went up later to shower and cool off the door into Pete's room was not only closed. It was locked. I marched straight into Tom's room, where he was trying to pull a fresh shirt over his sticky body, and demanded to know what was going on. But the light of my life merely glared at me.

"You keep out of this," he growled. "And let that room alone."

"I'm no snooper," I said tartly. "I merely wondered. If that thing's full of explosives, I'd feel better if it was in a bathtub full of water."

"Explosives!" He laughed—he has a very nice laugh—and rather unexpectedly came over and kissed me. "Well, you can call it that, my wilted darling. Take a shower and forget it."

Pete came home after dinner. Roy was not with him, and he looked tired and worried. I wasn't surprised when he went to see Pat as soon as he had bathed and shaved, but he seemed depressed when he returned, although he said Mrs. Wilson was better. He was puzzled, too, about the car incident.

"It doesn't fit," he said morosely. "Nothing fits. Why the fire? Why steal the car and then leave it? Unless—"

He didn't finish that. He went up to bed, but hours later I heard him going out again, and I was not entirely surprised the next morning to see his door open and the suitcase gone from his room. He himself was at the breakfast table when I went downstairs, and he was looking as pleasant and innocent as though he had spent the night in gentle slumber. It was Mother who added to my bewilderment.

"Did you see Lindy?" she asked him.

"I saw her. Yes."

"Did she talk?"

"No. It's what she wouldn't say that matters."

Well, Lindy is our colored laundress, and all at once I was filled with fury.

"What goes on?" I inquired. "Is this a guessing game, and am I supposed to guess? Or am I merely a stupid fool, too dumb to be told anything?"

Mother opened her mouth to speak, but Pete gave her a warning look.

"I merely wanted to ask Lindy a question," he said mildly. "She wouldn't answer it, so that's that."

"And I suppose you took your washing to her in that suitcase," I said. "You should have emptied the bricks out of it. Lindy's particular about washing bricks."

Mother looked startled.

"What washing?" she inquired. "And what about bricks?" But the grapefruit came just then, and there was no more chance to talk.

The day passed somehow. Mother went to the club for bridge in the afternoon. The fighters were still shooting overhead, and the dirigible passed low over the treetops. Far out in the Gulf a few bombers were dropping practice bombs. They would peal off from the formation, dive, level off, and leave behind them what looked like small geysers in the sea. And Pete spent the afternoon simply loafing, if you can call it loafing when a man sits still for a minute and then jumps up and looks at his watch.

At five o'clock he got his bicycle and went to get some cigarettes, although the house was full of them, and at six he was back, looking as if he had lost all hope of heaven and pretending that the parcel he carried was tobacco. He went upstairs to where Tom had been taking a shower, and through the open window I heard him talking.

"What the hell am I to do?" he said. "There it is! Absolutely foolproof. Look at it."

Tom apparently looked. I couldn't hear what he said, but Pete was excited. I could hear him well enough.

"Look how it shoots up here. And here," he said. "You get it, don't you? Only I wish to God I knew the exact time. When did that bridge game start? And how long was Bill Smith in the Pass searching for the body? It didn't take long, of course."

That was all I heard, for evidently my suspicious lord and master had noticed the open window. He slammed it shut, and left my particular world to chaos and to me.

Pat's mother died that night. She was already gone when Lulie ran over just after dinner, and we all went to the Wilson house. Pat was in the lower hall when we arrived. She looked dazed, but calm.

"She didn't suffer," she said. "She merely turned over in bed and—went. Perhaps it's better. She hated being helpless."

I said all the proper things, but I don't think she heard me. She said her mother had been all right that day, but that she was tired after the doctor left that afternoon. He had taken an electrocardiogram, and it had exhausted her.

She didn't really break until Tom and Pete came in. Then, as though it was the most natural thing in the world, she went to Pete, and he put his arms around her and held her. That was when I wandered into the living-room and saw Pete's suitcase. As I've said, I'm no snooper, but it wasn't locked, and what was inside it was not laundry.

Some time later Tom and I left them together and walked home. Tom was having one of his taciturn

195

fits, but I didn't intend to be put off any longer.

"I suppose it's the best way out, isn't it?" I said casually. "It solves Pete's problem, anyhow."

"What problem?"

"Pat. He's crazy about her."

"I don't know what you're talking about," Tom said, in his best War Administration manner.

"And the Negroes knew it all along, didn't they? That's why they burned the garage. To prove it."

"To prove what?"

"See here," I said, "I'm not deaf or dumb or blind. That electrocardiogram machine was a lie detector, wasn't it? The doctor put it on her and then asked the questions Pete gave him. That's right, isn't it? And the Negroes knew Mrs. Wilson could get around when she wanted to. That broken hip was healed long ago. Only they were afraid to talk, so I suppose they burned the garage to scare her into running out of the house and giving herself away. That's why they saved Pat's car."

"You're guessing, darling," Tom said, with masculine superiority. "You haven't an ounce of proof."

"Haven't I? What about Roy's gun?"

He stopped and looked down at me.

"What about Roy's gun?"

"She knew he had it. She sent Lulie off, and she fixed it so that Mary Pearl went with her. Then she went to Roy's house and shot Hugh from the porch. Only she didn't have time to put the gun back. She put it behind some books in the library."

Tom looked dazed.

"How on earth do you know all that?"

"Because I saw Roy find it that night. He thought at first that Fanny had done it, so he took the gun to the basement and cleaned it. Later on, I suppose, he

196

suspected the truth. He probably knew Mrs. Wilson could walk. He knew a lot of things besides shells."

Tom stood gazing down at me. Maybe there was love and admiration in his eyes or maybe he was just a male, irritated that a female had put something over on him. I'll never know.

"I suppose," he said, still trying to be superior, "you know why she did it. Or has that escaped you?"

"Maybe it was this south wind," I said. "And, of course, she didn't like him. But anyhow she didn't want Pat to marry anybody. That's why she played helpless. She wanted Pat to stay with her. And, of course, there's the money too."

"What money?"

"Pat gets half of it when she marries. Hugh knew it, of course."

That, I think, was when he gave up.

"Then Pete—"

"Certainly. Pete, the old college chum! Pete with a red carnation in his buttonhole so you would know him! Pete will marry money, my beloved. Only he doesn't know it."

It was dark, but I think he had the grace to blush.

"Colonel Peter Randolph of the Military Intelligence, my dear," he said. "Gardiner knew a lot of stuff. When it looked as though he had been murdered, they sent Pete here. That's all."

"And who suggested that?" I asked sweetly.

He didn't answer. He stuck a finger in his mouth to wet it and held it up in the air.

"By God," he said, "I believe the wind's changing."

The
Burned
Chair

1

Jessica overslept that Sunday morning. It was almost eight when she wakened, which was not surprising since she had had very little sleep for the three preceding nights.

She went in her nightgown to Tommy's room next door, and stood looking at him. He was sleeping soundly, but it always seemed to her when he had a return of his South Pacific malaria that he still showed the yellowish cast of the Atabrine they had given him.

She was tempted to touch his forehead to see if the fever had broken, but she did not. He looked young and helpless lying there, and very thin. Thinner than he had ever been since the days in the hospital when he first came back to her after their brief marriage. She had a lump in her throat as she went back to dress. There was no time for a bath. She dressed hastily and ran a comb through her short reddish hair. Even so, without make-up, she was a very pretty girl. Not that she noticed it then, or cared. It was only important if Tommy liked the way she looked.

The big house was still quiet as she went down the stairs. The millionaire colony was slowly dying, of two wars and high taxes. But its houses remained, huge and burdensome to those who still came to spend the summer in them. Some day, she thought, she and Tommy would have a little place of their own. Without his family. Just the two of them, and maybe later on—

The house faced on the bay, and she could hear a small surf rolling in. She had no time to look at the water, however. She went back to the kitchen and opened the door to the porch, to find the milkman there with his rack of bottles.

"Same amount as usual?" he inquired.

"I suppose so," she said vaguely. "You haven't heard of any local people to come in and help, have you?"

He gave her a quick admiring look. Not many young women could look like that without make-up at eight o'clock of a hot July morning. But he shook his head.

"I been asking around," he said, "but you know how it is. They've got families of their own, and the ones that haven't are already working for the summer folks. I'll keep on trying, Mrs. Jewett."

She watched him drive off, and then turned back to the large old-fashioned kitchen. It was almost a week since the staff Julia had engaged had decamped in a body. The house was too big, they said, the place too remote and lonely, and frantic calls to New York had brought no results. As neither Julia, Tommy's older sister, nor his brother Henry's young wife, Marian, could cook, the kitchen had fallen to Jessica. Since Tommy's illness, however, they had had to manage, much to Marian's fury.

"I can fry eggs," she said, "but I simply refuse to wash pots and pans."

The evidences of that refusal were in sight, and Jessica surveyed them with distaste. Even in order the kitchen always daunted her—the butcher's block, a relic of the generous days when beef was bought by the side, not the ounce; the vast coal range, the wall rack with its incredible numbers of mysterious implements hanging on it, the great kettles for soup and for boiling whole hams. The only modern touch was a small two-burner gas stove on a table, which at least made the breakfast coffee.

She was putting on water for the percolator when Henry came in. He wore a dressing-gown over his pajamas, and he evidently had a heavy cold.

"Cough waked me," he said. "Only hope I don't give the damned thing to Marian. She's afraid of colds. I slept in the East Room last night. How's Tommy this morning?"

"Better. It looks as though the fever's gone. I gave him a capsule at ten, and I think he slept all night."

He gave her a quick glance. He was a big man, dark where Tommy was fair, and with none of Tommy's good looks. Just now he looked impatient.

"I wish he'd get over the thing," he said. "It isn't enough that he gets shot. He gets this bug, too. And battle fatigue, or whatever they call it, on top of the rest."

She flushed resentfully.

"He never had that," she said. "He was exhausted, hurt, and sick. After all, he's been in two wars. And another thing, Henry, I wish you'd stop treating him like your little brother. He hates it and so do I. He's twenty-nine, and if ever a man had a right to call himself a man, he has."

He looked surprised.

"Sorry, redhead," he said. "He's always been the kid to me. After all, I'm twelve years older." He coughed again, and glanced at the stove. "I imagine you've had a tough time all week, Jessica. Who's been carrying the coal for the monster?"

"I've been doing it. I didn't mind."

"What's the matter with the gardener?"

"He has a bad back. Or didn't you know?"

He grunted skeptically.

"Well, I haven't," he said. "I suppose, servants or no servants, you'll need the stove for Julia's idea of a Sunday dinner. So here goes."

He picked up the two empty coal pails and started for the cellar stairs. She watched him as he went. He did not look well, she thought, this older brother of Tommy's, with his big heavy body and red-rimmed eyes, and not for the first time she wondered why Marian had married him. She was twenty years younger, and came close to being a beauty. Security perhaps, she thought. She had been a dancer in a nightclub, and Henry's solidity and background must have appealed to her.

Down in the cellar Henry was shoveling coal. She made the coffee and got out a cup and saucer for him when he came up. Then she went out and stood on the kitchen porch. Across the lawn stood the next house, built much on the same pattern, as though the architect had run out of ideas. Both were huge, with vast echoing halls and majestic staircases. Both had long service wings for the ten or more servants of the turn of the century. And both faced on the water, with drives leading in from the village street and enormous stables which now served as garages.

The old flower gardens were largely untended now, although a few roses and delphiniums persisted. She might cut some, she thought, for the sick old man next door. That vast dreary house—

She was still standing there when she heard the nurse scream.

2

Nothing happened at first. Then Miss Scott, old Mr. Jewett's nurse, appeared at the terrace of the other house and waved wildly to her. Jessica ran to the head of the cellar stairs.

"I'm afraid something's happened to your father, Henry," she called. "I'm going over."

The nurse had disappeared when she got there. The terrace door opened onto old Mr. Jewett's ground-floor bedroom, the room he had used ever since he had his stroke. But to her surprise the bed was empty. She ran through the connecting door into the living-room and stopped, staring. Miss Scott was in the center of the room wringing her hands and muttering.

"But I don't understand," she was saying over and over. "Why did he come in here? Why didn't he ring for me?"

There was no question about it. Old Horace Jewett was dead, and he had not died peacefully. He was half in, half out of the big white upholstered chair which overlooked the sea, his body twisted as though he had tried desperately to get out of it and failed. His wheelchair was some distance away and overturned, and the telephone was on the floor beyond his reach and sitting upright.

Jessica went over and touched him. She had been a nurse's aide during the war and she knew death when she saw it.

"He's been gone for some time, Scotty," she said. "After all, we expected it, didn't we? Sooner or later?"

Miss Scott roused herself.

"Not like this," she said stubbornly. "And not with his family over there next door, and nobody with him. I said I didn't want the responsibility, not the way it was, with him partly paralyzed. And he didn't ring the bell last night. He didn't."

Jessica paid no attention to Miss Scott's frightened indignation. It was an old story. When Horace Jewett was able after his stroke to be brought to the summer place he had chosen to live in what had been his wife's morning room on the first floor, where his chair could be wheeled out onto the terrace. But one season of the late comings and goings of his family had been all he could take. He had bought the big house close by and installed them there, much to their resentment.

"I want you near," he said, "But not on top of me. I haven't got long, and I need peace and quiet."

It did not look, however, as though he had had it when he died. Jessica looked around the room.

"Did you open the window, Scotty?" she said.

"No," Miss Scott said dully. "He must have done it himself. He could, you know. It's a casement."

The servants were in the hall by that time, all three of them staring in avidly, and Jessica went over to them.

"I'm sorry," she said. "Mr. Jewett is gone and there is nothing you can do. Except to make some coffee. The family will be over."

She closed the door firmly and looked once more at the dead man. It was obvious that he had wheeled himself into the room and managed with his one good arm to get into his big chair. Then somehow the wheelchair had slipped away from him and upset. The window, however, puzzled her. It was wide open; and last night had been foggy and cold.

But she had little time. Henry was coming in through the bedroom, as she had come. He had waited, she thought, to wash the coal dust off his hands, but he looked profoundly shocked.

"Good God!" he said. "So the poor old chap's finished at last." Then he seemed to realize the oddness of the situation. "What on earth's he doing in here, Scotty?"

Miss Scott did not answer. She was collapsed in a chair and crying, her shoulders shaking. Henry turned to Jessica.

"I've called Julia," he said, "and Marian. But Tommy was still asleep. I didn't wake him."

Jessica nodded, but her feeling that something was wrong persisted. Not only was the window open, but the lights had been switched off. Surely if he had come in for any purpose he would have snapped the switch between the two connecting rooms. And why had he come? Not to read. There was no book near by. To telephone? But why, when he had not even rung for Scotty?

"Did you turn off the lights?" she asked the nurse.

"No," Scotty said drearily, without looking up. "I've touched nothing."

Julia came in then. She wore a housecoat over her nightgown, and when she saw her father's body her handsome, rather hard face set in grim lines.

"So he's gone," she said. "I suppose we had to expect it. Better call Doctor Marlow, Henry."

Automatically she reached down and set the wheelchair upright. Then, still without any show of

207

emotion, she replaced the telephone on the table where it belonged.

"We'd better get him back into his bed," she said. "He looks dreadful like this. His face—If you'll bring his chair, Henry—"

Jessica was startled. Already there was a sort of order in the room. Henry had stooped and picked up something from the floor and put it in his pocket, and Julia was closing the window. She spoke, for the first time since Julia's arrival.

"But you can't do all this," she said. "I don't think he just—died. I don't believe he came in here alone, to sit by that open window in the dark. Why should he? It was cold last night, and foggy. He hated fog. And that chair, beyond his reach and upset. I think you ought to call the police."

Only then did she see the door to the hall opening, and a maid with a tray standing there, her mouth open.

Julia waved her away furiously and slammed the door.

"I hope you're happy," she said, her voice bitter. "Now it will be all over town. But don't make any mistake, Jessica. Father died of a heart attack, as we've expected for years. Or of another stroke. And he's going back to his bed, where he belongs."

But there was definitely an air of uneasiness in the room. Jessica stood defiantly, her slim young body stiff with suspicion.

"I still think it's a matter for the police," she said. "Why was he here? Who was he seeing? And why was he trying to get out of that chair? He was trying, desperately. Look at him!"

The scene, acrimonious as it was, was broken by Marian. She came in, took one look at the body, and slid to the floor in a dead faint. Julia eyed her with distaste.

"Get her out of here, Henry," she said coldly. "This is no time for hysterics. Put her in Father's bed in the next room. She'll be all right."

Henry gathered up his wife tenderly. There was always something of wonder in his face as he looked at her, Jessica thought, as though he still could not realize why anything so precious married him.

"Better come and look after her, Scotty," he said. "She's had a real shock. She's not used to death."

Jessica found herself still rigid. Old Horace Jewett continued to lie half in and half out of his chair, and except that his eyes were closed he might have been watching them all. She had thought that people mostly died with their eyes open. At least that had been her own small experience. As a rule, too, their faces looked peaceful, the lines smoothed out, as though death had wiped a kindly hand over them. This one did not.

She looked up to see Julia's gaze fixed on her, hard and suspicious.

"We can look after things here, Jessica," she said. "You'd better go back to Tommy. All this wild talk about the police! I suppose we had to expect that from your father's daughter."

Of all the family Julia, Jessica knew, was the only one who had resented Tommy's wartime marriage. She returned Julia's stare.

"I should think," she said, "that you would want to know why your own father died—"

"I know how and why my father died."

She left then, going out by the hall so as not to disturb Marian. But she glanced in as she passed the door. Henry was stooped over the bed, and Scotty was

209

fixing a glass with something in it. She felt alone and discredited, as though Tommy's family had finally rejected her and she would never be one of them.

Back at the house again she went through the kitchen. The coal was there, but the stove was still cold and menacing. She was surprised, too, when she went upstairs to find Tommy still asleep. He looked better, however, and she remembered their brief honeymoon before he went to Korea, when she would waken early and look at him, for the sheer joy of knowing he was there, big and strong and vital.

This was to have been their second honeymoon, this summer at the seaside, to finish his long convalescence. He had been excited about it. His leg wound had healed so that he only limped when he was tired or worried. And the nervous symptoms had almost disappeared.

"We'll sail and swim," he told her, "and I'll get back to normal. God, I'll be glad to see the old place. I spent every summer there for years. It will be a rest for you, too, honey. I've been a chore long enough."

She had agreed, of course. Anything he wanted was all right for her. But she was not so sure about his family. She had not known them very well. When she and Tommy came East that spring they could not find an apartment, so they had lived in two rooms in a residential hotel, and once or twice Tommy's father had asked them to dinner in his tall, gloomy house in the East Sixties, to which Julia had retired after her divorce some years before. But Henry and Marian, since their marriage, lived in a whirl of Café Society and she saw more of their pictures in the newspapers than of them.

She had had great hopes of this summer, nevertheless. For Tommy was still not quite his old self. They

210

had kept him too long in the tropics during the Second World War, and Korea had not helped. Once or twice the malaria had come back. Then, during the feverish stages, he would call out to men whose names she had never heard. Or he would try to get out of bed and go somewhere. It frightened her, but when she told him he would give her his endearing grin.

"Must have dreamed I was back with the fellows," he would say sheepishly. "Sorry, darling. I know I'm a damned nuisance."

She was thinking of that now, for the summer so far had not been an unqualified success. For one thing, Horace Jewett had wanted Tommy eventually to go back to the mill, and Tommy had resented it. He wanted to strike out on his own, not to be only his father's son; and just before the malaria hit him again there had been something of a quarrel.

"Do what?" said Horace. "What else are you fitted for, except killing?"

"I'd like to write," Tommy said. "It's been in my mind ever since I left college."

"Write!" said Horace contemptuously. "That's the refuge of a man who'd rather wear out the seat of his pants than the soles of his shoes. Don't be a jackass."

That same night Jessica had wakened to find Tommy shaking with a chill, his face livid, his hands cold, his nails blue. It was followed in due time by the usual fever, which for some reason persisted, and by a mental confusion which puzzled Doctor Marlow.

"Apparently he thinks he's back in the hospital again," he had said to Jessica. "What's he doing? Escaping? From what?"

"He and his father differ about some things," she said evasively. "It couldn't be that, could it?"

211

"Don't ask me about the psychiatric effects of wars. Most men have some sort of unbalance for a while, I suppose. Give him time. That's all he needs." He had eyed her. "Not worried about money, is he? The old man has his own theories about that, I understand."

"He has some his mother left him. They all have. We manage all right."

3

She was thinking over that talk as she went upstairs to Tommy's room. She would have to tell him about his father when he wakened, but what was she to say? That she had suggested the police? She couldn't do that, with old Horace pulled up in his chair, the window closed, and everything neat and tidy before the doctor could get there.

She couldn't tell him all at once anyhow, weak and ill as he had been. But she had a brief respite. Tommy was still asleep when she got there, his face relaxed and quiet. She bent over to straighten the tangled bedclothes, and remained stooped and staring. There was something small and yellow on the carpet, the capsule which was his sleeping pill and which he had not taken, after all.

She was puzzled. Why, then, was he still sleeping? But a moment later she knew the answer. It was there, at the foot of his bed. His bedroom slippers were wet and bedraggled, and the cuff of the one pajama leg she could see was damp and dirty. Some time in the night Tommy had wakened and gone out.

All at once she was frightened. Desperately frightened. Had he had a return of the nightmares when he was killing Japs, and blundered in on his father? Perhaps frightened him into a heart attack?

She was still standing there, bewildered and uncertain, when she heard Henry coughing in the hall. Stooping quickly she picked up the slippers, but she had no time to hide them. Henry was in the doorway, still in his dressing-gown, his face sober and unhappy.

"Have you told him?" he asked in a low voice.

"No. He's still asleep."

He grunted.

"It's just as well. The police chief's over there. Afraid you've started something, Jessica. What the hell made you do it?"

He did not reproach her, however. He moved away along the hall, to dress, she thought; to see the thing through, whatever it was; to bring home his young wife, lest she be contaminated by any trouble. And to pretend he had not seen those slippers of Tommy's, or her own frightened, agonized face.

She retrieved the sleeping pill from the floor and flushed it down the bathroom toilet. Then she carried the slippers down to the kitchen and hid them in a closet. After that she lit the big coal stove and, waiting until the oven was warm, placed them in it to dry. She was still there when she heard Tommy's bell ring. They all rang bells, the Jewetts. They had been raised that way. They rang and someone came running. But this time she did not go all the way up to his room. From the stairs she called "Tray coming up" and went back to the kitchen again.

She fixed his breakfast—orange juice, a boiled egg, some toast—and felt her hands steadier as she worked. When she carried the tray in to him he was sitting on the side of the bed, looking around him.

"Where the devil are my slippers?" he inquired.

"Around somewhere. Get back into bed so I can put down this tray. Had a good sleep, didn't you?"

"I slept to hell and gone." He put his legs back into bed and smiled up at her. "Well, a nice good morning

214

to you, Mrs. Jewett. And how's the family slavey today? No kisses?"

She stooped over and kissed him. This was Tommy. Not some creature crawling around in the night, but Tommy himself. A Tommy who did not know his father was dead, or that the police were around. A Tommy who liked two lumps of sugar in his coffee, and his eggs four minutes, and who was eating, really eating, for the first time in days.

"Get the tooth mug and have some coffee with me, darling. It's superlative. Just like my wife used to make."

But when she was settled on the foot of the bed, tooth mug in hand, he said, "I had the damnedest dream last night. I was out somewhere in the mountains, and I was lost. Dreamt I walked for hours and couldn't get back."

She steadied her voice.

"Where did you go? In the dream, I mean?"

"How do I know? Look, do I imagine it, or are you pretty serious this morning?"

She took the tray away before she spoke. Then she told him, as simply as she could, what had happened. He took it quietly enough, but his tone was bitter.

"So he's dead," he said, "and the last time I saw him I told him to go to hell. That's a fine thing to remember!" He drew a long breath. "I hope it was easy, poor old boy. He didn't suffer, did he?"

"I don't think so," she told him, thinking of the twisted body in the chair. "I don't know the details. Julia's over there, and Marian. Henry's here to get some clothes. He was in the cellar in his dressing-gown getting coal when the news came."

He lay back and closed his eyes. The news had helped her in one way. He had forgotten about the slippers. But she remembered them. She would have to go down and get them out of the oven. Without speaking she picked up the tray and slipped quietly out of the room.

The kitchen was hot when she got there, and she put down the tray and hurried to the oven, only to hear a mild voice at the open door.

"Morning, Mrs. Jewett. Guess the folks are having breakfast at the other house. Mind if I come in?"

It was the local chief of police, a tall rangy man in a blue uniform, with an automatic hanging from his belt. His name was Fenton, and during the bootlegging days he had built a reputation for shrewdness which still persisted. He had not waited for an invitation. He was already in the room.

"Bad news about the old man," he said. "Suppose it was to be expected, but death's like that. Never welcome. Mind if I smoke a pipe?"

Her knees were shaking, but she steadied herself.

"No," she managed. "My father always smokes one when he has a problem to think out."

"Kind of a big bug out there on the Coast, I understand."

"He's a criminologist. In San Francisco."

"So you might say you're a policeman's daughter," he said. "That's mighty interesting." He had filled an ancient pipe and was busy lighting it. "Family here didn't like it much, eh? Snobbish lot, these summer folks."

"I married Tommy, not his family," she said rather sharply.

"Well, Tommy's a good kid," he observed. "You did all right. I used to take him fishing. Hear he had a bad time in Korea. Got shot in the leg. Malaria, too. How is he this morning?"

"Better. He ate some breakfast."

216

But he was not listening. He had put his pipe aside and was looking at the range.

"That's a pretty big fire, isn't it?" he inquired. "Kind of early for the Sunday roast, too." He got up leisurely and crossed to the stove. "Ought to do something about the dampers," he said, and without warning opened the oven door.

"I see," he said. "Got wet, did they? Now that's right curious, isn't it?"

He was still looking at the slippers when Henry appeared. He had taken time to dress in a dark suit, and Jessica thought he might have been outside the door long enough to hear what was going on. Anyhow, he did not look at either of them. He went to the stove and jerked out the slippers.

"Damn it all," he said. "I clean forgot them. Now I suppose they're ruined." For the first time he seemed to know the others were there. "Sorry," he said. "I got them wet on the grass this morning and put them there to dry. That stove thinks it's Vesuvius." He held the slippers cautiously and started for the back porch. "I'll put them with the trash," he said, and disappeared in good order. The chief's eyes followed him.

"Now that," he said, "is what I call quick thinking."

He did not explain, and Jessica sat down to relieve her shaking legs. The chief smoked quietly for a minute or two. Then he shook the dottle out of his pipe and put it in his pocket.

"Just why did you want the police this morning?" he inquired. "Here's a simple case of an old man dying in his chair. According to Marlow, it was his heart. But according to town talk, you yelp for me. Just why?"

217

She hesitated.

"It looked queer, that's all. I'm sorry now."

"What looked queer?"

He could get it, she knew. Scotty would tell him if she didn't. And just because Tommy had been out that night meant nothing. She had been a fool about the slippers.

"He was half out of the chair," she said. "The lights were off, and the telephone was on the floor, where he couldn't reach it. His—his eyes were shut, too, and his wheelchair was overturned. But mostly it was the window. It was wide open beside him. I've thought of that since," she added. "Maybe he needed air and opened it himself. He could, you know. He had one good arm."

Fenton was calmly refilling his pipe.

"That isn't the way I found things, Mrs. Jewett," he said slowly. "Somebody had evidently been doing a lot of tidying up. He was in his chair, all right. Kind of hunched up, but that's all. And the window was closed. What about those slippers?" he said suddenly. "I'll bet Henry never got those big feet of his in them. Whose are they? Tommy's?"

When she said nothing he got up and picked up his cap.

"Just a chance the nurse made a mistake in his medicine," he said. "She broke her glasses a day or two ago. So I wouldn't worry too much. I understand Tommy gets delirious now and then in these attacks of his. But that doesn't mean he'd kill his own father."

"Then—you think somebody did kill him?"

"Darned if I know. The family has shut up like a clam. Marlow says it was heart, and the nurse is hysterical. But sure as hell some one was there last night, either when he died or afterward. Maybe he

218

opened the window, but I doubt if he closed his own eyes or shut off the light. "

She watched his tall angular figure as it went stiffly down the porch steps and around the corner of the house. She was quite sure he was looking at the slippers, and equally sure he would take them away with him.

4

She was washing the dishes from Tommy's tray when Henry brought Marian home that morning. They walked very slowly, his arm around her, and because it was nearer they came by the kitchen porch. When he saw Jessica he shook his head at her, as a warning not to refer to what had happened. But Jessica had no idea of mentioning it.

"Well, wouldn't you know!" Marian said. "Those idiots of servants over there are packing up to leave. Julia asked them to come here, but they turned her down cold."

Jessica looked at her. In spite of her tone she looked pale and shaken. What make-up she had put on was badly smudged, or gone altogether. It made her seem older.

"Is there any coffee left?" she inquired. "That swill they had over there was awful. And I suppose you're happy, Jessica, wishing the police on us."

Jessica was putting on the coffee to heat. She did not turn.

"I'm sorry about that," she said. "I don't think it did any harm. The doctor says it was his heart, doesn't he?"

She was aware that Henry was watching her.

"He might have had a shock of some sort," he said deliberately. "The door from his bedroom to the terrace was unlocked. No one ever locks anything around here. If someone walked in on him and startled him—or even attacked him—"

"Who on earth would do that?" Jessica was aware that her voice was high, almost shrill. But if Henry was intimating that Tommy was guilty, she was ready to scream him down. He said nothing more, however. His cold was worse, and he was coughing again. When the coffee was ready he waited for Marian to drink it and then he carried her slowly upstairs.

"I'm putting her to bed," he said. "Marlow's coming over to see her, after he sees Tommy."

Was he warning her, she thought, about Tommy? She must see him and prepare him. Before she had time to go upstairs, however, she heard him coming down. He came slowly by the back stairs, and he had managed to shave and get into slacks and a shirt. But his face was grim as he held to the side of the door.

"Why, Tommy!" she said. "What are you doing, all dressed like that?"

"The funeral baked meats!" he said. "Set out to garnish forth the marriage feast, or however it goes. Where the hell are the rest of them? You all alone here?"

"Sit down," she said. "People have to eat, you know. Julia's at the other house, but the servants are leaving. And Marian's upstairs. She fainted this morning."

"She would," said Tommy bitterly. "Why don't you ask me what I mean by the marriage feast? Don't you know that we've all come into the hell of a lot of money? The poor old boy's heart stops, and so we're rich. Hurrah! Hurrah!"

He wobbled to a chair and sitting down hauled a

handkerchief out of his pocket.

"Oh, for God's sake!" he said, and dabbed furiously at his eyes.

She knew he wanted no sympathy. She wanted to go over and touch his hair, to show that she understood. But she knew he hated breaking down like this, and that every man in grief had to be alone. When at last he put the handkerchief away and looked at her she was taking the Sunday roast beef out of the old-fashioned icebox. She avoided his eyes, but she knew he was watching her.

"What's happened to my slippers?" he inquired. "Did I go out last night? Is that what's scared you, making you look like a scared redheaded rabbit? I did, didn't I? It wasn't a dream, then."

But she realized that he did not relate it to his father's death; that he saw in it only a relapse to his earlier condition, a condition they had both thought and prayed was over. She put the roast on the table and going over to him put her cheek against his.

"It was only the fever," she told him. "Don't worry about it, darling. If you'd taken your pill it wouldn't have happened."

"I'm not going through the rest of my life on dope," he said. "That's final, my girl."

He seemed relieved, however. He offered to shell the peas for her, and Marlow scolded him for being out of bed, but found his temperature normal. Neither of them mentioned the death, nor did the family when they finally sat down to dinner. Henry, having carried a tray to Marian, chewed stolidly through the meal. But Tommy ate very little, and Julia hurried to get back to the other house.

"What's the rush?" Henry demanded. "There's nothing we can do until tomorrow."

"I'm closing the room over there," she said tartly. "Since Jessie made that silly speech of hers, crowds are wandering around all over the place, and trying to look in the windows. A reporter from the county seat, too. I shut him up in a hurry."

Tommy ignored the reporter.

"What speech?" he inquired. "What's all this, Jessica?"

No one answered him, and Henry spoke quickly.

"How about the house, Julia? Think we can sell it?"

"I don't know. It's too late to rent it for the summer. Anyhow, people don't care for a place where there's just been a death."

"Lots of fine stuff in it, of course. Marian says she would like some of it. We're taking a larger apartment, now we can afford it." Henry finished his apple pie and put down his fork. "What about Scotty?" he asked. "What's to become of her?"

"I imagine Doctor Marlow will have a case for her," Julia said indifferently. "She's going to the Inn for a few days' rest."

Tommy had listened without comment. Now, however, he looked at Julia.

"This ought to be a break for Don Cameron," he said. "You've collected a lot of alimony from him for the past five years, and he's been pretty much of a gent about it."

Julia eyed him coldly. "That's my business," she said.

"It's his, too. You've damn near busted him. The third vice-president of a bank doesn't get much salary. What's the idea? So he can't marry again?"

"You don't need to be common, do you?" Julia snapped, and pushing back her chair left the room

223

and slammed out of the house.

Henry raised his eyebrows.

"Why bait her like that?" he inquired. "She hates Cameron, and you know it."

"Look," Tommy said. "She's got a vile temper at times. She walked out on him in a fit of jealousy five years ago and beat it to Reno. If you ask me, she's still in love with the guy."

But he was looking exhausted again, and after the meal Jessica coaxed him to bed. She came out of his room, closing the door behind her, to find Henry waiting for her in the upper hall. He was holding something in his hand.

"Sorry to do this, Jessica," he said cautiously, "but I think you'd better have it. It's Tommy's fountain pen." He held it out to her, but she did not take it at once. "I found it on the floor by Father's chair this morning. No need to talk about it."

She took it unwillingly.

"I don't understand," she said. "He hasn't had it for days. Not since before he got sick, I know. He said he'd lost it."

He shrugged.

"That slipper stuff didn't go over very well with Fenton," he said. "If he learns about this—"

"Are you saying Tommy was in his father's room last night, Henry?"

"I'm saying it looks like it. I'm saying maybe they quarreled again. And Dad couldn't take it."

"I don't believe it," she said stoutly. "Maybe Tommy did go out. He was feverish. He may have wanted the air. But he loved his father. Sometimes I think he was the only one who really did. And there couldn't have been a quarrel. Mr. Jewett knew Tommy was sick."

In the end, however, she took the pen and put it in

224

the desk of the small room upstairs where Tommy had made a tentative start on the book he hoped to write. He might not notice it. He used a typewriter. But she would have to think up something in case he did.

It was then she realized her hands were shaking.

5

Jessica was downstairs again in the kitchen, clearing up after the dinner, when the chief came back. He walked in and sat down, eyeing her appreciatively.

"Well, I guess we're all washed up," he said. "No marks on the body and everything hunky-dory. I've been talking to the nurse. He sent her up to bed at ten o'clock last night, saying Henry was coming in to talk to him. She left a bottle of Scotch beside the bed and a hypodermic fixed for him. Seems he took his vitamins that way. Did it himself, too. Said she hurt him. See the hypo this morning?"

"It wasn't in the living-room. I didn't go into his bedroom."

He took out his pipe again. "All right," he said. "But I wish someone could tell me what in time took Horace into that room last night. He wasn't reading. No book near him, was there?"

"No. I didn't see one."

"Marlow says he died about one a.m. That's the hell of a time for a man to be out of his bed, sitting by an open window on a foggy night, and in the dark, too. Think any of the family went over there after Henry left?"

"I wouldn't know. I went to sleep early."

"How about money? He's left a pile of it, you know. Any of them hard up?"

"I don't think so. They all had some income from

226

their mother's estate, and Henry managed the business after his father had the stroke. He drew some sort of salary for it. But Mr. Jewett was pretty strict about money. He said he wanted his children to learn the value of a dollar before they got what he would leave them."

"So Julia had the income from her mother and her alimony. She was doing all right. And Henry had the same, minus the alimony and plus a salary. What about that wife of his? Married him for money, of course. Spend a lot?"

"I think she's extravagant," she said unwillingly, "but that's about all. She went over to see Mr. Jewett every day, and I think probably he slipped her a small check now and then. He knew Henry was crazy about her."

Fenton smiled.

"Kind of leaves you and Tommy out on a limb, doesn't it?" he said. "Poorest of the crowd, aren't you?"

She flushed.

"We get along all right," she told him. "We have each other. That's all we want."

He nodded.

"Thought I'd better tell you," he said. "I've got those slippers locked away in my safe. Nobody's business, far as I can see. Not yet, anyhow."

He got up and put on his cap. It always looked too small for him, and he slapped it down with his fist.

"Well, that's that," he said. "I see you don't mind dishpan hands. My wife never used to, but lately she's been hearing about them on the radio. Got herself a pair of rubber gloves, by gosh, and you can hear china smashing all over the place. Suppose I could see Henry?"

But Henry, summoned to the kitchen, was little or

227

no help. He had left his father about eleven, going out by the door to the terrace and closing it behind him. They had talked business, and he had poured a drink for his father. He didn't take one himself. As to the terrace door, he did not know whether it locked itself behind him or not. Probably not. On hot nights it often stood wide open. But why all the questions anyhow? he wanted to know. He hadn't been over to the other house after he left it. He was tucked up in the East Room, nursing his cold.

"Mind saying what the business was about?" the chief inquired.

"Estate matters," Henry said stiffly.

"Father take his vitamins while you were there?"

"No. The syringe was ready, but he didn't use it."

Still pretty much on his dignity, he picked up a coal scuttle and went down the cellar stairs. Fenton waited until he heard the sound of the shovel. Then he smiled quizzically at Jessica.

"I'm just a hick policeman," he said, "but I wonder what a fellow like your father would make of all this. Nobody murdered Horace Jewett, but there's some funny business going on. And how."

It was hot that evening. What small breeze there was came from the south, and after a supper of cold roast beef and salad the family gathered on the porch. There was little conversation, however. Julia was tired and sat with her eyes shut. Tommy sat on the steps, his head against Jessica's knees. Only Marian, driven from her room by the heat and nestled against Henry on the broad seat of the swing, talked at all. Already she was planning to move into a larger apartment, and her voice sounded young and excited.

It was Tommy who finally protested.

"For heaven's sake, Marian!" he said. "Can't you

228

wait until he's buried?"

Henry moved resentfully, but before he spoke a figure loomed out of the darkness. It was Doctor Marlow. He took off his hat and wiped his forehead, staring into the porch.

"Sorry to bother you," he said, "but I've got an unpleasant job to do. Are you all here? The family, I mean."

"Yes," Tommy said. "Get it over, Marlow. What's the trouble?"

Marlow stood where he was, on the path, his tall figure only faintly outlined in the gloom.

"I don't like it," he said, "but I think the town's gone crazy, and Fenton hasn't helped any. The plain truth is that my telephone's been busy all day and my office has been crowded. People have got the idea that Mr. Jewett was poisoned, and nothing I can say has any effect."

Julia moved abruptly.

"That's ridiculous," she said. "It was his heart. We all know it."

"They won't believe it. Not since Tommy's wife asked for the police. I suppose you know what they want—post mortem examination."

"Good God!" Tommy said. "Can't they even let him rest now? I'm against it, Marlow. Let him go in peace."

But it was not so easy as that. Public suspicion had been aroused, and old Horace had been a summer resident for almost fifty years. Moreover, he had donated the library to the town. In the end Julia and Henry agreed, and Tommy found himself in a hopeless minority. After Marlow promised to bring a good toxicologist the next morning from the county seat he left them there, quiet and uneasy.

229

Tommy, Jessica realized, was profoundly shaken. She bent over and put a comforting hand on his shoulder.

"It won't matter to him, darling," she said. "I'm sorry I started all this."

"You must have had a reason. What did you see? Why did you want the police?"

But the others were listening and she did not dare to say.

"I think it was because the window was open," she said evasively. "I suppose he did it himself, for air."

It was after they went upstairs, however, that the situation between them became critical, for it brought up again the matter of the slippers, and finally she had to tell him.

"I put them in the oven to dry," she said, as casually as she could. "Then I forgot them, and they're ruined. I had to throw them out."

He was dragging his shirt over his head. He gave it a final jerk and stared at her.

"You threw them out! Do you want everybody to know I was off my rocker last night? Who saw them?"

She could not tell him about Fenton, so she lied.

"Only Henry," she said. "And he won't talk."

He dropped down on the side of his bed and held his head in his hands. She sat beside him, putting an arm around his thin body, and felt him shiver at her touch.

"I thought I had it licked," he muttered. "How long is it going on, Jess? I was scared to hell in Korea, but who wasn't? If after all this time I have to fight the thing all over every time I get sick I'd better be locked up somewhere. I'm not safe even to have around." He lifted a haggard face. "Do you think I scared Dad last night?"

"Of course not," she said sturdily. "How could

230

you? His own son. He wanted to see you anyhow, Tommy. Said he had found something of yours that would interest you. I don't know what it was."

Her matter-of-fact manner quieted him, and soon after he went to bed he was asleep. But Jessica herself slept badly. The day had been a series of shocks, culminating in the request for a post-mortem. She knew the others blamed her, and even Julia's iron nerves betrayed her the next morning, when Henry appeared in the kitchen for a tray for Marian.

"I really think," she snapped, "that however besotted with love you may be you could see she at least gets up for breakfast these days. It's bad enough having things the way they are, without that."

"She only has black coffee and orange juice," said Henry defensively.

"She also has two perfectly good legs to come down and get them," Julia retorted. "I'm not interested in her keeping her figure. I couldn't care less about it."

There was a sort of anticlimax at noon, however, when the report came from the post-mortem. Horace Jewett had died of heart failure. There was no sign of poisoning, and although the toxicologist had taken some samples away with him, it was unlikely that anything further would be discovered.

The funeral was to be the next day, Tuesday, and Marian drove that afternoon to the county seat for appropriate mourning, coming back with her car laden with boxes. The servants next door had gone, and Julia spent the remainder of the day closing the living-room and bedroom of the house. Henry nursed his cold, wrote out telegrams to all and sundry, and sent his coat and Tommy's to the local tailor's for black mourning bands. Only Tommy seemed to be fretting, and once Jessica saw him going

231

back to where the trash was kept.

The cans had been emptied, however, and he came back with a curious set look on his face.

There was nothing she could do except to keep the house running, to order meat and groceries, to cook and wash dishes. Yet she found the easy acceptance of everyone that Horace had died a natural death hard to take. She could still see the room on the morning before, with his body twisted in an agonized attempt to get out of the chair, the telephone upright on the floor and beyond his reach, the open window, the lights shut off. And Henry, Henry picking up Tommy's fountain pen from the carpet.

He suspected Tommy of something, of frightening his father, or quarreling with him, and so bringing on the attack. But when she asked him bluntly if he did so he only looked uneasy and irritated.

"For God's sake, Jessica!" he said. "Can't you let well enough alone? Do you have to go round playing the sleuth like this? Haven't you had a bellyful of it?"

"I'm not letting Tommy think he walked in on his father and scared him to death, Henry. That's what he's afraid of."

Henry looked uncertain. Then he seemed to make up his mind.

"All right," he said stiffly. "If you insist, I think that's exactly what he did. I've done my best. I saved you about those damned slippers, but that's as far as I go. I've told you it was Tommy's fountain pen I picked up off the floor. Now run to the police and see what it gets you."

She stood very still, and his face softened.

"Don't worry," he said, more normally. "Matter of fact, I didn't think about Tommy until you began to stir things up. It's all over now, anyhow. Forget it."

She shook her head.

"It's not over, Henry," she said. "Not as long as you feel the way you do. And one thing is sure. Tommy couldn't have had the pen with him that night. He went out in his pajamas. Why would he carry a pen?"

"Why would he go out at all?" Henry countered. "One makes as much sense as the other."

6

When night came she was too tired and too uneasy to rest. Tommy had finally been induced to take his capsule and was sleeping comfortably. She had moved back into their room, and as she lay in the next bed she could hear Henry saying a prolonged good night to Marian, and Julia wearily climbing the stairs. As the night air cooled the house, she could hear it beginning to creak, after the manner of old buildings everywhere, but it sounded eerie, as though ghostly figures were moving about. Outside, too, every now and then a sleepy gull meowed like a cat, and through the open windows she could hear the soft murmur of the sea.

But her anxiety would not let her rest and finally, despairing of sleep, she got up, put on a dressing-gown and slippers, and went downstairs. Perhaps a walk along the shore path would help, she thought. There was a bench there, between the two houses, and she could sit and listen to the water. She did not, however. Almost without volition she found herself on the terrace outside the room Horace Jewett had converted to a bedroom after his stroke.

To her surprise she found the French doors unlocked, and a moment later she was inside the house. She had no idea why she had come. She was even a little frightened. She had not brought a flashlight, and the darkness daunted her. But the electric current had not yet been shut off, and she found the switch and turned on some lights.

The bedroom was much as it had been, but the bedclothes had been taken off and a sheet covered the mattress. The pillows under it gave an uncanny effect of a body there, however, and she found herself shivering. But it was the living-room which shocked her: the ghastly white of the furniture, covered for the winter, the newspapers over the books on the shelves in the corner where Horace had so often sat, and the mothflakes lavishly sprinkled on the carpet. It bore no resemblance to the room where she had seen the body, and she realized that any hope she might have had of finding anything important was gone.

She did not go in at once. She had turned on the switch by the door—the switch Horace should have used and had not—and stood there staring. Then she saw that someone had been there before her. Someone had walked over the mothflakes, and although a hasty effort had been made to eliminate the marks they were still there. They led from where she stood to the corner where the old man had died in his big chair, and she saw, too, that the papers covering the books had been disturbed. They certainly did not look like Julia's careful protection, and going to the corner she found two half-burned matches, as though whoever had been there had not dared to turn on a light.

Suddenly she wanted to get out of there. It was as though something evil lurked around the room; around all the great empty house indeed. She almost ran outside, closing the doors behind her, and hardly taking a full breath until she was close to the bench. Then she stoped abruptly. There was a man sitting there in the faint moonlight, smoking a cigarette.

He got up and took off his hat.

"Good evening," he said pleasantly. "I'm trespassing, I suppose, but I knew this bench well at one time, and the room at the Inn was hot." He eyed her speculatively. "I imagine you're Tommy's wife. Right?"

"Yes," she said, her voice uncertain. "You—you startled me."

"I didn't mean to. I'm Donald Cameron, and at one time I spent my vacations here. As you may know, I am—I was—married to Julia. Isn't this rather an unusual hour for you to be out?"

"I couldn't sleep," she said simply.

He laughed a little.

"I see. So you go to the room where my revered ex-father-in-law died! Not a cheerful excursion, I imagine. Won't you sit down? It's too nice a night to spend in a house."

She could see him better now, a tall man with an agreeable voice, but she did not sit down.

"You were over there yourself, weren't you?" she said. "I saw your footmarks in the mothflakes."

"My dear girl," he said, "I was not over there. If you doubt me examine my shoes. No mothflakes. Anyhow, I'm no ghoul. Why should I go there?"

He was quite definite. He had only reached the bench when he saw the lights go on. His car was back on the street. If she still doubted him she could feel the radiator.

"If it's still hot," he said amusedly. "It's been half dead for the last five years."

But while he talked he seemed to be eyeing her curiously.

"Just what took you over there?" he inquired. "Leave something you forgot? Or do you think—well, I gathered at the Inn that you asked for the police. One of the servants heard you, apparently.

Why did you do that, Mrs. Jewett?"

She was still suspicious, however. It was long after midnight, and an odd hour surely for him to be in that vicinity.

"Can't we both sit down?" he inquired. "I'm a little tired myself. My car broke down and I had the devil of a time getting here. Not that you'll believe me, of course, but it happens to be true."

She sat down unwillingly, and he lit a cigarette and gave her one. She relaxed somewhat.

"If you came to see Julia," she said, "she's in bed. She's had a hard day."

He seemed to be smiling.

"As a matter of fact I came to attend the funeral," he said. "I was rather fond of old Horace, in spite of the alimony he got out of me. Look here, why did you ask for the police? You sound like a sensible young woman."

Somehow his very frankness inspired confidence. She found herself giving in, to her own surprise.

"I don't know, I can't think why he went into the living-room alone that night. He wasn't reading. There was no book around. And the lights weren't on. He hadn't rung for his nurse, either. There was a bell beside his bed."

"His nurse, that would be the Scott woman," he said reflectively. "I saw her at the Inn. She took rather a bad turn in the dining-room tonight. I helped carry her upstairs."

"Scotty! She's sick?"

"She's all right now. Doctor Marlow said it was a diabetic coma, or something. That's one reason I came here so late. Thought she was a goner at first."

"Diabetes. I didn't know she had it."

"No, I don't suppose she talked about it. Any idea who it was in the other house tonight?"

237

"I can't imagine," she said, rather tensely. "Everybody was in bed when I left."

He laughed again, his light, amused laugh.

"So I'm still a suspect of some sort," he said. "Julia will come into a lot of money, she won't need the alimony any more, and after her usual generous fashion she will set me free. That's the idea, isn't it?"

He got up and stood looking down at her.

"Only you don't know my Julia," he went on. "And I gather no one murdered her father. All of which lets me out nicely. Now it's time for beautiful young women to be in bed. That's not a hint. It's a statement. I'll wait here until you're safely inside."

She wondered about that later. What did he mean by safely? Did he, too, think there was something strange about old Horace's death? But she had no chance to talk to him again. She saw him the next day at the funeral, a tall, slightly balding man who shook hands formally with the family—including Julia—after the service and then disappeared. She looked for him at the cemetery, but he was not in the small decorous crowd around the grave.

The weather continued hot. In New York the temperatures rose into the official nineties, and even Marian, anxious to find the new apartment, seemed reconciled to staying where she was. On Wednesday Henry left for the city, and a young woman from the local real estate office began to inventory the house next door. Marian was indignant that morning when she heard.

"You're simply playing into the hands of Washington," she told Julia angrily. "They'll tax us up to the hilt. Why not get a moving van and take out the best pieces? No one would ever know."

"I'm not bucking the Federal Government," Julia told her dryly. "If you want to end up in Atlanta,

I don't."

She had not once mentioned Don Cameron, although Jessica had seen him shaking hands with her at the funeral.

Room by room now the empty house was being closed. As fast as it was inventoried the furniture was covered, the hangings taken down, folded, and put away. By Thursday the work was done. A local carpenter had boarded up the windows, the chairs were gone from the terrace, and the house stood dreary and forlorn, with only a crow or two stalking across the lawn and the incessant noise of the sea gulls its only sound.

But Jessica had at least some relief from the hot kitchen. A local woman had agreed to come in for a few hours each day, and what with Henry gone, with Marian at the Club pool, and Tommy definitely on the upgrade, she went that afternoon to see Miss Scott.

She found her sitting on the Inn porch, alone and looking rather lost. Looking odd, too, without her familiar glasses. She smiled, however, when she recognized Jessica.

"How nice of you!" she said. "I feel so badly about the funeral. I missed it, you know."

"I'm sorry you were sick."

"I'm all right now," Scotty said, rather hurriedly. "It wasn't anything, really. The doctor thought it was shock. Finding the—finding him the way I did. And then your suggesting the police, and the way people here looked at me that night. As though I had killed him!"

"They know better now."

"I suppose so. But Chief Fenton was in to see me this morning. He wanted to know all about that night. I couldn't tell him much. All the family except

Tommy had been in during the day, and Mr. Jewett seemed to feel fine. He got a letter in the afternoon mail that seemed to upset him, but he didn't say anything about it. After dinner he sent for Henry, but he and Marian had gone to the movies. It was ten o'clock when Henry got there, and Mr. Jewett sent me up to bed. I left the Scotch for him, and his hypodermic ready to use."

"And that's all?"

It seemed to Jessica that Scotty hesitated.

"I don't want to make any trouble," she said slowly. "Nothing will bring him back. But I didn't see his vitamin bottle the next morning."

"His vitamin bottle?"

"That's what he took in the hypo. B-one, you know. It was in a rubber-tipped vial, one where you put the needle through the rubber top. He should have had it before dinner, but he was upset. Anyhow, he liked to do it himself. He could, if it was ready for him. He always said," she added drearily, "that it hurt less when he did it. He took it in his thigh."

Jessica's voice was tense.

"Did you find the syringe?"

"Yes. It was beside his bed. He had taken the hypo, all right. It had been used."

"What became of it, Scotty?"

"I cleaned it in alcohol and put it away. Why? They didn't find any poison, Jessica, and you can't fool with those bottles. The rubber cap's sealed on."

But her expression had changed. She looked suddenly doubtful, and Jessica wondered if she had thought of something. If she had she said nothing, and Jessica changed the subject.

"What about the letter?" she asked. "You say it worried him. Did you find it later?"

"It wasn't in his room. I suppose he gave it to

240

Henry. Usually he did that, kept the mail in the drawer of the bed table, and handed it over when Henry came for week-ends. There never was very much, of course."

"Look," Jessica said, rather desperately. "Tell me exactly what was on or in that table, Scotty, when you left him to go to bed."

Scotty looked surprised.

"Well, there was his reading lamp, of course, and the Scotch and his glasses. That's funny. He didn't have his glasses on when I found him. I never thought of it."

"And what else?"

"His hypodermic syringe and his watch. That's all I remember. Of course, the drawer was different. He kept his personal checkbook there, and somebody's fountain pen. It wasn't his. I don't know who left it."

Jessica drew a long breath of relief.

"It was Tommy's," she said. "Scotty, why would Mr. Jewett wheel himself into that room and take Tommy's pen with him? Did he mean to write something?"

Scotty looked doubtful.

"There was no paper around. Maybe he meant to dial the telephone. He always used a pen or pencil for that."

"That's all, then?"

"Well, he kept Tommy's old geometry in the drawer. I don't remember anything else."

"What about Tommy's geometry?" Jessica asked sharply. "What was it doing there?"

"I found it one day behind the books in the living room, when I was looking for something to read. There was a funny drawing in front of it, like a cartoon. It was supposed to be Mr. Jewett, grinning and showing his teeth, and it said: 'Father's new uppers and lowers. The better to bite you with.' He thought it was funny. He was keeping it to show Tommy when he got better."

"Tommy would like to have it, I know. Where did you put it, Scotty?"

Scotty looked vague.

"I don't remember seeing it again," she said. "I suppose someone picked it up and put it away."

Well, that was the natural thing, Jessica thought. No use adding to the mystery, if there was one. Everything was apparently cleared up. The toxicologist's further report had revealed no trace of poison anywhere. She was being a fool, she felt. If only she could be certain Tommy had not seen his father that night—

She kissed Scotty good-by and went thoughtfully home, taking the shore path which passed the other house. She stopped and looked at it. Surely the book must be there somewhere. Books did not vanish. And Tommy would want it, she knew.

Rather reluctantly she turned and went up the path. Probably she could not get in. Julia had taken the keys. But she found the kitchen door unlocked and she opened it and stepped inside.

Except for the light from the door the room was dark, and she felt a faint repugnance to going farther. To her relief, however, the electric current was still on. She lighted the back hall and, snapping switches as she advanced, found her courage coming back.

But it was not pleasant. Over everything was the smell of Julia's mothflakes, and another odor she thought was like that of old burned wood. It grew stronger as she advanced, until it was overpowering when she reached the front of the house. Her eyes were smarting, too, and she began to cough, as though the air was bad.

242

She opened the door to the living-room and turned on the lights. She did not go in immediately, however. She stood there staring incredulously. The room was much as she had last seen it, with one exception. It was filled with smoke, and Mr. Jewett's big white chair was gone, or largely gone.

It had been dragged somewhat out of its corner by the window, and what was left of it was only its charred and ghostly skeleton. The rug had been turned back, but the floor boards beneath where it stood were badly scorched, while overhead the high ceiling was stained almost black.

7

The whole thing seemed impossible, without sense or reason.

She looked around, remembering the room as it had been left, the shrouded furniture, the newspapers covering the books. But, although the rest of the room was much the same, there were no newspapers on the books now. They had been dragged off and thrown into the fireplace. Whoever had done it, and she was sure it had been deliberate, was taking no risk that the flames would spread.

Julia was on the porch when she hurried home. She looked tired and discouraged, but she received Jessica's news with complete incredulity.

"Burned!" she said. "How could it burn? I don't smoke, and the room's been closed anyhow."

Only when she saw it did she believe it, but even then she refused to see any sinister aspect in it. She was willing to blame the carpenter, or the girl who had made the inventory, and when Jessica remarked that it had not spread she said scornfully that with the house closed there was no air to feed it. Not until Jessica brought in the fire extinguisher from the hall and showed it was empty did she throw up her hands.

"All right," she said. "Somebody started it and then tried to put it out. I'll grant you that. But who?"

"Somebody who didn't want the whole house to burn," Jessica said obstinately. "Somebody who had to burn the chair and nothing else."

"But why the chair?" Julia seemed dazed. "Just because Father died in it—"

"Why did he go in there that night?" Jessica insisted. "Why didn't he ring for Scotty? What was he doing in that room, Julia? Was he seeing someone? Have you thought of that? Someone not necessarily in the family. He had some reason for going there. I'm sure of that."

"If you think he saw Don Cameron," Julia said stiffly, "just forget it. He wasn't here that night. And there's no need to tell the village about it, Jessica. Or the police, either. There's enough talk as it is."

"I intend to tell Tommy," said Jessica, equally stiffly.

"All right, but, for God's sake, keep Marian out of it. It would be all over the Club by morning."

Rather to Jessica's disappointment Tommy took the chair rather lightly. He went over to look at it and came back cheerful enough.

"Funny as all hell," he said, "but no mystery, darling. Records of every fire department show what cigarettes can do. We'd better agree not to smoke in bed any more. What were you doing there anyhow?"

"I was looking for your geometry," she told him. "Scotty says she found it and gave it to your father."

Tommy whistled.

"So he saw the picture I drew in it!" he said. "Golly! I hid it for years. He used to scare the be-jesus out of me. Did you see it?"

"I didn't look, after I saw the chair."

So the mystery of the chair, if there was one, was cheerfully ignored by the family, and the next two days were quiet. Tommy had gone back to his desk and was much his old self again. Julia managed to get rid of the burned skeleton somehow, the other

245

house was definitely closed, and on Saturday morning when Henry arrived he brought with him old Horace's lawyer, a man named Willis, to read his last testament. It was much as they expected. The estate was divided equally among the three heirs, except for a sizable sum to Scotty. And there was a rather touching codicil about Jessica.

"To my beloved daughter-in-law, Jessica Waring Jewett," it said, "I bequeath the sum of fifty thousand dollars, free of tax, for her own personal use."

Jessica found herself softly crying, and Tommy reached over and took her hand.

"The fine old boy," he said quietly. "The decent fine old boy!"

It was after Henry had driven the lawyer to the late train that night that Tommy, restless after the strain, decided to go to the other house to hunt for the geometry. Julia objected.

"I've got everything in order," she said, "the books covered, everything. The current is off, too."

But he was insistent. He found a flashlight, got the keys, and started out. That was at half past ten, and Jessica did not go with him. Instead she wrote a long detailed letter to her father. She had already wired him about the death. Now she put in the letter the whole story, her own early suspicions, the failure to discover any poison in the body, the burned chair, even Scotty's collapse and coma, and her feeling that the nurse knew or suspected something she had not told. She felt slightly sheepish when she finished, so she added a postscript. *If I'm being a fool, better wire me.*

It was midnight when she put an airmail stamp on it and carried it to the corner postbox. Then, hearing Tommy whistling, she waited for him at the path. He drew her arm through his.

"What are you doing, out at this witching hour?" he asked.

"Mailing a letter to Father," she admitted.

"Still the little chip off the old block, aren't you?" he said. "Sorry to be so late, darling. I was looking over the books. Some of them were interesting, but— no geometry."

It was not an alibi, they were to learn the next day. A killer may whistle on his way from the kill. He may even kiss his wife, there in the open, with the sea splashing softly against the rocks, a sea which probably even then was washing a body against the village pier. For there was a body.

It was Scotty who was dead. Scotty, whose neatly clad corpse was found by a fishing boat at daylight on Sunday morning.

The people who ran the Inn did not even know she had left it. The night had been hot, and she had been sitting on the porch when she was last seen. Just when or why she had gone to the pier nobody knew, unless it was to find a breeze.

There was evidence, however, that she had not been alone. The pier was dark at the end, where there was a bench, but a boy and girl, out in a canoe, had heard voices there the night before. They were not certain of the time—between eleven and twelve, they thought—or whether the voices were male or female, but they were sure they had heard them.

Fenton had sent for the district attorney as soon as the body was recovered, and he came over at once from the county seat. A small, dapper man, he grinned when he saw the chief.

"Kind of stirring things up around here, aren't you?" he said. "Bad for the tourist business, you know. The State won't like it."

"We'll get plenty of publicity, if this is a murder," Fenton said dryly.

"Well, is it or isn't it?"

"I thought maybe you'd know. I think it is."

They brought in the boy and girl, but they could add nothing to what they had already told.

"Were they quarreling?" the district attorney inquired.

"I wouldn't think so. Just talking," the boy said. "We went on, and we didn't hear any splash."

Scotty had drowned. There was no question of that. Her lungs were full of salt water. But also there was a deep cut in the back of her head, as though she had been struck with something sharp. The district attorney—annoyed at losing his Sunday off—examined the cut as she lay in the town mortuary.

"Maybe she hit the pier as she went in," he suggested.

"Not if she was at the end of it," Fenton said. "Those boards are out over the piling. You ask me, she was knocked out and shoved. And you ask me again, she knew something she was holding back about old Jewett's death."

"It might be a suicide. She had a good chance to do Jewett in, if he *was* done in. He left her some money, didn't he?"

"Women just inheriting money don't jump off piers," Fenton said trenchantly. "Anyhow, she was taking a case for the doc here in a day or two. I've got some kids diving off the end of that pier. Maybe they'll find something."

The district attorney lunched with Fenton at the Inn that noon. The people there could throw no light on what had happened, nor did Miss Scott's room. A few bottles in the medicine cabinet, a minimum of street clothes but several fresh uniforms, a box of face

248

powder, and a comb and brush were all they found, outside of the bag in which she carried her hypodermic case, some bandages, adhesive tape and surgical scissors, a bottle of grain alcohol, and so on.

But over one small vial the district attorney hesitated.

"Was she diabetic?" he asked. "Or was this for old Jewett?"

"Hers, I guess," Fenton said indifferently. "Horace had plenty of trouble, but not that."

They learned only one other thing at the Inn. Scotty had been depressed for the last day or two, and sometime late on Saturday afternoon she had used the telephone. No one knew whom she had called, and the telephone operator in the village said some summer people were getting up a dance, and she had been too busy to notice. Fenton took the district attorney back to his small brick office next to what was locally called the firehouse, and the latter gentleman prepared to go. He was at the door when two or three boys in wet bathing-suits came in. They stopped sheepishly in the doorway, and pushed one of their number ahead. He had something in his hand at which Fenton gave a long stare.

"So you found that?" he said.

"Yes, sir. Just off the pier."

"All right, son. Put it on the desk, and here's a quarter apiece."

They retired in good order, and the district attorney smiled and put down his hat.

"So that's it!" he said. "Nice work, chief."

Fenton said nothing. He sat gazing at the golf club before him. It was an old-fashioned midiron, and there were three initials stamped in the metal head. He drew a long breath and unlocking a drawer of his desk took out a pair of leather bedroom slippers, shrunken and hard.

"The club," he said heavily, "belongs to Tommy Jewett. So do the slippers. He wore them out somewhere the night his father died, and his wife tried to dry them in the oven."

The district attorney looked interested.

"His wife?" he said. "I thought she was the one who wanted the police."

"That was before she found the slippers," Fenton said heavily as he got up. "I hate like hell to do this," he went on. "Boy's got a fine war record. Just getting over another attack of malaria, too. But no matter what killed old Horace this is murder. We got to bring him in for questioning. It don't look too good."

But Tommy, when he arrived, simply looked blank when they showed him the club.

"What *is* all this?" he demanded. "Sure it's mine if my initials are on it. Or it was. I haven't seen it for years. I've been playing other games than golf."

"Know where it was?" Fenton inquired.

"Maybe at the Golf Club. Maybe in the other house. My sister Julia may know if it was there." Then he saw the slippers, and stiffened slightly. "I don't get it," he said. "What are you doing with those things?"

The district attorney had been watching him. He ignored the slippers when he spoke.

"I'm sorry, Mr. Jewett," he said, "but there's a possibility Miss Scott was murdered. Struck on the head and thrown off the pier. That club was found in the water near where she must have been when she was attacked."

Tommy reached abruptly for a chair and sat down.

"Murdered!" he said thickly. "But who would kill her? She hadn't an enemy in the world."

"That doesn't follow. She may have known

251

something dangerous to someone else. Mr. Jewett, I'd like to go back to the night of your father's death. According to the chief here, you were out of the house that night. Were you?"

"My wife thinks I was. I don't know, myself. Sometimes when I have a fever I think I'm back fighting somewhere. I got out of the hospital once or twice that way. It raised the devil of a row." Then the import of the question struck him. "Look," he said. "The hell with all this. I didn't kill my father. Nobody did. And I haven't seen Scotty since the funeral. My wife knows where I was last night. I didn't go near the pier. I went over to the other house to look for a book."

"What time was that?" the district attorney asked smoothly.

"I don't know. It was after Henry had taken Willis, Dad's lawyer, to the train. After eleven, I imagine. I hunted around a bit, but I didn't find what I was after."

Fenton looked up sharply.

"So Henry was out, too, was he?"

"You can't pin anything on Henry, if that's what you think." Tommy's tone was truculent. "Why would he kill anybody? He liked Scotty, as we all did. And he drove straight back after he left Willis at the train. I heard his car come in."

They went over the evening with him, Julia reading downstairs, Marian in bed with a detective story, Jessica with him, and his own restlessness.

"What was this book you were looking for?" the district attorney inquired.

"Nothing much. A school geometry of mine. I just wanted to see it again." They looked a trifle blank at this, and he explained. He'd been there an hour or more just browsing around. Then he'd gone home.

"My wife wanted to go with me," he said, "but I wouldn't let her. She's been overworked for the past two weeks. Now I wish to God she had."

They let him go then, and from the window Fenton watched him get into his car.

"I'd hate to think it was that boy," he said. "Known him all his life. Now Henry, Henry's different. Made a fool marriage, for one thing. And he did some mighty quick thinking when I found those slippers in the oven. Claimed they were his." He grunted. "Well, there you are! Not an alibi in the crowd, but as sure as hell one of them killed the nurse. And if I didn't know better I'd say the father, too."

"The nurse knew something. Is that it?"

"I'll bet ten dollars she knew how and why Horace Jewett died. It preyed on her, probably. She had kind of a funny spell at the Inn the other night, and there's that telephone call of hers yesterday. If we knew who that was—"

"Any chance the autopsy on the old man missed something?"

"Not a hope. The fellow Marlow brought in took some things away with him. Couldn't find a trace of poison."

To Jessica the next day or two were things of pure horror, not relieved by a wire from her father on Tuesday evening. The local office of the telegraph company was closed, and the message was telephoned over.

Suggest search for vitamin bottle. Also further talk with nurse. What is her physical condition? Wire complete details and be careful yourself. Love. Dad.

The irony of the sentence about Scotty's condition brought tears to her eyes. But her great concern was Tommy. That he was under suspicion was certain, in spite of his refusal to believe it. For Henry's alibi had apparently stood up. He had taken Willis to the train, and so far as they could discover had come directly back. Asked if he had detoured to the town pier, he told Fenton not to be a damned fool. He'd picked up the tennis pro and brought him into town. As to the golf club, Julia had a faint recollection of some old clubs in the attic of the other house, but said she would not know if one was missing.

In the end she unwillingly gave Fenton a key to the kitchen door of the other house, and he took Tommy with him. The clubs were there in the attic, rusty and forlorn, in a shabby canvas bag. They were all marked with Tommy's initials, and the midiron was missing.

Tommy could only shrug and repeat what he had said about it. But in a corner he discovered what Julia had done with the burned chair. It stood there, gaunt and ugly, and Fenton stared at it while Tommy explained.

"Pity it can't talk," the chief said. "It might have quite a story."

But apparently Horace Jewett had not been murdered, and Scotty had. After all, plenty of chairs burned. As long as people dozed off in them or left lighted cigarettes in them—

Fenton shrugged and went down the stairs, carrying the rest of the golf clubs with him.

The inquest over the body was held by the county coroner on Wednesday, in the empty schoolhouse. It took on some of the attributes of a social occasion, for the summer colony, bored with its usual diversions of bridge and sailing and golf, turned out in numbers. Long before the hour the street was cluttered with gleaming cars and station wagons, and Jessica found herself fiercely resenting the

254

Very little developed, however. The body had been identified and the jury had seen it. The fisherman who had recovered it testified to that extent. The young couple in the canoe told of the voices they had heard, and Doctor Marlow stated that, while death had been caused by drowning, the head injury had been—in his opinion—caused by a heavy blow.

"From something with a sharp edge, doctor?"

"Almost certainly. Yes."

"I show you this golf club, found in the water near the pier. Could it have inflicted the injury?"

"It could. I cannot say positively, of course."

If he saw Tommy's initials he ignored them, according to the request of the authorities. As a result, the jury brought in a verdict of homicide at the hands of a person or persons unknown, and the party—as Julia sourly termed it—was over. Evidently Fenton and the district attorney, for all their suspicions, had as yet no case.

Throughout the proceedings Tommy was stiff and silent. Marian had hysterically refused to go, and Henry sat alone, looking stern and unhappy. Only Julia was herself, rigidly handsome and coldly detached. It was not until they reached the pavement that Jessica saw Donald Cameron. He melted away in the crowd, however, before Julia saw him, and Jessica did not mention him.

To her relief everybody in the house retired early that night. No one wanted to talk, and the cloud which hung over them was almost tangible. Henry, getting up from a table where nobody ate much, made the only comment.

"For a family of killers," he said dryly, "we certainly look the part. I never saw a lot of guiltier faces."

Jessica waited until the house quieted down that night before she showed Tommy her father's telegram. He looked astonished.

"Vitamin bottle?" he said. "Are you sure you got that right?"

"I am. They mailed me the wire. Here it is."

He read it and looked up.

"What's this about your being careful?" he said. "And what does he mean about Scotty's condition? She's dead, which is the hell of a state to be in. See here, darling, does he think you're in danger? What on earth did you write him?"

He listened while she told him of her talk with Scotty, and her feeling that the nurse at one time had looked disturbed.

"Her expression changed," she said. "She looked thoughtful and then—well, scared."

"That was about the vitamin bottle?"

"Yes, I think so."

"Did you ask Julia if she'd seen it?"

"No. Scotty said it was missing that morning. She looked for it."

But the day had been long and exciting, and Tommy looked exhausted. She got him to bed finally, but as usual with her now she found herself sleepless. At one o'clock she got up, put on her dressing-gown and slippers as she had once before, and taking a flashlight went down to the kitchen porch. There was a chance that the trash from the other house had not yet been removed. In that case the bottle might still be there. In any event she intended to find out.

She had meant to go by the path, but she did not. In the faint moonlight she saw two people on the bench there, and one of them was Julia. As Jessica watched she got up suddenly.

"I don't believe it," she said sharply. "Even if you're right, it doesn't matter now."

"I'm not so sure of that. All I'm saying, my dear girl, is that if you need me at any time I'll be here."

"Why should I need you? There's no case against anybody. And I'm not your dear girl. That's over."

Julia walked rapidly back to the house, and as he lit a cigarette Jessica recognized Cameron. He waited until the front door closed, then he took the path to the drive and the village street. Jessica stood still on the kitchen porch as he passed it, and apparently he did not see her. But he walked slowly, as though he were thinking, his head down, the cigarette unheeded in his hand.

She waited until his footsteps died away before she moved. After that she went on, using her flashlight when she needed it, until she found the small housing which held the garbage and trash cans from the other house. But when she opened the doors it was to have all sorts of boxes, discarded clothing, papers, old letters, and so on come tumbling out about her feet.

She stared at them in dismay. It would take a week of time and good daylight to find a small vial in that chaos. She could not even replace the stuff. And as if to add horror to her confusion, someone at that moment put a hand on her arm and another over her mouth.

9

"Don't scream," said a voice. "No use waking the neighborhood. Or being scared. It's only me."

The hands were removed, and Cameron was standing beside her.

"I saw the flash from the street," he said, "so I walked back. What on earth are you doing here?"

She felt dizzy with shock. She put a hand against one of the doors to steady herself, and he put an arm around her to hold her.

"Sorry," he said. "Too much going on around here to have you yelling for help at this hour. Besides, I have an idea Fenton's got somebody keeping an eye on the place. What are you after, anyhow?"

"A bottle," she managed to gasp. "Mr. Jewett's vitamin bottle."

He freed her abruptly.

"Now see here, Jessica," he said. "That doesn't make sense, and you know it. You're after the letter, aren't you?"

"What letter?" she asked shakily.

He did not explain. Instead he took her by the arm and led her to the kitchen steps close at hand. He waited until she sat down, then he stood looking down at her.

"I wonder," he said. "Are you as innocent as you sound? Or are you and Tommy playing a game of some sort? I'm damned if I know. What's this about a bottle?"

"There's no game," she protested. "I've got to prove Tommy didn't kill his father or Miss Scott. I must. That's all."

"Pretty much in love with the guy, aren't you? What's that got to do with all this?" He motioned toward the trash a few feet away. "Or, for God's sweet sake, a bottle?"

She wondered how much she could trust him. Somehow there in the dark he looked tall and rather menacing, and she was still suffering from shock. He might be a suspect himself. Certainly he had been around off and on ever since Mr. Jewett's death; on the bench the night someone had trampled Julia's smoothly placed mothflakes, at the funeral, at the Inn the night Scotty collapsed, at the inquest, and now.

She felt suddenly panicky. She tried to get up, but he bent down and put a hand on her shoulder.

"We'd better have this out," he said "I'm not going to hurt you. Get that out of your pretty head. But I want to know what brought you here at this hour, Jessica. Don't tell me it was vitamins. I don't believe it."

She was at his mercy, she knew, in spite of what he said. His voice was calm and reassuring, however, so in the end she told him about her letter to her father with all its details, and his telegram that day. He seemed to know who her father was, and as she went on he sat down beside her and lit a cigarette. It was over the telegram that he showed surprise.

"Scotty's physical condition?" he said. "What did he mean by that?"

"I don't know, unless he thought she was tired enough to have made a mistake."

He nodded.

"Gave the old man something else instead of his regular stuff, you mean. But he wasn't poisoned. Or was he? After all, someone had a reason for getting rid of the nurse. That's certain." He got up and dropping the cigarette stepped on it to kill it. "Maybe your dad has something, after all. Suppose we look for that bottle. How big was it?"

"It was a vial, really. Quite small. I've seen it often. It had a rubber top cemented on."

"Well, there's nothing like trying," he said, rather hopelessly, and fell to work.

An hour later they stood in the midst of Julia's carefully stored discards from the house and stared at each other. There was no vial in the heap around them. There were bottles of every sort, from empty catsup ones from the kitchen to liniment and other medicine ones from the sickroom. But of the vial of vitamin B-1 there was no sign.

In the failing light from Jessica's flashlight Cameron looked dirty and disgruntled.

"So that's that," he said, in disgust. "Only there's one funny thing about it. It ought to be here. Julia's made a clean sweep. So—where is it?"

They were both electrified when a brilliant light was turned on them, and a voice spoke from the darkness behind it.

"What's all this? What's going on here?"

Jessica recognized the voice. It was George Higgins, one of the extra policemen Fenton hired during the summer, and as he lowered the flash to the piled-up rubbish around them she could see him more plainly. He was holding the flashlight in his left hand, while the right rested on the butt of his gun. Cameron, however, had had a minute to rally.

"It's all right, officer," he said urbanely. "This is Mrs. Jewett. She's lost a wrist watch, and we've been

260

looking for it."

"Funny hour for a thing like that," Higgins said suspiciously.

"Not so funny. She couldn't sleep, so she decided to look for it. I was passing by when I saw the light and thought I'd better see about it. My name's Cameron, if it interests you. I'm a friend of the family here. I'm staying at the Inn."

Higgins seemed doubtful.

"Ought to run you in, making a mess like that," he said. "Miss Julia's going to have a fit. Mean to put it back?"

"I was just wondering about that." Cameron's voice was still urbane. "You might know somebody who would take on the job for, say, ten dollars. And not talk about it. You see, Mrs. Jewett's husband gave her the watch. She doesn't want him to know it's missing." He pulled out a wallet and extracted a bill from it. "Here it is," he said. "Pass it on if you find someone."

He was shaking with suppressed laughter as he took Jessica back to the other house, for behind them Higgins was already at work, his coat off and the flashlight resting where it would do the most good. But at the kitchen porch he became serious again.

"I don't like it," he said. "I don't like any of it. No more running about at night, young woman. I think your father's right. And if you ask me, we're up against a killer with no more conscience that that doorknob there."

She overslept the next morning, not waking until she heard Henry's heavy steps carrying Marian's late breakfast tray up to her. Tommy's bed was empty, and she saw that he had abandoned his customary slacks and had put on a suit. It was not like him, and she felt uneasy. It was ten o'clock by the time she had

261

dressed hurriedly and run to Marian's room. Henry was still there, but his cold was worse and he was standing by the open window coughing while Marian watched him, her face sulky.

"I've told you to get out before you start that," she was saying. "Those things are contagious, and you know it."

Jessica stood waiting until the paroxysm was over. As usual Marian in her bed was as luxurious as Marian anywhere. She wore a soft silk jacket, and she was surrounded by small lace and colored pillows. The tray was beside her, and she was holding a coffee cup when she saw Jessica.

"Come in," she said. "If you want Tommy, the police sent for him late last night. It doesn't mean anything," she added casually. "Who would want to get rid of Scotty? These small-town hicks make me sick."

Henry had got his breath. He wiped his eyes and looked apologetically at his wife.

"Sorry, sweetheart," he said. "I didn't have time to get out. But Marlow thinks I'm not contagious now." He saw Jessica, and his big, heavy face clouded. He tried to reassure her, however.

"I wouldn't worry about Tommy," he said. "He'll be back soon. Just some points Fenton wanted to clear up. That golf club, you know. No fingerprints on it, but he used to lend his clubs to all sorts of people. Probably it hasn't been in the other house for years."

"He used them himself until the war, didn't he?" This was Marian, faintly malicious. "He'd have missed it, wouldn't he, if it was gone then?"

For once Henry was annoyed with her.

"You let the police handle this, my girl," he said. "Keep out of it."

Marian was not easily subdued, however.

"They can have it," she cried carelessly. "Only I'd like to know what Jessica was doing out last night. What was it, Jess? I heard you slipping in about half past two. You wouldn't have a boy friend somewhere, would you?"

Jessica's patience suddenly snapped.

"No," she said. "If you must know, I was out looking for a vitamin bottle. And if that isn't enough, I think Henry's father was poisoned, just as Scotty was murdered."

For just a moment she was aware of them both staring at her, and that Henry's face was suffused with rage.

"Don't be a fool," he said thickly. "That's crazy talk. What's come over you, Jessica? Do you want to hang your own husband?"

"I don't think for a minute Tommy did it," she said, "but I'm not so sure about some other people I know."

She turned abruptly and went back to her room, leaving a heavy silence behind her.

10

Scotty's funeral was held that afternoon. If Horace
had drawn a crowd, poor Scotty, alone in the world
and largely friendless, drew a multitude. The village
streets were parked with cars, and the cemetery later
overflowed. But Tommy was not there. Jessica,
telephoning frantically, learned that he was at the
county seat and being held for questioning, whatever
that might mean.

She was terrified when she heard, but had she
known it, the questioning, as a matter of fact, was
getting exactly nowhere. Tommy was surly and
resentful.

"Why in God's name would I kill the woman?" he
demanded. "I barely knew her until we came here
this summer. She seemed a decent sort, and my father
was completely dependent on her."

The district attorney looked tired. The day was hot
and he had taken off his coat and hung it neatly over
the back of a chair. In a corner a police stenographer
was making the usual pothooks, but there were long
pauses when he had time to mop his face. Fenton's
tongue was dry from too much smoking, and he got
up and getting a paper cup of water at the cooler,
drank thirstily.

Only Tommy looked cool, but it was the coldness
of rage. He had run out of cigarettes, but he was
asking no favors.

The district attorney stirred. The back of his shirt was stuck to his chair, and he scowled.

"Has it occurred to you, Mr. Jewett," he said, "that she might have been killed because she knew something about your father's death?"

"I thought he died of heart failure. Maybe you know something I don't."

There it was. They still knew nothing about Horace's death, and this good-looking boy was aware of it. They had no case, against him, against anybody. If they could only prove he had been on the pier that night—

"About these night walks of yours, Mr. Jewett," he said. "Do you care to explain about them?"

"No," Tommy said defiantly. "Why should I?"

"But you do take them now and then?"

"I've been known to when I had a fever. Does that prove anything? I don't get up and kill people. That's fantastic."

The district attorney consulted a paper on his desk.

"Isn't it a fact that in the Second World War you were lost in the jungle in Burma for some time?" he said.

"If you want my record, you can get it from the Defense Department," Tommy said stiffly, and getting to his feet picked up his hat.

"How about taking me home, Fenton?" he said. "I have a wife. And this could go on for a month and get nowhere."

They eyed him cautiously. This tall young man staring at them defiantly looked every inch a soldier. He held himself like one, and none of them there would have cared to tackle him, sick as he had been. He looked cool and uncompromising—almost dangerous—after nearly a day of interrogation.

They had not put him in a cell, of course. He had

slept what remained of the night before in a hotel room, with Fenton snoring in the next bed. Now they knew they could not hold him any longer, unless something new turned up.

"Suppose we compromise," the district attorney suggested. "You and the chief here get dinner somewhere. Then you can telephone your wife. And—well—we'll see how things look."

Tommy nodded, as though he could not trust himself to speak, and Fenton got up.

"This meal's on the county," he said. "Let's go."

He mellowed somewhat over a highball, did Fenton. He was tired, and as he watched the set face across from him, decidedly uneasy.

"Look, boy," he said. "Nobody's trying to railroad you anywhere. You know that. But what gets me is why that nurse had to be killed. What's behind it? Nobody gains a thing so far as I can see. She was an inoffensive sort of woman, wasn't she?"

"She was. Quiet and kind," Tommy said, with stiff lips. "We all liked her. Don't ask me for a motive. There isn't any. It looks like a lunatic." He smiled faintly for the first time that day. "Unless you think I'm one," he added. "The district attorney intimated something of the sort, didn't he?"

Fenton looked shocked.

"Of course not," he said. "He was just making conversation."

At which Tommy suddenly and wholeheartedly laughed.

To Jessica the day had been endless. It was after Scotty's funeral, when there was still no word from Tommy, that she wired her father. *Miss Scott dead. Murder suspected. Tommy being held. Can you come on?*

She felt rather better when she had telephoned it.

The village woman had taken her afternoon off, and she and Julia got the supper. Nobody was hungry, however, and Henry was still indignant with Jessica after the morning. At eight o'clock he decided to go to the county seat, and they heard his car drive away. Evidently he or Marian had told Julia about what Jessica had said, for she, too, was cool and silent, but not until the last dish had been put away did she bring it up. Then she slammed the door to the hall to shut out the sound of Marian, who was singing at the piano, and confronted Jessica.

"What in the world got into you this morning?" she demanded. "Do you like to make trouble?"

"It's already made, isn't it?" Jessica said. "Only Tommy had nothing to do with it. If you think I'm going to let them hold him for something he never did you're crazy."

Julia sat down heavily.

"He was out of the house about the time Scotty was killed, Jessica. That's the trouble."

"So was Henry. So, as far as I know, were you, or Marian. And you know perfectly well where he went. He was over at the other house, looking for that book of his."

"But why?" Julia said, a note of desperation in her voice. "Why was the book important? I didn't see it when I closed the house. I told him so. But he had to go and look, with that golf club in the attic and everything! No wonder they're holding him." She got up. The noise from the piano was deafening, and she frowned.

"Why on earth doesn't that girl stop her cater-wauling!" she added impatiently. "We might at least preserve a sense of decency around here."

She banged out of the kitchen, leaving Jessica to finish the cleaning up, and a moment later silence descended on the house. She heard Marian slam the piano shut and run upstairs. She heard Julia leave by way of the front porch, probably for the path by the water. And all at once she felt lonely and a little frightened. She remembered Henry's face that morning, ugly, almost threatening. And she thought of Don Cameron and Julia on the bench, and of him later, diligently helping her search through that mass of rubbish.

Perhaps he had a reason of his own for that search, she thought. Perhaps, after all, he had found the vitamin bottle, too. He could have found it and slipped it in his pocket. After all, he would almost certainly profit by both deaths, by Horace's because of Julia's inheritance, by Scotty's if she knew or suspected how he died. If there was something wrong with the vial, he would want it, of course.

She cheered up, however, when she heard Tommy's voice over the telephone.

"I'm on my way, darling," he said cheerfully. "They've apparently decided I'm a right guy, after all."

"Have you had anything to eat?" she asked.

"You sound just like a wife! I have. Both food and drink, on the county!"

But his voice changed subtly when she told him Henry was on his way to see him.

"We'll look out for him," he said. "Love and kisses, as usual."

Then abruptly he hung up. It was not like him. It was as though he did not want Henry to meet him. But that was impossible. He and Henry—

She went thoughtfully back to the kitchen. It was a cloudy night, threatening rain, and as she stepped out onto the porch with the garbage pail she found herself in complete darkness. Afterward she was to remember feeling her way toward the steps and reaching for the railing, but from that time on her mind was a blank. She had no recollection of any attack, of hearing footsteps or seeing any movement. One minute she was standing on the porch. The next, when she opened her eyes, she was in bed and a frantic Tommy was holding her hand and was calling her name.

"Jessica! Jessica!" he was saying over and over. "For God's sake, speak to me! It's Tommy."

"Get away from her, you young fool," Doctor Marlow said. "Didn't the war teach you anything? She needs quiet, and I'm seeing that she gets it."

She was aware of a needle pricking her arm, and because by now she trusted no one she tried to pull away from it. Her reflexes, however, were no good. If this was death she thought dully, it was a pleasant one.

As it happened, it was not death. She wakened in the morning only to a headache and a substantial bump on her head. Tommy, fully dressed, was asleep in a chair by the window. He looked crumpled and weary, so she let him sleep until Marlow arrived.

He jerked awake then, but the doctor merely ordered him downstairs for breakfast, examined the bump, felt her pulse, and then sitting down by the bed smiled at her.

"Gave yourself quite a knock, didn't you?" he said. "That's what you get for going around in the dark. Now I think I have some good news for you."

"I don't think I fell," she objected, ignoring his news. "I was reaching for the railing. I know those steps. I ought to, after the times I've used them."

"But you see," he said patiently, "no one had any reason to attack you, Jessica. Why should they? After all, there have been no murders. None at all." His voice was cheerful. "As a matter of fact I should have known it all along. In a way I blame myself," he went on. "I recognized Scotty's symptoms when she collapsed at the Inn. The plain truth, Jessica, is that she was a diabetic, and she had to take insulin to control the condition. Only she hadn't been getting it. She'd been getting Mr. Jewett's vitamins instead."

"Are you saying they'd kill her?" Jessica asked.

He smiled gently down at her.

"No, but her own drug killed Horace Jewett. It's like this," he continued, "and I don't take any credit for it. Your father suggested it by wire to Fenton. Insulin would be fatal to anyone with a bad heart. And it wouldn't show up in the post mortem. She obviously mixed the two vials, poor woman. Remember she'd broken her glasses, and the two are not unlike. She must have realized what she'd done after her own attack, so she killed herself." He got up, looking brisk and rather smug. "So there you are, my dear. An accidental death and a suicide."

She did not believe it. She did not believe one word of it. She tried to shake her head, but it hurt, so she desisted.

"You'll be all right," he said, picking up his bag. "No concussion, no anything. Just keep quiet for a day or two. That's all."

He was at the door when she spoke.

"Then who pushed me down the steps last night?" she asked.

He looked annoyed.

"Hasn't what I've said registered at all? I've told you, Jessica. It was dark. You fell, and that's all there is to it."

11

She lay back on her pillows after he had gone. Let it go at that, she thought wearily. Tommy was safe. They were all safe. Only she was sure she hadn't fallen. And Scotty hadn't burned the chair, or hit herself on the head with Tommy's golf club. She tried to remember the vitamin bottle as she had often seen it in Horace's room. Surely it was labeled. How could Scotty even without her glasses have made such a mistake? Or had she? Had someone else done it? It wouldn't be hard to put a hypodermic needle through the rubber cap, draw out the vial's contents and inject the other drug into it.

Only that meant it was premeditated. Someone had planned it, perhaps for days or weeks. Someone, too, who knew enough to make such a plan. Scotty would know the danger, and she was garrulous at times. If she had told about it—

But Jessica was still incapable of any prolonged mental effort. Her head ached, and the ice bag on it bothered her. She lay there with her eyes closed listening to the sounds of the house around her, the woman in the kitchen washing up after breakfast, Henry coughing and Marian protesting, the soft rustle of Julia's dress as she came to the door to see if she was all right, the sound of Tommy in the bathroom shower.

They were all normal people, she thought tiredly.

They did not kill, or plan to kill. And her father had suspected something from Scotty's collapse at the Inn. That was what he meant about her condition. If, for instance, her own bottle had been filled up with the vitamins from another one—

He knew so much about murder, her father.

Tommy had finished and was coming in. There was certainly a change in him. He was still thin, but the sick man of the past few days had become the definite, slightly arrogant young officer she had married. The one who had said, "Listen, my girl. We're getting married, and there isn't one damn thing you can do about it."

Only what he said now was different. He draped his costume, a bath towel, around his waist and sat beside her on the bed.

"All right," he said grimly. "I heard Marlow's story downstairs. He likes it. I don't. You've got eyes like a cat. So who pushed you last night? Who was around the place?"

"Only Julia and Marian. Henry had gone to meet you."

"Sure of that, are you?"

"I heard his car drive out."

He made no comment. Instead he went to his coat and pulled a telegram from his pocket.

"From your father," he said. "It will tell you what he thinks about Marlow's accidental death and suicide!" He sat down beside her and opened it. "'Insist you leave at once and come here,'" He looked at her. "And it's just what you're doing," he said. "As soon as you can travel."

"I'm doing nothing of the sort, Tommy. You know that I'm not leaving you. Not ever."

"I know you're a damned sweet stubborn little fool," he said, and drew her close to him.

But later on he released her and sat upright.

"Look here," he said. "I've been thinking a lot about Dad. Why did he wheel himself into the living-room that night, Jessica? Was he meeting someone there?"

"No," she said positively. "When he saw anyone he always had a rug over his legs. He didn't have it when I saw him."

He was silent, thinking.

"Of course," he said, "if he felt sick, and Scotty didn't hear the bell—The phone was on the floor, wasn't it? Suppose he dropped it?"

She did not answer. It had not been dropped. It had been carefully placed where he could not reach it. She knew that. She stirred uneasily.

"Maybe Scotty's bell didn't ring that night, Tommy. Have you thought of that?"

He stared at her.

"Why not?" he said. "Do you mean to say he was delierately cut off from help?"

"It wouldn't hurt to look, would it? You may not find anything, of course. If that's the way it was, it's probably all right now."

"Probably," he said, and let it go at that.

He had not forgotten it, however. Her headache was better, and in the afternoon he carried her downstairs to the porch overlooking the sea. The weather had cooled, and he tucked her in her chair with pillows around her and a blanket over her knees. The house was quiet now. The family, relieved of its anxiety about her, had scattered. Julia had gone to a meeting of the local hospital, Marian was asleep upstairs, and Henry had taken his car and gone off somewhere.

But Tommy did not stay with her. He disappeared into the house, to come back with a bunch of keys in

273

his hand.

"Thought I'd look into that bell matter," he said. "You're all right out here, and the gardener is over there trimming the shrubbery. I'll tell him to keep an eye on you."

It was very peaceful out there. A man was fishing for flounder from a rock not far away; a chipmunk ran across the porch railing, saw her and turned back; and a cat was sitting under a tree, pretending innocence of a bird's nest overhead. She was dozing a little when she heard Tommy come back. Something was wrong. His face looked bleak as he held out his hand to her.

"Bit of cotton still stuck to the clapper," he said. "It was shut off, all right." He sat down on the porch step and stared out at the sea. "Who did it, Jessica? Who wanted him out of the way like that? You've been suspicious all along, haven't you? That's why you asked for the police."

But she didn't know. She told him how she thought it had been done, deliberately done, but that was all.

"I guess your father was right," he said heavily. "I'd better get you away from here. You're dangerous to someone, and you don't even know it."

Neither of them had noticed George, the gardener. He had stopped his pruning and in his overalls and wiping his face with a huge bandanna, was coming across the lawn. At the foot of the steps he stopped.

"Hope you folks'll excuse my appearance," he said. "I was trimming back that spirea by the other house, and I came across this. Looks like it fell off the living-room window sill. It ain't hurt any. No rain lately."

He held out a book, and Tommy took it and looked at it.

"Thanks, George," he said. "I've been hunting for it. It's an old schoolbook of mine. I'm glad to have it."

George retired in good order, and Tommy stood turning over the leaves. On one of the end pages was the cartoon of his father, and he eyed it somberly. Then he handed the book to Jessica. But as he did so a letter dropped to the floor, and he stooped and picked it up. The envelope was missing. Only the folded paper remained, but Tommy's face grew stiff as he read it.

He did not show it to Jessica. He folded it carefully and put it in his pocket. And he did not speak. He stood staring out at the water until Jessica made an effort to get up and go to him. He rallied somewhat then.

"Just a business letter from the bank," he said. "From Don Cameron, as a matter of fact. I suppose that's why he's been hanging around. No need to mention it to anyone," he added. "It's not important any more. If you're all right, I'll walk up the shore path a way. I need some exercise."

She watched him cross the lawn, and for the first time in months she saw he was limping again. Not much. Just as though he was tired, or worried. His shoulders were drooping, too, his head was down. The letter, she thought. It had been a blow of some sort.

He was still in sight when she heard Marian's voice behind her.

"What's the matter with Tommy?" she said lightly. "You two have a fight? He looks like it."

"He's upset. George found his geometry in the shrubbery under his father's window."

"Why should that upset him? He's been hunting the darned thing for days."

275

She picked up the book from Jessica's lap and riffled through it.

"Nothing here," she said casually. "Maybe it's this picture. I expect the old boy blew his top when he saw it. Well, I'm off to the hairdresser's and the Club. Henry's taken that cough of his to the doctor's. I threatened to leave him if he didn't."

She dropped the book back into Jessica's lap and disappeared toward the garage. But Tommy's short walk seemed to have prolonged itself. Jessica was still alone when she heard a car stop, and Don Cameron came around the corner of the house. He greeted her cheerfully.

"So you're all right!" he said, shaking hands with her. "That's fine, but don't tell me they've all left you. Where's Tommy?" He sat down and dropped his hat on the porch floor. "Understand he's been acting like a wild man since someone hit you. Or did you fall? That's Marlow's theory, you know."

"I didn't fall," she told him. "I think someone pushed me. I don't know."

"Maybe you're meddling too much."

"Maybe I am," she said soberly. "Tommy's gone up the beach. The gardener found his geometry in the shrubbery over there, and it had a letter from you in it. It seemed to upset him."

Don did not reply at once. He sat looking out to where the gulls were trailing a fishing boat, and a large black dog was wandering along the path. His face was grave.

"I see," he said, and got up abruptly. "Maybe I'd better go after him. Anybody here to look after you?"

"I don't need looking after."

"I think you do," he said decisively. "Mind if I help you upstairs and into your room? And see here," he added, "I think things are going to happen today.

I'd feel a lot better if you'd agree to lock your door until Tommy gets back. Don't open it for anyone. And that means anyone."

"But I don't understand," she said, bewildered.

"Do you need a brick wall to fall on you?" he said impatiently. "Someone's already tried to put you out of the picture. Do you want it to happen again?"

"It would be rather neat, wouldn't it, if that person happened to be you?"

He stared down at her, then he laughed, the light ironic laugh which always annoyed her.

"Well, it might be at that," he said. "Only I'm no bungler, my dear girl. I don't kill when a gardener with a pair of pruning shears is keeping an eye on me."

He was not gay, however, when he helped her up the stairs and into her room. His face was grave and thoughtful.

"I'm damned if I see how you come into it," he said soberly. "Any idea yourself?"

But she was still not sure of him. She shook her head, and as she closed the door and locked it he was still standing there, as though unwilling to leave her.

After a while she lay down on the chaise longue. She felt exhausted and puzzled. What did she know? she wondered. They would all know now that old Horace Jewett had been murdered, and how. They would know, too, that Scotty's bell had not rung that night. But would they know who had gone back into that house of death, after it was all over, turned off the lights, and even closed the sightless eyes, as though they could not bear to see them?

Was it the book? Did someone think she had found the book and the letter? Had her things been searched? She thought not, but she could not be sure. Or was it the chair? Had there been something about

277

it she was supposed to have seen? Why was it burned? And suddenly things fell into focus, the white chair and the fountain pen. Horace could have known he was dying and written something on it. A name? Or message? No one now would ever know.

Was she supposed to have seen it, the night she went into the room, where someone before her had left prints in the mothflakes?

The time dragged on. By seven o'clock Tommy had not come back, and she found her nerves were failing her. The big quiet house seemed to be closing in on her, and the locked door, with someone perhaps outside waiting to kill her. She almost screamed when she saw the knob slowly turning.

"Who is it?" she called breathlessly.

"It's me, Jessica," Julia said. "I was afraid you were asleep. I've brought you your supper. Why on earth is your door locked?"

Not anyone, Cameron had said. But surely he had not meant Julia. She got up on shaking legs and opened the door.

"I'd like to know where everyone is," Julia said. "Henry and Marian are probably drinking cocktails somewhere, but Tommy is usually on time. Where did he go? Do you know?"

Jessica had recovered somewhat, although she was still trembling.

"He went up the beach," she said. "Don Cameron went after him. I don't know why."

She sat down on the chaise again, and Julia pulled over a low table and set the tray on it.

"I've had about all I can take," she said slowly, picking up the knife from where it lay beside the plate. "About all I can stand," she repeated. "If only you hadn't called in the police—"

It was then that Jessica screamed.

12

Five men were gathered in Fenton's office late that afternoon. The district attorney was there, Fenton himself, Tommy and Henry Jewett and Don Cameron. There had been six, but the gardener George was already gone. Henry was huddled in a chair, his head in his hands. Only once or twice did he look up, as Fenton spoke to him.

"You say your father was willing to overlook what had happened? Did you discuss that with anyone?"

"No. I had no chance that night."

"You didn't know Miss Scott was a diabetic?"

"No."

"Or the effect of insulin on a damaged heart?"

"How could I? I'm no doctor."

"But someone knew. You realize that?"

"I don't realize anything. I don't see how anyone would know. Unless Scotty told them."

As the story unrolled, however, he tried to pull himself together. It was all there, the old man's failure to get help, the probability that he heard his killer coming back and had thrown the book with the letter out the open window. There were even a few exhibits on the desk in front of Fenton, the vial of Scotty's drug from her suitcase and shown to be largely water, Tommy's shrunken slippers and golf club, and the letter from the bank.

Fenton picked up the letter and glanced at it.

"What became of the checks this mentions?" he asked.

"I burned them when I got home. He gave them to me, and I burned them. In the kitchen stove," Henry added wearily.

"Just why did you do that?"

"I didn't want them around. I should think that's obvious."

"Mr. Jewett, did you kill your father?"

"No. For God's sake, no! I still don't know who did it."

"You still refuse to tell us about those checks. But has it occurred to you that if you had explained about them that night your father might not have been killed?"

"How do you know that? Anyhow I couldn't, I tell you. I couldn't. I was feeling pretty sick about everything. I don't believe it even now. You've got nothing to go on. How do I know Scotty's bell was muffled? That's pure guesswork. A bit of cotton! What does that mean? And a burned chair! For Christ's sake, why burn a chair? What good would that do?"

The district attorney spoke then. His voice was stern.

"It might," he said, "if something was written on it, Mr. Jewett. Your father was an intelligent man. And he did not die at once. He knew something was wrong, but he had time and strength enough, when he could not reach his nurse, to wheel himself into that room and to try to use the telephone to call the doctor, probably. Only, according to Jessica Jewett, the telephone had been carefully put where he could not reach it."

"I didn't notice that. I wasn't noticing much that morning. My wife had fainted, and I was looking after her." He added, avoiding Tommy's eyes, "There was a fountain pen on the floor."

"Whose pen? Your father's?"

"I don't know. Just a pen."

"I hope you're telling us all you know, Mr. Jewett." The district attorney was still stern. "Remember, your father's death was carefully planned and carefully carried out. The same is true of the Scott woman's. And there has been a definite attempt since to destroy all possible clues. If you can help us your duty is to do so."

Henry only shook his head, and Tommy got up and going over to him put a hand on his shoulder.

"I think he's taken about all he can," he said determinedly. "And I agree with him. You have no case yet. Certainly not against him. If he made a mistake of judgment, it can't be held against him. He killed nobody. I'm taking him home."

Henry got slowly to his feet. He looked dazed, and with Tommy holding his arm he moved automatically toward the door. No one said anything as they went out. The door was open, and the three men watched in silence as they got into the car standing there.

Then Fenton moved.

"Tommy's right, of course," he said heavily. "It could be any of them. Even his wife. She got a wad of money by the will. Or his sister Julia. Or it's as the doctor says and the Scott woman made a mistake and then killed herself."

"Banging herself on the head with a golf club first and then jumping into the bay!" Cameron said scornfully, "And you can leave Julia out. She has a bad temper at times, but I managed to control it for a good many years."

Fenton eyed him shrewdly.

"You've been seeing quite a bit of her lately, haven't you? How about the alimony you've been paying her? Horace's death ought to let you out of most of it."

"That's my affair, and hers," Cameron said coldly. "And in case I'm also a suspect, I didn't get here until after Horace Jewett died. I can prove it, if necessary."

"Alibis are a dime a dozen," Fenton said. "But so far I don't figure you in the case. Maybe I'll change my mind." He got out of his desk chair and picked up his cap. "Guess I'll go over there," he said. "Time somebody did a little talking."

He left them there and got into his shabby old car at the curb. He was not surprised when he reached the Jewett house to find that Tommy and Henry had not arrived. They would drive around, he thought, until Henry had recovered somewhat. He parked the car and going around to the front porch found the door open and stepped inside.

He was just in time to hear Jessica's scream.

He took the stairs two at a time, to find her cowering on the chaise longue, and a dazed and shocked Julia, knife in hand, standing as though she were paralyzed and staring down at her.

"What the hell's the matter?" he demanded. "What are you doing with that knife?"

She seemed unable to speak, but she held out the knife to him. He took it and examined it. It was a dull silver one, the blade blunt, the cutting-edge dull. He looked down at Jessica and smiled grimly.

"She couldn't kill you with this," he said. "Looks as though it wouldn't cut a piece of steak."

"Scrambled eggs and salad," Julia said thinly. "I didn't think she needed it. I just picked it up, and she—"

"Screamed," said Fenton. "Don't tell me. I heard

her." He looked at Jessica. "Where'd you get the idea she was after you?"

She tried to explain: Cameron's telling her there was a killer loose, and to lock her door, and about the attack on her two nights before. Julia stood stiffly until she had finished. Then she turned to Fenton.

"Isn't it time we ended this?" she said bitterly. "You know who's guilty. So do I. I've tried to protect my own brother, but it's no use any longer."

Jessica sat up, her face horrified.

"Not Tommy!" she gasped. "It couldn't be Tommy. I don't believe it. Never."

But Fenton had heard the men arriving below. He turned and went quickly down the stairs, and Julia followed him. Jessica could hear them, Fenton's asking them to go into the living-room, and Marian's arrival, rather noisy, from cocktails at the Club.

"What's all the shootin' for?" she asked gaily. "It looks like a party."

Jessica got up. It was going to finish now, and Tommy must not be alone. He would need her. She went quietly down the stairs and into the room. Only Marian was seated, with a cigarette in her carefully manicured fingers. Julia and the men were all standing, Henry staring out a window at nothing, Fenton stern and forbidding in front of the empty hearth, and Tommy, looking sick and white, near the door. She went in and slipped her arm through his.

"It's all right, darling," she whispered. "I'm here. It's all right."

He squeezed her arm but said nothing. And then Fenton began to talk.

There was a certain dignity about him as he did so, his gaunt face unhappy but determined.

"I think Julia is right," he said. "It's time we all got together and went over this thing. A little while ago Henry said we had no case. That we didn't even know there'd been a murder. He's wrong, but I'm going to go back a bit. We know from Don Cameron that several checks on Horace Jewett's personal account had been forged, and for considerable sums. It became necessary then for Horace to die before his bank statement reached him.

"As it happened, the bank didn't wait. It suspected the forgeries and sent the checks in an enclosing letter to him. I think he knew pretty well who was guilty, and that night he sent for Henry. Whether he told him his suspicions or not I don't know. But I *am* sure that talk was overheard.

"I think Henry was pretty badly worried. The checks were out of his father's checkbook in the drawer by the bed, so it looked like a family matter. I gather that Mr. Jewett wanted no scandal about them, so Henry burned the checks that night.

"He made a mistake then. He could have cleared everything up that night. But he didn't, and by morning it was too late.

"Remember, the death had been planned for some time. It was to occur before the checks reached the old man. But nothing was left to chance that night. The wrong drug in the vitamin bottle. The bell muffled in the nurse's room. The telephone in the next room out of his reach. And by that time he knew he was dying.

"But he was smart. Horace Jewett always had been a smart man. He'd put the bank's letter into a book and took it with him into the living-room when he went to call the doctor. As it was planned, he couldn't call the doctor. He was alone and helpless. But one thing he could do.

"He could reach the window, and he did just that. He opened the window and threw the book outside.

Why? I don't know. Probably because he heard someone coming. For someone did come. Someone who came to see if the plot had worked, who found him dead or dying, who did not like the open eyes and so closed them, and who on leaving him there made a mistake and turned out the lights.

"That is what Jessica here saw the next morning, the closed eyes and the lights off. She's a policeman's daughter and he'd taught her to observe things like that. She's been a bigger help than she knows, for when he wired her he wired me, too. He suspected the Scott woman of having had a diabetic coma, and he reminded me that insulin given hypodermically is poison in heart cases.

"On the day she was killed I saw Miss Scott and warned her to be careful. She was shocked. I think she had told someone about the drug, but she denied it, and in the end that denial killed her.

"So, one way and another, we began to piece things together. It wasn't easy. Tommy'd been out the night of his father's death. Seems he does that now and then when he has a fever. I wired his hospital on the Coast. He and his slippers kind of complicated things. It seemed like the Scott woman had telephoned the person who killed her and made an appointment for that night on the pier, but we couldn't trace the call. And the bank reported that the total of the forged checks was less than five thousand dollars.

"That was a fleabite to Horace Jewett, but he was strict about money. You all know that. There was always the will to remember. He could change it any time.

"But somebody had to have cash, and in a hurry. Why? Bills? Stores don't dun people like this family. So what? Gambling? The stock market? Old debts? I put my bet on gambling, and I think I was right."

He looked around the room. No one moved. Henry still kept his back to the others. Julia was white and looked sick, and Marian was lighting a fresh cigarette. Jessica, looking at Tommy, saw his eyes fixed on his brother.

"So you see," Fenton went on, "we had got that far, but there we stopped. We needed someone who saw who was with the Scott woman the night she was killed. We had plenty of alibis, but none of them were worth anything. And we needed someone who knew who went into the other house after Mr. Jewett died and turned out the lights. Someone who had planned his murder and went over to see how it had worked."

He glanced at the window.

"How about it, Henry?" And when Henry did not turn, he went on. "You didn't figure on a murder, did you? But I think you know who was out that night. After all, you had good news. The checks were destroyed. So I think you went to your wife's room, when you couldn't sleep. You wanted to tell her your father wouldn't prosecute, that it was all over. Only—she wasn't there."

Henry did not turn. He stood, his heavy shoulders sagging, still staring out at nothing. It was Marian who got out of her chair, her face convulsed with anger.

"Lies!" she screamed. "All lies and guesses! You can't prove a thing. Tell them, Henry. Tell them you know I never went out that night."

But Henry did not move or speak. Marian ran to him and caught him by the arm.

"Don't be a damned fool, Henry," she shrieked. "Tell them I was asleep, in bed."

Then, and only then, he shook his heavy head.

"Sorry, baby," he said huskily. "You see, I saw you

coming back. Only I couldn't believe—"

He did not finish, and Marian let go of his arm. Viciously and unexpectedly she put the end of her burning cigarette against his hand, then she turned and made for the door. Fenton started for her, but Tommy barred the way.

"Better let her go, chief," he said quietly. "I think she knows the answer."

Henry still did not move when he heard her car driven furiously away. He did not speak until Tommy went to the portable bar in the corner and pouring out a sizable Scotch put in his hand. Then he took a long breath.

"Thanks, old man," he said.

No one seemed surprised when Cameron came in, took a look at the room, and going to Julia put his arms around her. Or that Julia held to him almost fiercely.

"I've been an awful fool," she said brokenly.

"Then there is a pair of us, my dear," he said, and managed to smile down at her.

Jessica suddenly found her legs would not hold her. She sat down, while Tommy bent over her.

"What did you mean, she knows the answer?" she asked, her voice tremulous.

"Wait and see, my darling," he told her. "It's out of our hands, anyhow. Remember, she tried to kill you, too."

"But why? What had it to do with me?"

"Perhaps she knew you had a smart father," he said.

They learned Marian's answer soon after he had taken her upstairs to bed. Fenton was on the telephone, and his report was brief.

"Drove smack off the end of the dock," he said. "It will be a good while before we get her. Hours

287

too late.''

The house next door was very quiet that night. In the footman's rest off the hall, that niche where in former times a gentleman in livery had waited for callers, a field mouse was busy making a nest in the upholstered seat. In the drawing-room, where a chair had been burned, there was still a faint reek of smoke, and over it all lay the scent of mothflakes and the damp cold of empty houses everywhere.

Jessica lay still in her bed. It was over at last. Some day Henry would be able to face his world once more, and Julia had learned her lesson. What really mattered was that Tommy was himself again, and safe.

As he undressed she looked at his tall, thin body, his tired face, and his mop of unruly hair. She had fought for him so long, praying for him through the war, waiting and watching in the hospital on the Coast, and now here.

It was queer, she thought. Men! They got themselves inevitably into trouble, but they always expected some woman to stand by. And the women did, and loved it.

He caught her eyes and grinned.

"Suppose I dream again tonight," he said. "Think I'd better tie my big toe to the foot of the bed?"

"No," she said seriously. "You won't do that any more. You've been scared about a good many things for a long time, Tommy. Your father, and maybe even Henry, and, of course, the war, and that you might be lame for life. But there's nothing to be afraid of any more. It's all over. There's only you and me, darling.''

"Just you and me and the bedpost," he said lightly. But his face was thoughtful as he kissed her.

288